D1593968

A BESPOKE MURDER

An absolutely gripping cozy murder mystery full of twists

JEAN G. GOODHIND

A Honey Driver Murder Mystery Book 12

JOFFE BOOKS

Joffe Books, London
www.joffebooks.com

First English edition published in Great Britain by Joffe Books in 2023

First German edition published by Aufbau Taschenbuch in Germany as Mord in Anzug in 2014

Cover art by Dee Dee Book Covers

ISBN: 978-1-80405-860-2

CHAPTER ONE

There was something erotic about a man wearing tight britches and knee-high riding boots.

'He's *very* fetching.'

Honey Driver reined in her hormones before giving the highwayman another once-over. His britches were made of burgundy-coloured velvet, the antique type made from material that looked as though it could be used to cover an armchair. His black leather riding boots were the old-fashioned sort with extensions totally covering his knees. A white silk cravat fell in a frothy bow over the top of a gold brocade waistcoat. His frock coat was of navy blue wool, the colour matching his tricorn hat.

If that wasn't enough to set a girl's heart racing, he wore a mask over his eyes and a black kerchief over the lower part of his face.

In Honey's opinion he was every red-blooded woman's idea of a highwayman for whom one would willingly stand and deliver!

Unfortunately . . . he wasn't real but part of a shop window display, one of many entered for a competition. So far he was her favourite, sending her imagination into overdrive.

Pistol in hand, he was standing against a backdrop of dark hills and black trees. With the help of strategically placed spotlights, a pale moon threw silvery patterns across an indigo sky. Bespoke tailored tweed sports jackets, in autumn tones ranging from rust through mustard to dull red, framed the scene cascading from the top of the window to the bottom like huge autumn leaves, their shadows playing on the moonlit backdrop.

The highwayman's shadow, which should have been centre stage against the backdrop, was replaced by that of a noose hanging from gallows.

The scene sent a shiver down Honey's spine. She was fascinated. Up until this moment most of the shop window displays had been pretty, pleasant or highly artistic. The one at the toy shop had been animated thanks to tooting train sets and bouncing balls. Audio had also figured in the display though the tinny singing of a brace of dolls, teddies and plastic animals did grate on the nerves. The whole thing had been spoilt when a plastic Spiderman had fallen over and appeared to be looking up the dress of a plastic Lolita.

There had also been clowns; Honey disliked clowns. She much preferred highwaymen!

Thanks to the shadow of the gallows, this shop window display didn't resemble any of the other displays. It was artistic, yes, but just ever so slightly scary.

'Oh, yes,' she breathed, her eyes shining. 'I'm glad I came.'

She had had reservations when first asked to by Bath Retailers' Association — BRA for short — to judge Bath's best window display.

'I have to warn you I know nothing about what makes a good window display, at least not in a professional capacity,' she'd told Lee Curtis, one of the organisers. 'I just know what I like, I wouldn't want to upset anyone who knows a lot more about it than I do.'

It may have been her imagination but for a nanosecond she was sure she saw something furtive flick into his eyes before the usual blue blandness reasserted itself. Lee owned a shop himself, a place where you could buy saucy outfits.

She'd never been there, not fancying dressing up as a French maid or an old style nurse wearing starch and black stockings.

His nose quivered as he sucked in his breath.

'You shop, don't you?'

'Doesn't everyone?'

Why did she feel guilty about that?

'Of course you have. Ever window-shopped and been drawn to a very compelling display?'

Yes. That too. She nodded.

His chest expanded when he took another deep breath. His nose quivered again.

'That in itself qualifies you to tell us which one you like best.'

She had to agree that he had a point. Shopping was something she HAD to do. It was also something she'd been doing for years.

Amazed at how experienced she now appeared to be, she nodded. 'Yes. I suppose you're right. I'm very experienced on the shopping front.'

Lee had gone on to outline the details. The prize was £5,000 plus coverage in the local paper, possibly radio and TV too. Free publicity in other words.

So Lee Curtis had sworn her in — so to speak — as one of three judges.

The deal was that each judge would go round individually accompanied by Lee who was armed with a clipboard and pen, and that was what Honey was doing now. He asked her to rate the window displays after perusing each one, from one to five on artistic merit, lighting and which had made the biggest impression on her.

He had to do this three times with each judge gathering their impressions as he went. Honey's fellow judges were unknown to her, a necessary precaution to prevent conferring and thus accusations of favouritism.

'So why did you pick on me?' she asked brightly. 'I mean, it can't solely be because I window-shop; everyone I know does that.'

She'd hoped the reason might be that she was known as a person of impeccable taste, a pillar of the community and a fashion icon whose views were well respected.

Lee's pronouncement surprised her.

'Firstly, we thought a woman who liked shopping would be ideal. There were other candidates, but we decided it would be very useful having someone aboard with friends in the police force — just in case things get nasty. Some of our entrants are known to be bad losers, so if the police do have to be called to sort out a punch-up, we thought you being involved might make them come more quickly.'

'Oh!'

So! Nothing to do artistic merit; but the capacity to elicit a quick response from the local nick if things got ugly; such were the advantages of being Crime Liaison Officer for Bath Hotels Association. It must also be known, she decided, that she had a sleeping partner (literally) namely Detective Inspector Steve Doherty. If she got caught up in something she couldn't handle, he was the cop who rode to the rescue. All in all, it was not at all what she'd expected to hear.

Lee took her along to each window display, avidly scrutinising her face as he awaited her comments. He never moved as he did that; like a mother hen waiting to see if her first egg is going to hatch. She'd already judged six entries. The highwayman was the seventh — lucky number seven!

Up until the highwayman she'd been sold on the display in The Chocolate Soldier, a shop specialising in upmarket chocolates. The display had centred around a chocolate castle inhabited by chocolate people and guarded by chocolate soldiers; very apt considering the name of the shop. Lots of sparkly paper wrapping had been used to alleviate the varying shades of brown and the ivory tones of various white chocolates. The only flaw had been the little drawbridge going up and down worked by an electric motor. The place where the drawbridge was attached to the castle was beginning to melt thanks to the motor. Apart from that it was first class and was the only window display to make Honey's mouth water.

However, all that had changed since coming face to face with the highwayman.

'I do like this one,' she said to Lee.

'Artistic merit from nought to five? Nought being not artistic at all, going on up through to five — highly artistic. Pick a number.'

Honey folded her arms as she considered, narrowing her eyes and focusing on each part of the scene, how dramatic it was! And what did it mean? Wasn't that what those in the art world considered when they viewed a painting? What message did it send?

'It's such a dynamic contrast,' she said out loud as she tried to think numbers. 'I mean, tweed sports jackets are not that inspiring. Neither are the men who wear them.'

'I wear them,' Lee said tersely.

'I mean . . . respectable, upright citizens,' blurted Honey, in an effort to make amends. 'As opposed to criminal — which the highwayman obviously is, despite his dramatically romantic image. I really think it's sending some kind of message.'

Lee seemed reassured, his ballpoint pen hovering about halfway down the clipboard.

'I suppose so.'

She sneaked a sideways glance at him. His nose was sharp, his face bland and round as a pudding. She thought of all those sexy outfits, rubber and leather in his shop. Plus the DVDs of course. And the books. Xcite, Black Lace. He had the lot.

'So why didn't you enter the competition?' she asked him.

His pudding jaw tightened in his pudding face.

'Not family orientated,' he said through clenched teeth.

'Oh!' It was all she could say. All anyone could say. Her mind boggled at the thought of what might have appeared in his shop window. At present, she knew, it was blacked out, a lovely shiny sheen of black with swirls of gold around the edges. Nobody could peruse the goods by window-shopping.

'Right,' she said, tugging her attention back to the job in hand. 'Now what score shall I give it? It's got to be a five

— or is it a one? Sorry. I've forgotten which angle I'm coming from. Is one the highest and five the lowest?'

'No. You've got it back to front. Five is the highest score you can give.'

'Then I'll give it five.'

'Is that your honest opinion?' he pressed.

Suddenly she felt like the foreman of a jury with the power to send someone to the scaffold — or at least to jail.

'Yes. It is. I mean, he really is the stuff of erotic fantasy . . .'

Lee swallowed as though he were in pain. Oops! She'd said the wrong thing. Erotica was his speciality, or at least he thought so. Honey wasn't so sure. Leather posing pouches and crotchless knickers didn't do it for her.

She took another look at the shadow of the gallows then at the eyes of the highwayman. Painted eyes. Brown and outlined in black.

'Yes.' The highwayman was the stuff of fantasy all right. He'd certainly figure in her fantasies anyway.

She nodded. 'Yes. I think a five. It's interesting. It has a message, you know, respectably smart against dramatically dissolute.' She knew which she preferred but hey, what was the point in hurting hurt Lee's feelings?

Lee circled the five on his clipboard with a deft sweep of his Biro. 'If that's what you think.'

He didn't sound impressed by her analysis of the designer sending the public 'some kind of message'. She twigged he would have preferred a big-breasted woman wearing a tight bodice — nothing else, just the bodice.

Besides the 'naughty' shop he owned, that she recalled was named Leather Lovers, he also ran a gift shop with his mother, the sort of place where pale pink and blue predominate and painted cottages and fluffy teddy bears are the biggest sellers. If there was a message in that kind of thing, it was more likely to be love me, love my teddy. She didn't even want to think about what message a sexy scene in the window of Leather Lovers was likely to send. Feel the thrill? Sadomasochism is a punishment in itself?

She dragged her mind away from such thoughts. Concentrate! She needed to concentrate.

Pauling and Tern whose window they were assessing were a gentleman's outfitter of the old school; not for them the brash designer labels, sulky models in the windows and nerve-tingling techno music. Founded sometime around the turn of the century — nineteenth to twentieth not the most recent turn — Pauling and Tern were bespoke tailors producing beautifully cut garments from quality cloths and sewn by the ultimate in the tailoring trade. They counted royalty among their clients. Not for them the Friday night millionaire with a job in computers and a set of wheels that shot from standstill to sixty miles an hour in ten seconds. Pauling and Tern was more vintage Bentley than hot rod.

Waving a three-fingered goodbye and wishing the highwayman would wave back, Honey followed Lee out of the alley.

She glanced back at the narrow alley and the honey-coloured buildings, thinking how little must have changed in two or three centuries — except for the shop fronts that is.

In the past there had been more than one shop in Beaumont Alley, all having the elegant bay windows more usually seen on traditional Christmas cards and boxes of chocolates or in TV dramas based on the novels of Charles Dickens.

The bowed window of Pauling and Tern was all that remained of a gentler time when ladies in long dresses and bonnets and men in britches had strolled arm in arm over the flagstones and cobbles.

Few people frequented the alley nowadays preferring the new arcades and shops at the bottom of town.

But the tailoring shop had clung on to its secluded address. She could understand that due to the nature of its clients, the gentleman's outfitters preferred to be discreetly tucked away from the main thoroughfare. Their clients, people who valued their privacy, made appointments to choose fabrics or be measured up. Pauling and Tern didn't need to be part of anything. So why, she wondered, had they entered the competition for the best window display in Bath? It seemed out of character.

The next scheduled window display was a far trendier shop aimed at the young man not the portly gentleman. Even twenty yards away, she could hear the music blaring out and see the spotlights flashing on and off in the handsomely lit window.

Crowds of shoppers and tourists had crowded around the new shopping facility at the bottom of town where plate glass prevailed and piped music flooded onto the pavements.

Lee threaded his way through the people, asking them politely if they would be so kind as to stand back as judging was about to commence. In doing so he pointed at the sign in the bottom right-hand corner of the window which said, *Bath Shop Window Display Competition*.

'Roadrunner Race Boys have been shortlisted,' he announced loudly.

Honey didn't recall there having been a long list so couldn't see how he could have been shortlisted. He was just showing off.

Despite the racing car in the window, she knew that Road Runners and Boy Racers also dealt in specialist audio accessories for cars, i.e. anything to increase the rap in your car loud enough to make you deaf and available to all whether you were a fan of rap, garage or whatever, or not. Noise in general it should have been called.

Lee having cleared her way, Honey stepped forward.

Slap bang in the centre of the display was a Formula 1 racing car. It was bright red, surrounded by chequered flags and all the razzmatazz of the racing circuit. The lighting in the window was in stark contrast to that at Pauling and Tern, lots of flashing lights and no shadows at all. No sexy figure either. The racing car presumably filled that role.

'Well, hello to you!'

Honey turned to see the owner or shop manager approaching, rubbing his hands together and smiling smugly, as though he considered that winning was in the bag.

'De . . . light . . . ed,' he cooed in a voice as sweet and runny as treacle. His smile looked as though it were set in cement. His white teeth flashed like a great white shark about to eat breakfast.

Honey glanced at her clipboard. Julian Cunningham. Number one poser, she thought to herself. He had the right shop, the right background — car racing, though only on a local scale. She didn't need to know that he considered himself God's gift to women or that he spent his holidays on the Costa Blanca; it was written all over him. Everything from his highlighted hair down to his suede loafers shrieked poser.

He was wearing a linen shirt that was as white as his teeth, the cuffs rolled up to expose bronzed arms without a trace of hair, a feature owing more to waxing than nature, she presumed. A thick gold bracelet flopped around his wrist.

His jeans were yellow and hung low on his hips. His hair stood up in gelled spikes all over his head. The white of his loafers was as glaringly white as his shirt and teeth. In her opinion they were probably made of Italian kid leather, in which case they'd cost a fortune. Or they could have been designer knock-offs and bought anywhere in Spain.

His eyes raked over her. 'Hey! Babe! Why don't all the judges for this event look like you?' The voice was designed to disarm her. Instead it made her cringe.

'Perhaps you need new contact lenses,' she said, smiling sweetly whilst at the same time automatically giving him nil points for subtlety.

Others had tried to influence her decision — offering coffee, a glass of wine, a small present and chocolate of course. The chocolate had almost swung her, but she'd resisted. Nobody had been as oily as Julian Cunningham.

Honey stepped closer to the window.

'Is it real?'

Julian rolled his shoulders. His smile widened. 'Every inch of me, darling.' He leaned closer and whispered. 'You can inspect if you like. I'd certainly like to inspect you.'

'I meant the *car*. Is it a real racing car?' snapped Honey, the corners of her lips curling with contempt.

Despite Honey's clipped tone Julian Cunningham was unperturbed.

'It is indeed, sweetheart. Though there's no engine in it. Just the chassis. A classic chassis I might add.' He grinned at her and even attempted to tentatively place an arm around her waist. 'I have a weakness for a classic chassis.'

His inference was obvious, that she was getting on a bit but still in great shape. He might regard it as a compliment, but she absolutely did not. The anger travelled to her right foot which she lifted and stamped firmly on his truly gorgeous Italian — or Spanish — leather shoes.

'Ouch!' He hopped about on one foot whilst staring at his smeared loafers with dismay. 'Jesus Christ! Look what you've done!'

Honey glanced at the imprint of her boot on one of his white shoes.

'Take it as a warning, Mr Cunningham. The judges are not to be tampered with!'

With a toss of her head, she went back to inspecting the window. She had to admit it was a very good display and the public certainly seemed to appreciate it. She reminded herself not to be influenced by Julian. The owner had been unavailable at Tern and Pauling; not so at a number of other shops. However, she had not let either their absence or their presence influence her preference and she wasn't about to start now.

'It's a real racing car,' he said again. 'And there's a message.'

She nodded and muttered an unintelligible acknowledgement. Of course there was.

'Winner takes all,' he said, his hot breath blowing into her ear.

She felt like saying that she did not form any part of the prize for this competition, but knew it would fall on deaf ears. Julian Cunningham's ego was big enough to fill the

Albert Hall. He wasn't the sort to take no for an answer — despite having his foot trampled on.

In all honesty it was a good effort and deserved to be considered. But she didn't want to give him a five. Instead, she wanted to wipe that smug smile off his face. Giving him a high score in the competition would equate to him acquiring a high score with her. She could do without that.

And yet . . . there was no doubting it was a good display. If only it would disintegrate . . . Dark thoughts. Mary Jane, resident professor of the paranormal at the Green River Hotel, had mentioned at some time that if you think dark thoughts hard enough, they'll take root in the real world and happen. It wouldn't hurt to try — would it?

It was sudden, too sudden to be as a result of her thoughts surely.

The coloured lights, green, red, white, purple and blue, had been flashing in sequence for some time. Suddenly the lights flicked, fizzed and a shower of sparks fell directly into the driving seat of the racing car.

'My God!'

A picture of animated panic, Julian Cunningham threw up his arms and screamed something to somebody inside the shop as he leapt over the threshold. One of the chequered flags caught alight. Cunningham began leaping around inside the window with a fire extinguisher, screeching at everyone to get more fire extinguishers, to put out the fire before the car got damaged and his name was mud.

'Oh dear,' said Lee, curiously undisturbed by all the excitement and showing no inclination to assist in putting the fire out. 'I do hope he's got fire insurance.'

Honey shook her head. 'I doubt it. He spent too much money on those shoes and blond highlights.'

'Probably,' murmured Lee and they walked on.

CHAPTER TWO

Nobody had opened the curtains. That was the first thing the old man noticed. And nobody had brought him his breakfast. Seven thirty. It was seven thirty he expected his breakfast, not a minute earlier, not a minute later. He looked at the clock on the mantelpiece. He couldn't see it clearly but it looked like it could be gone eleven? If that was the case, where was everybody?

With painfully rheumatic hands, liver spotted with age, the skin as slack and wrinkled as that on a bad apple, he fumbled for his mobile phone and punched in his son's number. It didn't matter if his son was only downstairs, it had turned out to be the best method of getting hold of him. Saved him shouting. Saved him shifting himself from the bed.

A tinny voice told him the number he was calling was unavailable. The ungrateful scoundrel had turned his phone off. What was he playing at?

It occurred to him that Nigel had been evasive and even a little rebellious in the days before he'd been rushed to hospital. Damned hospital! He hadn't wanted to go, but then he hadn't wanted to grow old either. He'd never expected to grow old. Even in middle-age he'd been convinced that his faculties would remain intact and he would physically stay at that age, unchanged and unageing.

Things hadn't worked out as he'd planned. He'd fallen and broken his hip. On arriving home, he had then caught a cold that the doctor feared was turning into pneumonia. He'd suggested going back into hospital, but Arnold had held out.

'If I'm going to die, I prefer to do so at home.'

Not that he'd had any intention of dying. Defiant to the end — that's what he would be!

The doctor had persisted, but Arnold, despite being delirious, had won the argument, mainly because Nigel had sided with him.

'If my father doesn't wish to go into hospital, then we have to respect his wishes.'

Yes, thought Arnold. *What you meant, my son, was there might be more chance of me dying if I stay at home and that would, of course, be best for you. Everything would be yours then, wouldn't it, son? Or so you think.*

Arnold couldn't help chuckling to himself, his chest rattling with the effort. 'I'm stronger than you think,' he muttered and chuckled again. 'And just wait till you read the will! Just you wait!'

In the meantime he'd put Plan B into operation. If the mountain won't come to Mohammed . . . if they couldn't be bothered to come upstairs with his breakfast, then he'd have to go down. Fired up by the determination he'd had all his life, he repeated what he'd already said, shouting it at the top of his voice.

'I'm stronger than you think, my son. Stronger than you think. In fact, I might even outlive you. Now wouldn't that be a turn out for the books!'

He reached for his walking stick. It wasn't there.

He shook his head in exasperation. If he could just get up on his feet and get downstairs. Get to the shop. Tern and Pauling was *still* his shop. He prided himself on supplying tailoring of quality to those with status and money, preferably both. Those who had both status and money were his favourite customers because for the most part they also had manners. There were exceptions of course, one in particular . . . he pushed the vision of that man from his thoughts. Scoundrel! Cad! As for that son of his . . .

'Useless boy!' he burst out. 'Can't even get that right. Can't get anything right. No breakfast. No walking stick. Well I'm not so incapacitated that I can't descend those stairs and give you a piece of my mind!'

After pushing back the bedclothes, he shuffled to the edge of the bed, grumbling. Rearranging his unruly pyjamas, he slowly eased one foot over the edge of the bed, then the other. Finally he had both feet on the floor and within inches of his slippers. He could see that his walking stick had fallen across the fur lined moccasins his son had bought him last Christmas. Nigel, bought him slippers every Christmas, even though the old ones were never worn out. He got them at Harrods. By now, there should have been half a dozen pairs in the wardrobe, but there weren't. He presumed the old pairs went to charity, but didn't enquire.

He heaved a big sigh and muttered a few more unkind words about his son. He should have checked the position of the walking stick, making sure it couldn't possibly fall over. Why was he always in such a hurry? But there, that was Nigel. Too much like his mother. She'd never been methodical either. Good in bed though — if you can call submitting to anything he wanted as being good. On reflection she'd never shown any sign that she was as enthusiastic about his sexual demands as he was.

Bending down to retrieve his walking stick was out of the question. His back wouldn't stand for it and his hips certainly wouldn't.

With the resolve of one who always expects to come out on top and to have things done his way, he slid first one foot and then the other into his slippers. The walking stick remained in situ, lying across the tops of his feet.

Positioning himself just right he carefully raised his leg, at the same time reaching for his stick. His bones creaked and groaned a little, but determination won through.

Now to see what the young scallywag is up to, he thought to himself, indifferent to the fact that his son was fifty years of age and had a head as bald as a billiard ball. He was still 'the boy', the scallywag, the undisciplined disciple in the business of Pauling and Tern. Even his tailoring was inferior. He basically managed the business, taking care of banking and administration, and the high quality tailoring done by outside contractors.

All in all, his son was a great disappointment to him, a mummy's boy, he thought to himself. Mollycoddled. He'd done his best to rectify matters, but to no avail. Boarding school had tried to make him a man but he still bounded about like a common grammar school boy — even in his fifties.

It had been some weeks since Arnold Tern had been downstairs in the large Victorian house purchased by his grandfather back around 1900. The house was well situated up a side road not far from Victoria Park, close enough to see the trees though not close enough to hear the shouts of playing children.

The bedroom door was very wide and also very heavy. He eyed it accusingly as he opened it, wondering why he hadn't noticed it before. He'd get the boy to do something about it. The hinges might be altered to ease the weight.

Shuffling out onto the galleried landing, he looked over the banisters, one hand firmly gripping the handrail. His legs felt wobbly and so did his head, understandable seeing as he'd been in bed for weeks with some kind of infection that he refused to believe was pneumonia. From somewhere in one of the downstairs rooms came the drone of a vacuum cleaner.

The light from the glass upper half of the front door streamed into the hallway. It was the first daylight he'd seen for weeks; he'd insisted the curtains be kept drawn in his bedroom.

There seemed to be nobody else around except for Mrs Cayford, the cleaner.

He called his son's name. 'Nigel?'

There was no response. Not entirely surprising. It was quite possible that Nigel had an appointment with a client — they never called the gentlemen who came to be measured for suits, jackets or trousers, customers — the gentlemen they served were always referred to as *clients*. Esteemed clients. The client, or more likely their valet or agent as they now seemed to term them, would telephone to make an appointment. Not for them, hanging around in a shop all day.

He looked down the flight of stairs, debating whether it was worth going down. Nigel was undoubtedly in the shop. Those stairs; they looked so steep; such an effort, though for a moment it seemed they were coming up to meet him, blurring, swimming . . .

'Mr Tern?'

His shouted name was followed by the thudding of pink plastic Crocs as Mrs Cayford pounded up the stairs on stout legs, just catching him before he tottered over.

'Mr Tern, whatever are you doing out of bed?' she scolded. 'Now come on. Let's get you back there. No arguments.'

Edwina Cayford was a part-time nurse who came in to do their cleaning two days a week. She reckoned getting a break from working in the hospital kept her sane and solvent.

Nigel had suggested they get somebody who could come in for a few hours every day rather than twice a week, but his father was having none of it. He liked Edwina. Sometimes she popped in still wearing her nurse's uniform, though only if he asked her to. He'd licked his lips at the prospect. He loved nurses in uniform. There was something extremely attractive — sexy even — about a nurse wearing a dark blue dress with starched collars and cuffs and a belt that cinched in her waist. No matter her size, a woman couldn't help achieving an hourglass figure wearing a belt like that.

Unfortunately, he'd failed to take on board that nurses didn't wear such an inconvenient outfit nowadays. They wore what they termed 'scrubs', a tunic top and trousers.

He'd been totally dismayed when he'd seen her dressed like that.

'But what about your uniform?'

'This is my uniform,' she'd said with a smile. 'Things have changed, Mr Tern. The old uniform wasn't practical. This is better. Easily washed and dried and non-iron.'

Arnold Tern contented himself with eyeing the swell of her bosoms against the tunic top which he ascertained was a size too small. Same for the pants she wore, though he only ascertained that aspect of her anatomy when she bent over. The trousers were tight around her bum which was very round and filled them out nicely.

Apart from her more obvious attractions, Edwina cleaned the house in a very efficient manner, everything scrubbed and sparkling by the time she left.

'Now, go careful.'

She had one arm across his back, the other holding his arm around her shoulder. He liked the way she held on to him, gripping him with strong fingers, her plump arms holding him upright. She was good at her job was Edwina, both cleaning and nursing. That's why he liked her around; she was used to giving assistance to those who could not help themselves.

'Let's get you back to bed,' she said in a forthright manner that left no room for argument. Not that Arnold had any wish to argue. He liked her manhandling him.

'You have very strong arms,' he said to her. 'I like feeling them around me. If I was twenty years younger I might take advantage and get you into trouble.'

'Mr Tern!' she said, pretending to be shocked. 'You *are* a naughty boy!' she added, chuckling. She continued to guide him back to his bedroom and the warm bed he'd just got out of.

'I haven't had my breakfast,' he said to her. 'Nigel is under instructions to bring me breakfast at seven thirty. My stomach demands it. What time is it now?'

'Gone eleven thirty.'

'It's nearly lunchtime?'

'It is indeed. He must have forgotten. Never mind. I'll get it for you.'

'I like it when you get it for me.'

'I know you do, but no naughty business,' she said laughing whilst at the same time adopting an accusing expression.

'If I was younger . . .' he chuckled.

'But you're not,' she said as she bundled him into bed. 'He should have told me you hadn't had breakfast. I expect he forgot what with all the excitement this morning.'

Arnold's eyes lit up at the possibilities of what she was saying.

'Excitement? I take it my son has gone to the office?'

He always called the premises occupied by Pauling and Tern an office. Terming it a shop was far too common.

'I should think he has,' trilled Mrs Cayford. 'What a wonderful day this is!'

To Arnold's ears it sounded almost as though she were going to burst into song. What the devil was she so happy about?

The only reason he could think the day was so wonderful was the identity of the client his son had gone to meet. His old heart leapt with joy at the possibilities; royalty was the ultimate of course. No matter how rich the Russian oligarch and how much they wished to be anglicised, there was no substitute for the royal connection, the British royal family of course.

There was one prince above all others who favoured well-cut sports or hacking jackets. A man who rode to hounds — or did before fox hunting was banned. His heart swelled with pride.

'Ah! My son is meeting somebody very important today,' he said with an air of great satisfaction and also great reserve. Pauling and Tern never betrayed their clients' names.

'Indeed he is,' declared Mrs Cayford as she folded him back into the bed, turning the bedclothes tightly as nurses do.

'Wonderful,' declared Arnold promising himself to ask for all the details the moment Nigel was home. Efficient and sexually enticing as Mrs Cayford was, there were certain things one did not share with the hired help.

She drew back the curtains with muscular arms then bent to turn over to adjust the thermostat at the side of the radiator.

'I hope he was suitably discreet.' His gaze rested on Edwina's ample backside. In his mind he imagined it unclothed, round and glossy.

'I don't know about that, Mr Tern, but he was so sure he was in with a chance, and when he phoned and told me a few minutes ago . . . well . . . I was as pleased as he was.'

Arnold blinked. He was losing the thread here. What the devil was the woman talking about?

'Could you explain exactly where you think he's gone, Mrs Cayford?'

'Well yes, Mr Tern. He's gone to collect the prize. Isn't it wonderful? I must say I thought it was the best window display, though Bob's Boots was pretty good too. So was the chocolate shop . . . but there you are the window display at Pauling and Tern won the five thousand pound prize . . . Mr Tern? Mr Tern? Are you alright?'

Arnold Tern's lower lip trembled. His eyes stared straight ahead. If he had been fit and well he might have punched somebody — probably his son. As it was all he could do was sit like a boiling kettle, bubbling inside and in danger of steam coming out of his ears.

Edwina went downstairs to make his breakfast leaving him tucked up in bed, his walking stick and mobile phone close to hand. There was also a glass of water and tablets for his heart, his blood pressure, his cholesterol and his bladder. He couldn't take any of them until he'd eaten something, but his mind had shifted from all thought of food. Edwina had told him in more detail about the shop window display. She'd admitted going into town and staring at it for quite some time.

'It was lovely. A highwayman with a noose hanging in the background and all the jackets and coats looking like giant autumn leaves flying around the edges of the window.'

Arnold was dumbfounded. Pauling and Tern had never indulged in flamboyant window displays. In fact they'd never indulged in *any* window displays.

It was Pauling and Tern's remit to always be understated, subtle. Their clients expected total discretion. They were rich people, *titled* people, people who had no wish to be photographed whilst being measured for their latest hacking jacket or morning suit. People whose private lives could make headlines if anyone at Tern and Pauling repeated some of the secrets told to them whilst measuring a person's inside leg.

He attempted to tell her that his son had gone behind his back and that Pauling and Tern never indulged in window displays. In fact, they curtained their windows, as after all their clients did not window-shop. They made appointments.

He was not happy. Not happy at all. If he'd been well, he might have done something about it, gone into town and catch Nigel on his way to the bank with his cheque for five thousand pounds — wasn't that the amount Edwina had mentioned?

The pillows and mattress seemed hard as iron beneath him; he'd been ill so long and had no strength to do anything. The room was gloomy even though the curtains had been pulled open. Was it his imagination or was it getting gloomier?

'I'd like a massage when you can fit it in,' he called out to Edwina. Whether she heard him or not he couldn't tell. Either way she didn't answer.

A return to slumber was imminent. He couldn't fight it indefinitely, just long enough to eat some breakfast which of course was now brunch as the Americans called it. But first he had to make a phone call. Nigel had angered him. He'd done something likely to take the business into the realms of commercial tailoring, not the bespoke it had always been. Goodness knows who would come in demanding a fitting! Pop stars even! Footballers!

He would not allow it. Nigel might think he could take the firm that way, but he could think again.

Although he was getting on in years and his short-term memory was fading, his long term was razor sharp. He knew the number he wanted off by heart. A few false starts, hitting the wrong numbers, but eventually he got it right. Thank God he'd insisted on a phone with a larger than average dialling pad, a must to a man who needed reading glasses. No other glasses though. He could see distances fine.

The phone rang for some time before Grace Pauling answered.

'Grace?'

'Arnold! How nice of you to call.'

He doubted that she thought it nice. He could almost hear her teeth grinding. He could also imagine the look of surprise on her heart shaped face. The moment she'd picked up the phone she would have begun combing her polished fingernails through her soft blonde hair instinctively knowing he was going to say something she didn't want to hear.

'Are you in your office?' he asked.

'I've been for coffee. I'm on my way . . .'

'Never mind. I need to see you. I want to amend my will. Call round. Pronto.'

CHAPTER THREE

Grace Pauling turned off the power on her mobile phone. She'd had coffee and now she was here to drink champagne at the expense of Bath Retailers' Association.

'Sorry,' she said, flashing a controlled smile to the people around her as she pushed her way through the crowd. She needed to be at the front where he could see her. She desperately needed to speak to him. The wheelchair helped. People always stood to one side to let a wheelchair through.

Nigel and the people presenting the prize were lined up ready for speeches and pictures in front of the winning display. Her mind lurched at the sight of it. It was quite exquisite, masculine but romantic. Head turning in fact. She wondered who had created it. Certainly not Nigel. He didn't have a creative bone in his body.

She threw him a meaningful look, one that would leave him in no doubt that she wanted to speak to him.

The Chairman of the Retailers' Association, Fred Baker, was standing in front of the shop window. His belly bulging over the waistband of his trousers. His jacket was dark red, his trousers brown. Nothing much matched about his clothes, but all the same she still couldn't help comparing him to a ringmaster in the circus ring.

A titled lady from Gloucester was to present the award, but he was the one making the introductory speech and obviously liked the sound of his own voice.

'When it comes to window displays, Bath is full of winners . . .' his voice ricocheted off the smooth facades of the buildings edging in the alley.

Grace Pauling wasn't really listening. She felt tense and worried. She knew what was in Mr Arnold Tern's will. Nigel had always been the main beneficiary. So was she. Plus . . . She didn't want to think of the other beneficiary. A scandal in the making if ever there was. Stupid old sod. That's what Arnold was, nothing but a stupid old sod!

Nigel Tern looked as though he were totally immersed in the proceedings, if the wide grin on his face was anything to go by.

Grace Pauling wondered what he intended doing with the prize money; probably taking one of his women on a jaunt to Italy. The thought of it brought a lump to her throat. Of course with luck he might ask her. 'All the same lying down, Grace darling,' he'd said one night when his ardour had got the better of him. He'd been drunk but seemingly serious, telling her it didn't matter that she was in a wheelchair . . . Somehow she didn't think he'd invite her, not this time, even though airlines and hotels catered for the disabled.

Grace glanced at her watch. She hoped the presentation wouldn't go on for much longer. A probate solicitor, she had work to do. Drawing up wills was a lucrative business. Her clients were well-heeled types who preferred someone else to do the donkey work. They were not the type to browse online do-it-yourself sites, thank God!

With regard to the Tern family, her ties were closer with them than most. Her father, Josiah, had been Arnold's partner. Both her parents were dead now but she still held an interest in the Tern family's holdings and the tailoring business in particular. She'd promised her father she would never sell it and she wouldn't, not whilst he was still alive and not whilst Arnold was still alive either.

She managed to catch Nigel's eye. She smiled. He smiled back. She gave him a little wave. He looked away. The corners of Grace's mouth downturned.

A reporter from the *Bath Chronicle* took notes and flashed off a few photographs.

The applause was accompanied by the sound of champagne corks. Drinks were firstly handed round to those who had taken part in the competition including the sponsors. A few glasses were left over for some of the onlookers.

Grace declined a glass of the champagne she'd previously been looking forward to, her eyes fixed on Nigel. Jealousy boiled up inside her coupled with a keenness to stay sharp, to taste the bitterness. She watched as he knocked back more than one glass, his face immediately turning a deep pink. She also noticed that he was leering at one of the judges, a female one of course.

She looked to be in her forties, slightly younger than Grace. Dark hair, dancing eyes and a cheery expression. She also poured the champagne without spilling a single bubble.

'Hmm. A steady hand I see,' Grace muttered with a deep scowl.

Her comment was overheard. 'If you're referring to the lady pouring the champagne,' said an onlooker, 'her name's Honey Driver. She owns the Green River Hotel.'

'Does she, now?'

OK, so the good-looking woman was a hotel owner, not a grand hotel but of reasonable size and good reputation. What she knew about the retail sector Grace couldn't imagine. How come she was one of the judges? *She knows somebody*, Grace confided to herself. She obviously knows somebody and they owe her a favour.

She had to concede that Honey Driver was an attractive name; an attractive name for an attractive woman. Nigel certainly seemed to find her pleasing to look at, hovering over her, chatting amicably whilst knocking back more champagne.

Grace gritted her teeth.

The woman was looking laughingly up into his eyes, her head held back, her swan-like neck exposed.

Grace couldn't bear it. She had to break this up and Nigel's father had given her a reason to do so. He wanted to change his will. Well that should puncture any thoughts of passion Nigel might have in mind!

She pushed on the rims of her wheels. The wheelchair shot forward.

'Nigel!'

Both Nigel and Honey looked down at the woman who had forcibly pushed her wheelchair between them.

* * *

Retrieving her toe from beneath a wheel, Honey said, 'Excuse me. Have you passed your test for driving that?'

The woman in the wheelchair blanked her out, her face upturned, eyes fixed on Nigel Tern.

'If you can bear to drag yourself away from your five minutes of fame, we need to talk.' Her tone was sharp and extremely businesslike.

Honey took a step back. 'I'd better leave you in peace . . .'

Nigel pulled her back. His breath and his attention was all over her.

'Look, I'm having a party tonight round at my place. Next door to the shop. If you're free . . .'

She held her breath against the smell of drink.

'Sorry. I've got a hotel to run.'

'Shame. Perhaps some other time. Dinner perhaps?' He was all avid attention. He was that sort, she could tell, desperate to impress, to make her another notch on his stick.

Honey was under no illusion that Nigel Tern would leap all over her given the chance. She'd responded politely enough, but hey, this was her professional self shining through!

'I'm sorry. Perhaps another time.'

She threw her smile at him first then at the woman in the wheelchair. The blonde-haired woman was too fixated on Nigel Tern to notice.

'I insist . . .'

His grip was quite strong despite the softness of his hands, the lack of calluses, the well-manicured fingernails.

She pulled her arm free, saying more firmly, 'I really do have to go now.'

'Perhaps I can call in? Have a coffee? Perhaps you can even give me the room rate for the night.'

As if she would.

The woman in the wheelchair showed her impatience. 'Nigel,' she said sharply. 'Your father phoned me.'

Nigel managed to tear his eyes away from Honey. 'He's recovered?'

Although Honey wasn't beyond hearing distance, the woman glowered and threw her a warning glance.

'You'll be disappointed to know that your father has recovered,' she said. 'That's the good news. The bad news is that he wants to change his will.'

That was about as much of the conversation Honey could catch. She found it intriguing but it was none of her business so she turned away.

'So what do you think of the winner,' asked a man with shoulder length hair and scruffy jeans.

'I'd take him to bed if I could,' she joked.

He laughed. 'He's made of plastic. Stiff but not real.'

Honey grimaced. 'I've known a lot of men like that.' She turned and strolled to the edge of the window.

'Any more of that champagne?' asked a familiar voice.

John Rees was leaning against the drainpipe of the property next door to the shop looking slightly bemused. He had not dressed up for the occasion preferring as usual to stick to casual denim, his beard untrimmed and his hair in need of cutting. Rough around the edges perhaps, but incredibly attractive.

Honey held up the bottle.

'Allow me.'

Champagne bounced and eddied as the glasses were filled, the bubbles dissipating within a centimetre of the rim.

'So what's the frown in aid of?' he asked her.

She looked back to where Nigel Tern was having what seemed a deep conversation with the woman in the wheelchair.

Top prize for intensity went to the woman in the wheelchair. She looked as though she might bury him beneath a stone slab if he didn't listen to what she was saying.

'Do you know that woman?' Honey jerked her chin towards the woman in the wheelchair.

John had a discreet way of looking over his shoulder, making it seem as though he was really looking deeply into her eyes.

'Do you see her?'

John said that he did.

'Who is she?'

'Grace Pauling. She's a lawyer.'

'Really? How do you know that?'

'I had a run-in with her once over some property I wanted to buy. She was acting for interested parties. My lawyer and I had a meeting with her. No clients. She refused to say who they were.'

'I see. Big shot property lawyer.'

John frowned. 'No. She's not. My lawyer informed me that she's actually a probate lawyer — you know — drawing up peoples' wills and stuff. She only works in other realms for favoured clients — friends and family, I guess.'

'She must have been a good-looking woman when she was younger,' Honey remarked, turning back to study the woman, seeing that her expression was no less intense than it was a few minutes ago.

John gave Grace Pauling a swift appraisal which was followed by a so-so shake of his head.

To Honey's mind that meant he was undecided.

'I guess she's OK, and I don't mean I'm put off by the wheelchair. What I do mean is that she's not a patch on present company.' His grin was enticing, as was the wicked wink that followed it up.

Seeing as Doherty was her numero uno, she deflected the conversation. Best to be safe than sorry. Or something like that.

'Do you know why she's in a wheelchair?'

'Riding accident when she was a kid, so I hear.'

He tipped his head to one side. Grace Pauling was going at Nigel Tern hammer and tongs.

'By the look of her she's got the tailor by the balls.'

Honey winced. 'Rather her than me.'

John's grin widened. 'Some guys get all the luck.'

* * *

Tramping round the streets of Bath could be downright tiring if you were determined to take in all the sights en route. Poor tourists, thought Honey, her feet aching merely by trudging around the shops to judge a window display competition.

Her daughter, Lindsey, long-term hotel resident Mary Jane and her mother were all sitting drinking coffee in the lounge at the Green River Hotel. On seeing her approach they poured an extra cup.

'Had a good time?' asked Lindsey.

Honey flopped into a chair. 'Can I categorically state here and now that said judge, Hannah Driver, known as Honey to her friends, had nothing to do with the chocolate display melting at The Chocolate Soldier, and ditto the chequered flag catching fire at Road Runners and Boy Racers — though I did stamp on the owner's foot.'

Gloria Cross, Honey's mother, and now having remarried was called Gloria Stewart, peered at her daughter.

'Does that have some significance?'

'It did to him. His shoes were very exceptional. Italian I think. If they weren't Italian they were Spanish.'

'Shame to spoil Italian shoes,' said her mother before taking a sip of her coffee. 'They are the very best. I presume you had good reason.'

'I didn't like him.'

'Obviously, but Hannah, you can't go round stamping on men's feet just because you don't like them.'

'I realise that. Still, I doubt I shall be seeing him again.' Lindsey was straight to the point.

'So tell us who won.'

'Tern and Pauling.'

Lindsey sat bolt upright. 'Really? I'm surprised. I mean, I am really SO surprised. I didn't even think they had a window display.'

'Well they do now.'

'I would have thought Road Runners and Boy Racers would have been in with a chance,' Lindsey mused. 'I saw their window yesterday. I thought it was good. So the manager wasn't friendly, then?'

Honey grimaced over the edge of her coffee cup.

'Oh no, he was *very* friendly. In fact each time I looked at him I kept imagining him in a posing pouch!' She shivered. 'That's enough to put anybody off! Not that I allowed my instinct to interfere with my judgement. I was fair and impartial all the way through.'

'I liked the highwayman best,' said Mary Jane with a heavy sigh. 'He reminds me of Sir Cedric.'

She went back to dunking her biscuit in her tea, her pronouncement over. Honey and her daughter exchanged knowing looks. Sir Cedric was dead. He'd been dead for close on two hundred years but Mary Jane reckoned she communicated with him on a regular basis. Sometimes he even drank tea in her bedroom, it being very convenient for him seeing as he appeared to live in the wardrobe. Lindsey was of the opinion she was in love with him.

'He's too old for her,' Honey had pointed out.

'All in all, quite an eventful day,' Honey murmured now, her thoughts turning to the fact that more than one man had invited her out or made it very clear that they fancied her. It was great to be fancied once you were in your forties. She'd honestly thought all that would have been over by now. What an idiot!

Hotel guests Mr and Mrs Boldman came wandering in with squashed expressions and drooping shoulders.

'Can we have coffee?' she asked her husband.

'Sure. We can get coffee here.'

They said it loudly, not exactly asking for coffee but just making it obvious that they wished to be waited on.

'They're not from California,' whispered Mary Jane, seemingly in an attempt to defend her home state from aspersions. 'I think they're from Vermont,' she added as though that explained everything. 'And guess what, they don't like it here because everything's so old.'

Gloria shrugged. 'So why did they come?'

'It's the thing to do,' said Mary Jane. 'Something to crow about when you next meet up with fellow members of the country club or whatever. They're the kind of people who embarrass me.'

Lindsey got to her feet. 'I'll get it.' She swooped down on their own tea tray.

Unwilling to converse with her fellow countrymen, Mary Jane huddled into her chair. It was an effort to make herself small which was very difficult to do. Mary Jane was very tall.

'I think they'll try and join us.'

She was wrong. Instead, they asked her to come over and join them.

'You don't have to go,' said Honey to Mary Jane who grimaced before politely declining the invitation and stating her intention to leave soon.

Gloria diverted Honey's attention. 'Would you like to come to a flower arranging party?' she asked.

She was tempted to say no, but on reflection decided it might be a good idea. The hotel could always be improved with the addition of a large bouquet in a pretty pot or vase.

She nodded. 'Let me know the when and where.'

'I will.'

As they passed the couple from Vermont, the woman leant forward eagerly. 'Are you English?' she asked.

'Definitely,' said Honey. Her mother and daughter echoed their status; yes, they were English too.

Anyone with eyes to see — especially female eyes — would regard Mrs Boldman as a blonde bimbo — her husband certainly hadn't married her for her brains. Her boobs however must have cost him a fortune!

Before apprehending them, it appeared Mr Boldman had been doing his best to persuade his wife that loud criticisms should be kept to a minimum – and spoken more quietly. He returned to his line of argument as soon as Honey had confirmed her nationality, saying, 'Look, sweetheart, I was only saying that you should be more tactful . . .' His wife stared at him blankly. Honey guessed she didn't know what the word tactful meant and certainly didn't know how to spell it.

'Chorley, honey, I'm just little old me . . .' simpered the blonde wife.

The tone was sickly. Honey felt like throwing up. OK, she looked at least half his age, but she was no teenager. She'd probably had a face lift or two.

'Chorley,' she said again, 'honey pie. I've just one question for these people and seeing as they're English I'm sure they'll tell me how things hang around here.'

Honey gulped. How things *hang*? What was the woman talking about?

'Sweetie . . .' began the husband.

Sweetie ignored her honey pie. 'All I wanted to know was what possessed your royal family to build Windsor Castle so close to Heathrow Airport. It must be a nightmare.'

Grandmother, mother, daughter and Mary Jane headed for the door without answering. Mary Jane looked as though she'd swallowed a wasp, eyes bulging, mouth firmly closed. Gloria looked long suffering. Honey and Lindsey were almost choking, only just about managing to keep the laughter at bay until they'd made it to the hotel reception.

Once there, Mary Jane offered them cakes and coffee in her room. 'Although I do have something stronger. Armagnac I think. Cedric recommended it.'

There was something oddly reassuring about a ghost who recommended French brandy. Lindsey commented that Sir Cedric must have had it smuggled in from France seeing as there was an ongoing war on the continent when he was alive.

Honey thought that indeed Sir Cedric did spend a great deal of time in Mary Jane's room, he must have felt very much at home. He'd definitely feel at home with the furniture, bits and pieces that Mary Jane had added to the basic reproduction Regency style already in situ.

Honey's mother sniffed the air. 'It smells lovely in here.'

Lindsey sniffed too. 'Jasmine.'

Only Honey disagreed. 'Brandy.' Her nose WAS in the glass at the time.

'Mr Boldman owns a chain of department stores,' Mary Jane pronounced. 'Candy is wife number five.'

Lindsey, who was cradling her drink with both hands, shrugged. 'What's the point of getting married?'

'He gets her and she gets his money,' Honey pronounced. 'Things wouldn't be so cut and dried if they were merely lovers.'

'I've known lots of men like him.' Gloria pronounced grimly. 'Their brain in their pants. And they spend a fortune on Viagra!'

'Well that's guaranteed to make the heart beat faster!' Mary Jane proclaimed.

'Sure,' muttered Honey. 'All the way to the grave!'

On leaving Mary Jane's room Honey decided to check if there was any dust on the windowsills and on the table in front of the arched window. The cleaners sometimes forgot or would do if they thought she didn't check.

There was no sound from behind the closed doors of the rooms along the landing. Honey wondered at the quietness of it all. She was totally alone. Nothing was untoward except for the unexpected scent of jasmine. She looked for any flower displays that she might have forgotten about. There were none.

She stood a moment in front of the arched window at the end of the landing and sniffed. The smell was stronger here. Probably Candy Boldman had wafted along here earlier, she thought. That was before she reminded herself that Candy wore some pretty tangy fragrances, nothing as delicate as jasmine.

The smell was no more by the time she got to the head of the stairs where she paused and looked over her shoulder. She thought she saw the curtains at the arched window move, a gold tassel swing, the threads catching the light.

Just a draught of course. The old place was full of draughts. Still, the smell of jasmine was a little unnerving.

CHAPTER FOUR

It was five thirty in the morning when Charlie York pushed his street cleaning trolley into Beaumont Alley. Daylight was drifting in like a lifting fog and if you happened to believe in that sort of thing, you could almost believe there were ghosts peering from the parapets and windows of the ancient houses.

Charlie wouldn't have noticed if a raving banshee was hanging from the windows. He was whistling along to Sounds of the Eighties on his iPod, a present from his daughter last Christmas. He'd downloaded the compilation of the music of his youth from a word-of-mouth pirate source.

Not wishing to disturb anyone, he whistled less vigorously once he was in the heart of Beaumont Alley. Because Beaumont Alley was a block entrance, sounds — any sounds — ricocheted off the Georgian buildings. The five storey buildings rose like sheer rock faces to either side of him forming a blank wall on either side. At the far end they curved round to form a cul-de-sac.

A strip of sky overhead more or less matched the size of the paved ground beneath his feet. He pushed his broom to the beat of the music, short sweeps in time with the backing tempo, a long sweeping action matching a held note or a strung-out finale. He hummed instead of whistling, puffing between snatches of tune with the effort of sweeping and humming at the same time.

Beaumont Alley had more than its fair share of rubbish this morning, most of it tucked into the gutter, but quite a pile outside Pauling and Tern.

He hadn't read the *Bath Chronicle* yesterday, so knew nothing about the celebration in Beaumont Alley. He grumbled to himself about the extra mess, but hey, Bath was a city worth keeping clean.

His spirits were suddenly lifted by the next track on his iPod. Music kept him moving. Sometimes the work he did made him feel old; old and tired. He'd held this job down for some years now, never complaining about getting up early and walking miles to keep the city clean but of late he'd been feeling more weary.

'I should be thinking about retiring,' he muttered. He couldn't do that just yet. His pension pot just wouldn't be enough.

His thoughts were suddenly shafted, exploded like fireworks on Guy Fawkes Night. His favourite music exploded into his ears.

Adam Ant was singing the eighties hit, 'Stand and Deliver'. They'd been one of the New Punk bands back in the early eighties, a bit girly compared to some, he thought, but he'd liked them a lot.

He'd been a young man back then and a keen follower of the punk scene. The beat flooded his mind, taking him back to a time when he'd had no wife, no daughter, no rent to pay, no car to get road-taxed before he got nicked by the police. None of it mattered once Adam Ant was playing.

'Yeah,' he breathed. 'Adam is back!'

Adam and the Ants had been labelled romantic, more to do with their dramatic appearance than their music. The lead singer had looked and dressed a bit like Johnnie Depp playing Jack Sparrow in *Pirates of the Caribbean*. His dark, unruly hair had been slicked back into a thin ponytail, eyes lined with black make-up and colourful stripes across his face. He'd worn an old-fashioned military style coat with brass buttons and braiding, a silk sash around his slender waist and another around his arm. His britches were usually satin or velvet, his leather boots had reached high over his knees — just like a real highwayman.

Back in the day, the girls had gone wild over Adam Ant and on that count alone Charlie would have copied the look if he'd had the money. Trouble was he'd never had the money back then in his youth. As for wearing that kind of stuff now; he chuckled to himself.

His overalls were baggy, his coat was grubby and his steel toe-capped boots were killing him.

Bloody Health and Safety people and their rules and regulations; it wasn't them that had to tramp over the pavements for six or seven hours a day.

As the music took him the trials and tribulations of working for Bath and North East Somerset flew from his head. This morning nothing of that mattered.

Legs spread, shoulders back, he heaved his broom to waist level.

To an onlooker it was still a broom. To him it was a Fender Stratocaster and he was strumming it.

Eyes half closed and pursing his lips, similar but not quite like Adam, he strutted his way further into the alley, echoing every note with the movement of his fingers.

In his mind he was no longer Charlie York, a sanitation operative — posh speak for street sweeper — wearing big boots and scruffy working clothes. He was snake-hipped eye candy to all those screaming young girls out there. He could see their hands, fingers splayed as they attempted to touch him, to feel the magic and the body of their pop idol.

When he came to, he found himself standing in the gutter outside Pauling and Tern. The hand that had mimicked the final flourish was still raised above his head.

As his half-closed eyes slowly reopened, the smile of satisfaction fell from his lips.

If he'd been drunk or high on drugs, he might have thought his dream had become reality. But Charlie hadn't indulged in none of that stuff, not back then and not now. Still, he couldn't help questioning whether he'd had too many beers last night.

'What the bloody hell . . .'

The guitar returned to being a broom as he blinked to get a hold on what he was seeing. He paused, took a few steps closer. Then stepped back.

'Bloody hell! Adam!'

Still considerate of the neighbours, he'd kept his voice down. His eyes felt as though they were bulging out of his head. Adam Ant was in the window! Adam Ant!

But, no. He couldn't be.

He pulled his earphones out and silenced the iPod.

The scene before him held his gaze, his eyes growing rounder as he took in all its details — including the other body hanging from a noose just behind the highwayman's head.

'Bloody hell!' he exclaimed, and phoned the police.

CHAPTER FIVE

The atmosphere in Bonhams' Auction Rooms was tense. Good stuff was going under the hammer at more than reasonable prices. There were not so many people bidding as there should be. Some blamed the fact that Bath rugby team were playing a tense match in France. Half the city had gone with them, or at least that was the way it seemed. Whichever way the match went, the wine in France would be flowing. There were plenty in the auction room who wished them all good luck. They wished themselves good luck too. The low prices kept rolling on!

Honey Driver had done pretty well so far, but there was one more lot to go. She was on a high. One nice corset bought and another in the offing. Her hand was in rocket mode, ready to shoot up when the time was right.

Then Doherty phoned. She thought about ignoring it but she never could resist him.

'Honey.'

'Doherty. Steve. How do you fancy a Victorian corset?'

'Not my style.'

'It might grow on you.'

He chuckled. 'Only if you were wearing it.'

She smiled into the phone. 'Something up?'

Doherty had a distinct tone when he had something serious on his mind, differing from when he was being playful, romantic or simply tired out.

'I understand you were involved with this window display competition.'

Her attention on what was happening in the auction room was diverted. 'I was one of the judges. Somebody suggesting bribery and corruption?'

'Worse than that. One of the window displays has seen some live action — or rather dead action depending on how you view it. There's a dead body swinging on a rope behind Dick Turpin.'

Honey sucked in her breath.

'The highwayman! The one in the window of Pauling and Tern?'

'Right. Bespoke tailors. Expensive tailors. I certainly couldn't afford a sports jacket from there — if I should ever want one that is.'

Honey couldn't visualise Doherty in a sports jacket. Leather jacket, yes. It was almost easier to visualise a man hanging from a noose behind the highwayman, though far more shocking of course.

'Who is it?'

'Nigel Tern, the proprietor. Do you know him?'

'Not really. I only met him at the presentation.'

'First impressions?'

'He was coming on strong. I declined his various offers.'

Nigel Tern had not appealed to her at all, but there were bound to be women who he did appeal to. She expressed her opinion to Doherty.

'An ageing Romeo; well that's something to bear in mind.' His tone was caustic.

'So you're interviewing all the judges, including moi?' she asked, ignoring him. 'Anyone else?'

'The street cleaner who discovered the body. I'm also currently interviewing the staff. The, um, highwayman is not a suspect.'

'Why hang somebody in full public view? It's pretty obvious it won't take long to be discovered.'

'I know where you're coming from. But I think that's the point. Most killers go out of their way to hide their victim.'

'Unless they're your standard weirdo who feels he has to make some kind of statement.'

'I agree. The victim was hanging in full public view, though nobody noticed it until about five thirty this morning when the body was spotted by a passing street cleaner. You attended the presentation for best window display yesterday along with the other judges?'

'That's right. All three judges were invited. I didn't end up meeting them though.'

'We've got the names of the other judges. We'll be interviewing them too.'

Had John Rees been one of them? She didn't like to ask. Doherty ground his teeth whenever John was mentioned. He tried not to — that's how she knew he loved her.

'Can you tell me who they were?'

'In time. It sounds as though a good time was had by all. I understand John Rees was there.'

There it was; John Rees, her second choice if ever her relationship with Doherty floundered — though she was sure it never would.

'I told you I was doing it and did ask if you wanted to come but you were otherwise engaged.'

'Yeah,' Doherty replied sullenly. 'I was. Chief Inspector's orders. I was required to attend a talk by somebody from the unsolved crime unit about bonding with other agencies in order to better coordinate historical information.'

He didn't sound impressed, the statement delivered in a dull monotone.

'Shame. You would have enjoyed it. We drank champagne.'

'Really? We had tea and biscuits.'

'I take it they weren't chocolate digestives.'

'There were some, but I was late arriving. Some numpty clamped my car.'

'Whoops.' He paused before another comment came. 'So the highwayman won. I'm guessing you were swayed by the tight-fitting britches.'

'And the mask,' she quipped. 'If I'd been wearing one of those tightly corseted dresses from the eighteenth century my bosom would have heaved and then I would have swooned.'

'Don't do it just yet. You're a witness. I need to speak to you.'

'I dare say you do.'

Her attention hovered between what he was saying and what was happening at the auction. She had already won an all-in-one corset and brassiere from the forties, the kind that used to be called a 'corselet'. Now she was after another one, not really for her collection, but to wear. It was amazing what an old-fashioned corset did for the figure. Reinforced with elastic and sliver thin strips of metal, it smoothed lumpy bits and added shape where none existed. This one was made of satin and the bidding had reached forty-five pounds. She dropped her hand, surprised at herself for not yet asking the obvious question.

'So, any leads so far?'

'No. No obvious enemies, though rumour has it that he didn't get along with his father. And from what you say, and from other sources, there could be a few scorned women in the background. We'll have to check.'

'He asked me to a party to celebrate his winning, but I had to decline due to a previous engagement. Anyway, I didn't like him much.'

'You didn't mention him asking you.'

'What would be the point? I declined.'

'Of course you did.'

Honey recalled that Nigel hadn't seemed that upset that she'd turned him down. Not surprising. He'd struck her as the sort of man who keeps a little black book. She mentioned this to Doherty.

'I wouldn't be surprised if he also gave them marks out of ten. A low score can upset people,' she added. It wasn't just

Nigel Tern she was thinking of. She wondered about retailers unimpressed because they hadn't won.

'Your comments, though ever so slightly cynical, have helped. Anyway, somebody didn't like him. I need to speak to everyone who was at the presentation and also those who attended the party later. I understand they held it at the Cricketers Wine Bar.'

Honey wrinkled her nose. 'In that case I'm glad I didn't go.'

The Cricketers had a very modern décor that seemed to have little to do with cricket. Not that she minded that. She'd only ever been to one cricket match which she equated with watching paint dry.

'Apparently a fight ensued following a drunken disagreement.' He sighed heavily. She could imagine him grimacing at the prospect of a long day.

'Sounds like you're going to need cheering up when I see you.'

'Say something naughty.' He sounded only slightly better.

'I'm in a public place,' she hissed down the phone, turning away as far as she could from the people around her.

'Just hint at something.'

Honey was good at thinking on her feet, a skill acquired swiftly if you were to survive in the hospitality trade.

'OK. I'm bidding for a corselet. It's got suspenders and it's made of white satin. Very 1940s. I'm going to wear it. With stockings.'

His sigh whooshed down the phone. 'I feel better already.'

Once they'd discussed his schedule, Honey promised she'd be along to Manvers Street Police Station at two o'clock. The other judges were being interviewed around the same time.

Once she hung up, she craned her neck, looking around the auction room in an effort to work out where the bidding had got to and whether she had won the second item.

It was hard to get the vision of a hanged man out of her mind. She knew the background of the window display had something to do with it; lots of darkness. Lots of drama.

Her thoughts were interrupted by the auction house cashier, Alistair, a big red-headed Scotsman with a large beard and broad.

'I noticed you were on the phone, hen,' he called. 'I kept an eye on the bidding for you and bid on your behalf. Fifty pounds plus the usual fees and VAT all right with you?'

'Fifty!' She couldn't help sounding surprised. She'd fully expected the second corselet to reach one hundred, the same as she'd paid for the first one. 'Thanks a bundle, Alistair. I fully expected to pay more. Can I collect it now?'

'You can indeed. Robin's brought it over. I said I suspected you might be shooting off shortly on police matters. I saw you take a phone call and, based on your serious expression, made an assumption.'

She eyed him sceptically. 'Oh come on. A phone call's a phone call. You know something. News through the grapevine?' News in Bath travelled quickly. Sometimes she was almost sure she could hear the jungle drums.

'No, hen. BBC Bristol. They said a bloke's been found hanged in a shop window in Bath. No details other than that but I guessed where it happened.'

Honey pursed her lips. 'Quite an exit.'

'Makes me think he was taking the final curtain call.'

'You saw the window display?'

He nodded his big red head. 'I did. Did you know Dick Turpin never rode to London in the time they say he did. He'd have needed to take the one fifteen from Kings' Cross to get there in that short a time.'

Honey smiled. If anyone was likely to put things into perspective it was Alistair. He spoke solemnly but with humour. He was also a mine of information.

'Did you know the dead man?' She asked as she paid for and signed for collection of her purchases. It was always worthwhile asking Alistair if he knew someone or knew someone who had known that someone. Alistair had his finger on the more obscure happenings in Bath besides the wickedest rumours.

'Not really. I do wear sports jackets, though, but ones that I've had for years.'

He also seemed to know who bought what and where. People who attended auctions were a community unto themselves and as fond of salacious gossip as anyone.

'No gossip about him? Nigel?'

She eyed him from beneath her fringe. If there were any rumours abounding, they no doubt would have come to Alistair's bushy ears.

He looked disappointed, his equally bushy eyebrows meeting above his nose like two hairy red-headed caterpillars.

'It behoves me to admit that I have never heard anything of a criminal nature about the man.'

'He did invite me to a party and out to dinner if I couldn't make the party.'

'There's no mileage in that on the gossip front — unless it's salacious you're talking about.'

Honey raised her eyebrows. 'Was there gossip of a salacious nature?'

'Oh well . . .' Alistair made a moue shape with his mouth as he expelled a breath of air.

'Apparently he was a bit of a ladies' man and not just that; he liked to indulge himself. Lap dancing clubs, pole-dancing clubs, strip clubs — a bit of a champagne Charlie.'

Honey was well satisfied that gossip in the city agreed with her analysis of the man.

'With a view to maintaining your modesty, I've wrapped up your foundation garments. Wouldn't want all and sundry knowing what you're going to be wearing under your best frock do we now?' He grinned.

'I'm only considering wearing one of them. The other's for my collection.' She was about to leave, but she had a question ripe for asking.

'How did you know I was going to wear one of them?'

He shrugged, still smiling. 'Let's just say I know your taste.'

She was about to go when another question leapt out of her mouth.

'Am I ever the subject of gossip?'

The grin broadened, spread in amongst all that facial hair.

'I couldn't possibly comment — except to say that there'll be a queue forming if ever you and the policeman fall out.'

Honey felt herself blushing with pleasure. 'How big of a queue?'

He tapped the side of his nose. 'That's for me to know.'

She was going to add, 'and for me to find out,' but stopped herself. She would only know who was in the queue for her affection if she and Doherty broke up. She could see no chance of that happening and neither did she want it to.

Corsets tucked under her arm, Honey made her way back to the Green River Hotel. The news of the murder had come as something of a shock. A whole load of questions and possibilities were spinning around her mind. Why had he been killed? What was the point of leaving him hanging in a window? How many women had he pursued and conquered, and how many of them had he jettisoned? How many of those he'd spurned wanted to kill him?

She stormed on through the crowds of shoppers and sightseers. Many of them staring at the elaborate shop window. The Chocolate Soldier appeared to be doing very well; the owner-come-manager was outside among a group of tourists and a few children who she thought should have been at school.

Alan Roper was everyone's idea of Santa Claus; he had the white hair, the beard and twinkling eyes. He also had not seen his toes for a long time thanks to his rotund belly.

He was laughing and joking with everyone, pointing out the finer points of his window display.

Honey caught his eye.

'How's the drawbridge?'

His cheery disposition vanished at the sight of her.

'You were one of the judges.'

'That's right. I much admired your window display.'

'It didn't win,' he snapped.

She attempted to reassure him. 'It was very close.'

The glum expression was unaltered. 'But not close enough to win.'

Honey glanced at the crowd milling around the window display.

'Well you appear to be doing very well despite not winning.'

'Five thousand pounds would have been very useful,' he grumbled. 'Have you any idea of the business rates this building attracts, and that's besides the lease and the rent . . .'

He went grumbling on. Honey would have left then and there, but she had to know whether he'd heard about Nigel Tern.

'Did you know the owner of the winning shop is dead. Found hung in his own shop window.'

'Oh dear. I am sad!'

It was obvious from his tone that Alan Roper was being sarcastic.

'I'm surprised at your tone, Mr Roper. Whether you liked Nigel Tern or not, I think it insensitive that you're taking that attitude just because he won the competition.'

A pair of pale blue eyes glared at her. 'Is that what you think, that my attitude is coloured purely by him winning the competition?'

'Isn't it?'

'Damned right it's not!'

At his raised voice, a number of parents covered their children's ears. The kids grinned. This all looked like fun to them.

Although Alan's attitude was a little intimidating, Honey stood her ground. 'Do you mind enlightening me?'

The midsummer replica of Santa Claus spouted some very dubious swear words under his breath. The parents who had heard guided their kids away, their ears still covered with protective hands from his profanity. Howls of protest followed of course, but The Chocolate Soldier wasn't the only chocolate shop in town. However, it was the only one with a very fetching window display.

Alan narrowed his eyes and thrust his white beard in her direction.

'You ever heard of Rachman?'

Honey conceded that she had. 'He was a racketeering landlord years ago.'

'That's right! And the word Rachman became synonymous with property racketeering. Well, in Bath, Tern is the name synonymous with rip-off rents and leases. Tern doesn't just depend on his tailoring shop to make a living. Don't think that. He owns and rents out property. A lot of property!'

CHAPTER SIX

Honey's news that Nigel Tern was active in the property market as well as chasing women, was received with interest. Doherty promised to look into it.

Alan Roper's bitterness that he hadn't won the window display competition should not have come as a surprise either. She had been warned about poor losers. What had surprised her more was that a man who looked like Santa Claus could react like that. The image and the attitude just didn't match.

On reflection she was more than pleased that Julian Cunningham had been hit out of the running because a portion of his display had gone up in flames. Had it been an accident or sabotage? She hadn't considered the latter possibility at all up until now. And how about the drawbridge on the chocolate castle? Had somebody fiddled with that?

She made a note to ask the other retailers a few pertinent questions, like how many had encountered problems with their displays. It was very likely they would all have suspicions, purely because they hadn't won.

'Thank goodness,' she said to herself coming to a halt at the corner of Pulteney Street and Abigail Square.

The comment came spontaneously and made her feel somewhat relieved that she wasn't a shop owner. Being involved in the hospitality game wasn't the be all and end all, but at least she didn't have hang-ups about window displays; neither did she have to pay rent and her property was free-hold not leasehold; the latter she knew could be a minefield.

She stopped to breathe a deep sigh at the same time surveying the hotel she owned as though for the first time. It always felt like the first time when she did that. She loved the building so much.

The Green River Hotel dated from the eighteenth century and was four storeys high. It had a classical frontage complete with large windows gleaming from beneath carved pediments. The double doors were set back into a broad alcove flanked by Dorian pillars and the pillars were not original but found in a local reclamation yard by a previous owner and cemented firmly in place. Nobody had attempted to remove them and they did look as though they belonged. In fact Honey reckoned they garnished the building with an elegant grandeur. No doubt her hotel guest, Candy Boldman, would take the lot down, but then she was the sort to demolish the whole building replacing it with something made of blue glass and stainless steel.

However, something was missing. Nigel Tern had been murdered. Doherty had been in touch. But there was one person who had not as yet phoned her.

She ran her gaze along each set of windows as she waited for the call she knew would come. He was late. She counted to ten and reached number eight when it rang.

'Honey. I cannot believe this has happened and in the shop window of a very well respected gentlemen's outfitters. What is the world coming to!'

Chairman of Bath Hotels Association, Caspar St John Gervais was playing catch-up and sounded positively outraged.

The last comment was a statement not a question; Caspar was always appalled when a heinous crime was committed, more specifically when it was committed in Bath. He didn't much care if it happened anywhere else.

Lindsey had described him as being like a medieval lord overseeing his domain and protesting loudly when the serfs ran amok. Honey conceded that he had a point. 'It is a World Heritage site after all. And we have kind of cultured murders; the sort that used to be solved in a drawing room by amateur sleuths with names such as Hercule and Jane.'

Honey also conceded that Lindsey was right. Caspar fitted the picture. 'And he'd look OK in tights,' she'd added. 'Not so sure about chain mail and armour though.'

Honey was of the opinion he'd look better in flannels, a striped blazer and a straw boater — a 1920s gentleman at large and very at home in a drawing room.

But musing on Caspar's characteristics was not going to get anything done. She had a job to do. She was the Hotels Association Crime Liaison Officer and Caspar deserved to be kept informed.

'Yes, Caspar, it really is quite terrible and on this occasion, I feel very uneasy seeing as I was one of the judges.'

'Oh dear. I myself declined the invitation. Shopkeepers can be SO competitive!'

Honey did not voice the thought that hoteliers could also be pretty competitive.

'Exactly,' said Honey at the same time recalling that she'd been invited because of her affiliations with the police force.

'Do the police perceive that you know something?' asked Caspar in his most imperious voice.

Honey chewed her lip before answering. 'Perceive' was a definite Caspar word, much preferred over the more common or garden term of 'think'.

'I'm not sure, but I have to make a statement. I've an interview with the police at two this afternoon.'

'Are there any suspects yet?'

'Not as far as I know. I'll know more later. There are ongoing interviews of the staff, people who attended the presentation and the party at the Cricketers later, especially the latter. I understand there was a bit of a fracas and the police were called.'

The rumour mill had been rife with speculation and Honey's sources were only too happy to share their suspicions.

A stony silence ensued on the other end of the phone.

'I attended the party at the Cricketers.' His tone was sombre.

'Oh.' She paused. 'Of course you did.'

She should have known. Caspar was quite a gadfly when it came to parties celebrating something likely to make headlines in the newspaper, even if only the *Bath Chronicle*. If it made the nationals or some up market magazine's social gossip column, so much the better.

'Do you know what the disturbance was about?' she asked him.

'I would not bend so low as to fraternise with the more violent element of the clientele. Two shopkeepers who were bad losers I shouldn't wonder!'

'And you don't know who they were?'

'No,' he said with an air of finality. 'I left early.'

Obviously he didn't want to know. They were only shopkeepers after all. If they'd been titled or highly placed in the judiciary or the military, it might have been another matter.

'Pauling and Tern have a very upmarket client list,' he said suddenly, his voice full of concern. 'I will trust you to be discreet.'

'Were you a client of theirs?'

'They are exquisite tailors — or were. I haven't graced their doors since Mr Tern Senior, Mr Arnold Tern, retired and his son took over.'

'Oh, really?'

Honey detected a disdainful sniff before Caspar continued.

'I wasn't sure of the ongoing quality,' he said finally. 'I did hear rumours that Tern Junior wanted to make the business more accessible to the general public — people with money and no status. They are suppliers to royalty you know.'

It never failed to amaze Honey that Caspar had survived into the modern age, seemingly unaware that the world of class and titled gentry was near-extinguished. He was quite astute on the political correctness front however, because he ran a business; La Reine Rouge Hotel where guests of every persuasion, class and nationality slept enjoyed his elegant rooms and old-fashioned courtesy.

The fact that Nigel Tern owned a lot of property stayed with her. Was he a good landlord? Or not, in which case how many tenants, she wondered, had often threatened to do away with him. Still, that was Doherty's remit. In the meantime Caspar seemed the man to ask about the tailoring business.

'How long since Nigel Tern took over the business?' she asked.

'I can't be sure, but I think it is about two years. Mr Tern Senior had a stroke, I believe and is virtually bedridden. I don't know where he lives and what his other circumstances are. We didn't move in the same circles.'

'You didn't socialise with him.'

'I don't think Mr Tern socialised full stop. He was a very private man. In fact the only time we ever met was in the shop.'

'And his son?'

'I last met him with regard to furnishing me with a new evening suit. He asked how I felt about off the peg. I told him I had no knowledge or feeling for off the peg except for that I wouldn't be seen dead in it!'

She closed the call after promising Caspar that she would get back to him when anything substantial developed, i.e. the arrest of the perpetrator.

'Back to work,' she muttered as she slid the phone into her bag whilst getting a firmer grip on the corsets she carried under her arm.

She took another in-depth look at the edifice of the building she owned, relishing the balance it gave her between the solid and the sordid. If she'd been able to take another look at the shop window display at Pauling and Tern, she would have done. But that would no longer be possible. The whole area outside the shop would be cordoned off with police and fluttering incident tape. She hadn't known Nigel Tern but couldn't put his shop out of her head, especially that highwayman who had appealed to the dramatic side of her nature.

Never mind, Honey, she said to herself. Leave the problem at the door and go home. Put your feet up. Pour yourself a glass of something nice. She wondered if Mary Jane had any Armagnac left. Good thought.

Her gaze swept the windows of the hotel, from floor to floor. All the rooms would be cleaned by now, beds changed, carpets vacuumed, loo paper replaced. A taxi drew up outside the main door and two people got out, the boot was opened up, suitcases retrieved and taken inside.

The arched window above the front door suddenly caught her attention. A woman who looked as though she were wearing a nightdress, was looking out, staring across to the buildings on the other side of the road. Her arms were outstretched as though she were about to crash through the glass and fly.

Honey's breath caught in her throat. The arched window had a low sill and was situated on the second landing . . .

Oh my God! The woman was going to jump!

Racing into reception, she flung the corsets onto the reception desk and dashed up the stairs shouting at Lindsey to send Smudger the chef up to the second landing — pronto!

It must have been the tone of her voice, but Lindsey didn't hesitate.

The flight of stairs to the first landing was tough enough; the second flight to the second landing where the arched window looked over the street left her puffing and panting.

She leaned against the wall, the eggshell blue of the walls blindingly bright. A blue and white vase — suitably Chinese-looking — sat on the low sill of the window. It was large and had been put there to stop people clambering up onto the sill to look out of the window.

There was no one on the landing, certainly no night-dress-clad woman.

'What is it?' Smudger, pink in the face, probably because he'd taken two stairs at a time, appeared behind her.

Honey turned, sheepish. 'I was out in the street. I looked up and thought I saw somebody about to throw themselves out of the window.'

Smudger looked around, unfazed.

'Nobody here now.'

'No. I was mistaken,' she said uncertainly. 'It must have been the vase.'

'Or an unsettled spirit,' said Smudger with a chuckle.

She refused to respond to his wicked grin, disconcerted. She was sure she hadn't imagined it.

He stood there regarding her, stiffly white in newly laundered and starched chef's gear. 'You OK?'

She nodded. 'OK.'

'Right,' he said already turning to go back downstairs. 'Then I'm back to my *coq au vin*. No more hysterics please. It affects my creativity.'

'I promise. It must be this murder playing on my mind.'

Or the smell of jasmine in Mary Jane's room. And here. On the landing. It was back. She shook her head; she'd keep her thoughts to herself.

'Do you want me to mention it to Mary Jane?' Smudger asked, turning back to look at her.

Honey considered his suggestion to tell her permanent resident, professor of the paranormal and a fashion disaster on legs who believed she shared her room with a long dead relative. Finally she shook her head. 'No. I don't think so. I was mistaken. Anyway, one ghost in this hotel is quite enough to cope with.'

CHAPTER SEVEN

Honey was due to be interviewed at two on the dot. Accordingly, she glided in having attired herself in blue jeans and a black sweater for the occasion. Doherty wouldn't expect her to dress up.

'Am I the first?' she asked.

'First what?' replied the sergeant in reception.

'The first of the people who judged the window display competition.'

The sergeant shook his head. 'You've just missed the first. The other is due in at four.'

'Do you have their names? You know, just so I can . . .'

'I don't think the guv'nor would appreciate you fraternising with other witnesses, Mrs Driver. You know how he is.'

She sighed. Yes, she knew how he was. She knew things about him that nobody in the police force knew. Personal things. The fact that he snored when he lay on his back asleep, that his right hand fidgeted with his left ear, one arm thrown across his chest.

The object of both her affection and mid-dream fantasy awaited her in an interview room and hugged her before offering her a seat.

'Coffee?'

'No. I'm all coffeed up!'

He sat down casually, leaning forward, hands clasped, elbows on desk. The desk was old and made of wood. He had been scheduled to have a brand new metal one with a leather top, but had strongly resisted. He liked the old wooden one. It had scratches and dents which only added to its character — just like him.

'So,' he began. 'Tell me all about it.'

Honey leaned back in her chair, the heel of her right foot resting on her left knee.

'I was asked to judge a window display competition.'

'Did you think that unusual?'

Honey gave it her considered thought. She'd wondered herself why she'd been asked but the reasons the organisers gave seemed logical enough.

'No. Not really. I mean, I'm a woman. I window-shop. Who better to know a good display when I see one.'

She was repeating what Lee had said to her. It seemed a good enough reason. She did not mention his comments about her familiarity with the local police force.

'And you saw Nigel Tern?'

'I did.'

'Is that the first time you've ever met?'

'Yes, I think so.'

'When was the last time you saw the display at Tern and Pauling?'

'When the presentation was made; the judging happened before lunch, the presentation was done in the afternoon.'

'Was there anyone there who looked suspicious?'

Honey threw him a wry look. 'No. Not that I can remember.'

'Any obvious animosity towards Mr Tern?'

'I did keep a lookout for any sore losers, but there didn't seem to be any likely to take their grievances to the next level. In my opinion the only time animosity raises its head at such events is when the champagne runs out.'

A flicker of a smile lifted Docherty's mouth. 'And it didn't?'

'No. There was plenty enough for the judges, the well-wishers and the rest of the crowd.' Her thoughts went back to the tension she'd seen between Nigel Tern and the woman in the wheelchair. Although unsure of its significance, she decided to mention it.

'I did notice that Mr Tern and a woman seemed to be having a moment.'

'Really?'

'She wore a tight expression, not a hint of a smile. Nigel maintained a grim smile as though he were doing his best to look as though what she was saying to him was of no consequence. Nothing but tightness between them!'

'And you thought whatever was being said might be of some consequence?'

'Of consequence, yes, I did. Judging by his expression, he didn't much like what she was saying to him.'

'But you didn't hear what was being said.'

'No. I did not. All I was sure of was that it was not well received.'

'So you know who the woman was?'

'Yes. Grace Pauling. I understand she's the family lawyer — besides being the daughter of Mr Arnold Tern's deceased partner.'

Doherty ran his fingers over his pursed lips. Honey heard the familiar purr of three-day stubble. Steve hated shaving. And she hated him doing it. Stubble suited him. So would tight britches. And a mask and knee-length boots.

'I'm off to ask Mr Charles York a few more questions,' he said, interrupting her fantasy. 'He's the road sweeper who found the body. Care to accompany me?'

CHAPTER EIGHT

It was the smell of Charlie York's flat that reminded Detective Inspector Steve Doherty that he hadn't got round to washing the dishes this morning.

Honey noticed his hesitance. 'Anything wrong?'

He smiled at her. 'I was thinking of last night.'

The night before he'd tossed a salad, sprinkled it with Parmesan plus garlic-flavoured oil and set it in the centre of the table. Smoked salmon had been on the menu, Scottish of course. Norwegian was too salty. Butter, Gorgonzola and chunks of crusty farmhouse bread had been added plus a bottle of Italian D'Avola. Honey had stayed until late, an hour or two on the rug together, then a taxi back to the Green River Hotel.

Charlie York hadn't washed up either, though the smell was stronger so it was likely than more than a day or two had passed since he'd done so. One sniff and she perceived the prime suspects as being fried bacon, Cumberland sausages, eggs, fried bread and baked beans. They already knew that Charlie's wife had passed away some time ago and understood how it must be for the man, but still, although food smells were pleasant enough when fresh the smell became stale after a few hours.

However, Doherty, Honey knew, had been in enough stinks in his life to have perfected the skill of half closing his nostrils and taking shallow breaths.

Charlie showed them into his living room, moving a few days' worth of newspapers to give them room to sit down.

'It must have been quite a shock for you,' Doherty said once they'd declined a cup of tea and a slice of toast. Charlie had also presented a jar of thick cut marmalade, but Doherty was firm. When murder reared its ugly head he preferred to be lean and mean. Being hungry helped him do that. Besides it was long past breakfast time. He wondered whether Charlie was aware of that. Getting up early for work played havoc with a bloke's body clock.

Honey made the excuse that she was on a diet. She was always on a diet. It's something that became a permanent routine once you were over forty.

Charlie sank gratefully down into a chair, his hands wrapped around a mug of tea. Doherty noted it was decorated with a picture of Miss Piggy, pink and fat against a lime green background.

When he took a sip he made a loud slurping noise, his hands shaking slightly.

'It were a shock all right. At first I thought it were a great window display. Adam Ant! Who would have thought of decorating a window with him?' He shook his head. 'Amazing.'

Doherty frowned thinking perhaps that he'd misunderstood.

'Adam Ant?'

'Yeah. That's right,' said Charlie wide eyed as he nodded. 'Were you a fan?'

'No. I'm sorry, but I understood the window display was of a generic highwayman.'

Charlie shook his head. 'Didn't look like no highwayman to me. That were Adam Ant. It came to me at the same time as the tune on my iPod. I like a bit of music when I'm on me rounds. "Stand and Deliver" he was singing. Have you heard of it?'

Doherty said that he had though it was slightly before his time. The road sweeper had to be in his mid-to-late fifties.

Charlie continued to shake his head, his protruding eyes staring into space.

Although impatient to hear what Charlie had to say, Doherty knew better than to press him. The poor chap looked a bit shattered to say the least.

'You didn't see anyone around?'

Another adamant shake of the head. 'No. There's never anybody much around at that time in the morning. Not even the pigeons.' He chuckled before taking another sip of tea.

'Can you tell me at what point you noticed the body swinging from the noose?'

Doherty studied Charlie's features whilst awaiting a response. His attention was drawn to Charlie's ears which waggled as he prepared to answer. Tufts of hair stuck out from each ear, their colour and wiry toughness matching his eyebrows. He reminded Doherty of an alien from *Star Wars*, one of those who hung around in intergalactic bars and looked almost human.

Charlie heaved a big sigh. 'I didn't really notice the hanged man until the finale came.'

'Finale?'

'On my iPod. There was nobody around so I was doing a guitar solo on my sweeping brush. Being a kid again I suppose,' he added with a self-conscious chuckle.

Doherty managed a saturnine smile. Humour tended to take a back seat when his mind was stuffed with the intricacies of a murder investigation. There was so much unpleasantness to think about and what with the paperwork . . .

'So this was early morning?'

'About five thirty. There's nobody around at that time in the morning, you know, tourists and such like. That's what it's all about, keeping things tidy for them.'

'You obviously take pride in your work.'

Charlie nodded avidly. 'You bet I do. I want them tourists to go home with lovely memories of a clean, historic city not wading through Big Mac wrappers and cigarette packets.'

Doherty was impressed that a humble road sweeper could be so conscientious about sweeping the pavements and gutters.

'Is it always food cartons and cigarette packets?'

Charlie shifted in his chair. 'Not always. Other things get thrown away.'

'Have you ever found anything of value?'

Charlie shifted again and his bright eyes suddenly dimmed. Doherty waited, noting the caution that had come to Charlie's face.

'Go on. You can tell me. Finders, keepers.'

Charlie shrugged. 'Nothing special. Sometimes a few coins, even a bit of paper money. Not your hundreds and thousands mind. And not a wallet or purse! I wouldn't keep that. Not anything with a name inside it. I take stuff like that to the nick and hand it over to your blokes. I'm honest, I am. Always have been, always will be.'

'Did you find anything that morning?'

Charlie squirmed for a bit, his head almost rotating on his scrawny neck as he fought to overcome his natural distrust of policemen.

'A fifty pence piece. A few pound coins.'

'I see. You didn't mention them in the statement?'

'Was I supposed to?' His eyes flicked wide open. He looked worried.

Doherty thought about it. 'I only ask because it might have been dropped by the murderer and have his fingerprints on it.'

Charlie's jaw dropped.

'I 'adn't thought of that.' He sprang to his feet as panic set in. 'Look, if you want to rifle through what I've got in my pockets . . .'

His baggy trousers hung like a clown's — low on his hips and sagging at the knees. The coins jingled as he rummaged deeply into both trouser pockets.

Honey considered the rubbish lurking in those pockets and decided she would not offer to go rummaging in there herself.

'No need,' said Doherty getting to his feet. 'You found them before finding the body. There's nothing we can do about that. The evidence — if it was ever evidence in the first place — is contaminated.'

Doherty excused himself, thinking of how the solicitors at the Crown Prosecution Service would turn their noses up at the prospect of evidence fingered by a scruffy road sweeper with a penchant for cooked breakfasts and a nineteen-eighties' band leader they'd probably never heard of.

'Well he's definitely not in the frame. He's just the man who found the body,' said Honey later.

'I think so. Though he did fidget a bit when I asked if he'd ever found anything of value.'

'He could be lying, though there's no guarantee if he does have anything valuable that it's anything to do with the case.'

'True.'

* * *

Once he'd closed the door behind Doherty, Charlie drew the chain across and turned the catch. There wasn't much in the way of crime where he lived, but securely locking the front door enhanced his sense of security.

Assured all was safe and secure, he trotted back along the passage to his living room, heading for the painted pine sideboard that was set against one wall.

He'd rescued the sideboard from a skip early one morning, balancing it across his cart once he'd finished his shift.

It hadn't been easy, but with a bit of help from a friend he happened to bump into, he'd got the sideboard home before returning his cart to the depot.

The sideboard looked good — not too heavy, not too big. For the first few days he'd never tired of admiring it. He didn't do that now. There was something else he was desperate to admire.

On opening one drawer, he took out the watch he'd found in the gutter just last week. It was heavy and obviously expensive, the name Bulgari picked out in small silvery letters on the watch face.

Tentatively, he held it in both hands, his heart quickening with delight.

It had been hard not to brag to the policeman about this watch, but then if he had he would have lost it. Taking a lost wallet or purse to the police was one thing. A watch was something different.

Like a magpie, Charlie was drawn to bright things. If he had turned the watch in, it would have gone into the lost property department at Manvers Street Police Station never to be seen again — at least it wouldn't be seen by him. Probably auctioned off at a fraction of its value. Not that he had any idea of its value, but he'd heard it was what they did with lost property if it didn't get claimed. Even so, he guessed the price would still be beyond him. Street sweepers didn't earn enough to buy top of the range items like that.

He'd found the watch up the steps at the end of Beaumont Alley so that had to mean it was nothing to do with the murder. That's what he counselled himself. Deep down he knew he was doing wrong, but this was the loveliest thing he'd ever found . . . and he wanted to keep it.

CHAPTER NINE

It was two days later when Doherty phoned to invite her to take a look around the tailor's shop.

'I'll meet you there,' he said. 'Access shouldn't be a problem. After all you are a witness.'

Honey referred Doherty back to her interaction with a very pissed-off Alan Roper. 'Any news on how much property Nigel Tern owned?'

'The Tern Trust still owns a great deal of property. The old man set it up. It's early days, but I'm not sure the murder victim knew much about the trust, merely reaping the rewards.'

'Which were considerable?'

'And still are.'

Long shadows fell across Beaumont Alley giving it a rather secretive and even gloomy air. She guessed its shadowy aspects were much appreciated by the select band of clients the business attracted.

Walking hadn't taken too long. The city pavements were occupied mostly by tourists at present. All the locals were still on holiday.

Honey arrived on time and tossed her head on entering. Her newly cut bob, fresh from the salon, swung like a metronome, her hair glossy. Having it restyled made her feel good. She waited for Doherty to comment.

Despite the provocative toss of the head, Doherty didn't appear to notice. She should have known better. He was in crime-solving mode, every detail about the case logged just as efficiently in his head as on the police database. There was no room for anything else.

The interior of the shop was better lit than she'd expected and smelled of beeswax, odd seeing as most of the fittings seemed to be of dark grey and black metal.

'Hello! My name is Cecil Barrington,' said a little man reaching out to shake their hands.' I'm the senior assistant here.'

'Is there a shop manager?' asked Doherty.

'Mr Nigel managed the shop.'

Cecil Barrington had a pink face and white hair. He was also portly and dressed in a grey pinstriped suit with a white shirt, burgundy silk tie and black brogues. Pale blue eyes gazed through a pair of gold wire rimmed spectacles. His smile was hesitant, only to be expected in the circumstances.

'Thank you for seeing us Mr Barrington. Have you arranged for the other employees to be here with us?'

'Yes. Mr Papendriou is already here and Mr Rossini, the junior, has gone to fetch the morning papers.'

Doherty introduced Honey, outlining her part in both the competition for the best window display and the investigation.

'Ah yes,' said Mr Barrington. He didn't seem terribly impressed.

'You don't sound as though you approved of entering the competition, Mr Barrington,' she commented.

He winced at her question.

'I didn't think it was right for us.'

'But Mr Tern insisted?'

'Mr Nigel was not content to leave things as they were. He wanted more . . .' Mr Barrington took a deep breath '. . . pizzazz! He said he was tired of kowtowing and bowing to a rapidly shrinking upper crust.'

'And you didn't approve,' Honey ascertained.

'No. I did not. I happen to be proud of this firm's long-standing service to people of quality. I'm not sure I want to administer to the nouveau riche — five-minute celebrities with more money than talent!'

He shook his head as he spat his opinion. Honey decided then that he couldn't possibly be the murderer. He was too small and too old. Nigel had been hung and the coroner was convinced it was murder — knocked on the back of the head before being strung up, according to Doherty. She didn't think Cecil physically capable of such a crime.

'You've had a revamp since I was last in here,' said Doherty who had been wandering around the shop whilst Honey had questioned the elderly shop manager.

'It was redecorated several months ago,' said Cecil Barrington.

Honey detected a sudden tightness to his mouth, as though he'd just sucked on something bitter.

'It's very modern,' remarked Honey.

'Certainly a different style,' added Doherty.

Honey opened her mouth but Doherty predicated her question.

'No. I was not here for a fitting. Not personally,' he said before she could say anything.

The predominant colour in the room was grey; grey walls, a darker grey ceiling, recessed lighting adding attitude to a colour that might have looked dead otherwise. Here and there the various shades of grey were relieved by splashes of purple.

'I expected highly polished oak or mahogany, glass countertops and little brass bells all over the place for the customer to ring and summon service,' said Honey.

Cecil Barrington's tight little mouth tightened further. 'We used to have lovely wooden counters and handsome panelling. Traditionally tasteful.'

Doherty grimaced. 'That's what I remember. Wood, brass and glass. I came in here with the Chief Constable. He wished to impart the details of a case we were working on whilst being measured up for a morning suit; he was off to attend the palace for some award if I remember rightly. Or it could have been Ascot Races. He was dead keen on horse racing — the sport of kings.'

'I take it you provided the moral support?' asked Honey.

'No. I was there on a case. Time was of the essence. The crime details had to be relayed whilst his inside leg measurement was being taken.'

'That must have been a bit off-putting,' said Honey.

'Slightly. I've never been briefed by a Chief Constable in a state of undress before.'

Mr Barrington assumed a forbearing expression. He was evidently the sort of man used to coping with all kinds of people. Doherty didn't faze him.

'Did you attend the celebratory party, Mr Barrington?' Doherty asked. 'For the window display?'

'No.' Mr Barrington's jowls shuddered as he shook his head. 'I arise from my slumbers early and I retire by nine o'clock at night. I wished Mr Tern the best and was pleased he'd won the award, but I declined attending the party. I'm too old for that kind of thing. I wouldn't have fitted in, and besides I didn't approve.'

He pursed his lips like a petulant girl.

Doherty kept at the questioning. 'Can somebody verify you were in bed?'

He nodded. 'Of course. My wife.'

'Anyone else? I mean, did anyone see you entering your house?'

Mr Barrington frowned as he thought about it. 'Yes,' he finally said. 'People on the bus. I always take the bus to and from the shop. I have a bus pass you see. I'm over sixty-five.'

Doherty nodded. 'I see. Anyone else besides your fellow bus passengers?'

'Well. Let me see.' The senior shop assistant, who had probably worked there all his life, frowned as he thought about it. 'There was that young man from the garage beneath the arches. The young man who sings all the time. Ahmed something or other?'

'Ahmed Clifford. He looks after my car,' said Honey. 'He's a great one for keeping cars like my old Citroen going.'

Mr Barrington nodded. 'That's right. He was working on next door's car. It belongs to the wife of my neighbour and I believe it is quite old. Ahmed quite often comes round to get it started. Personally I think they should dump it and buy a new one, but there, who am I to criticise. I don't drive.'

'Would he remember seeing you?' Doherty asked.

'Oh yes. Very likely. I complained you see,' said Cecil pompously, his height seeming to increase as he proclaimed his displeasure. 'He was singing very loudly. I asked him if he could turn down the volume as I was a man of regular habits and retired early.'

'And he obliged?'

Cecil pursed his lips. 'No. He told me singing helped him concentrate, and anyway, it was early.'

'What time was that?'

'About six o'clock.'

'Did you notice what time he left?'

'Not really. I think it was before nine otherwise I would have still heard him. It was a warm night and I opened the bedroom windows to let some air in. My wife and I cannot bear a stuffy bedroom.'

'And you didn't leave your house whilst Ahmed was out front.'

'I did not.'

'So did you fall asleep after he'd gone home then?'

Mr Barrington ran the palm of his hand over his almost naked head. There was something about his lips and attitude that was almost feminine, like a pantomime dame.

'I'm sure he was gone home by the time I fell asleep. Both my wife and I slept well. I haven't been sleeping that well of late what with all these new ideas Mr Nigel insisted on.' Mr Barrington shook his head dolefully. 'If only his poor father could have seen it . . .'

'You mean Mr Tern Senior has not seen the new improvements?'

Mr Barrington shook his head and sucked in his breath in a disapproving manner.

'No. He has not. When I asked Mr Nigel whether his father approved, he told me that he'd given him *carte blanche*.'

'You didn't believe him?'

Barrington shook his head so vehemently that his flews fluttered around his collar.

'No. I did not.'

'Who else didn't like the décor — besides yourself that is?'

Mr Barrington frowned. 'Our clients. We were going to lose them. I am quite sure of that.'

Doherty straightened. He'd been obliged to look down at Cecil Barrington during the questioning which had resulted in a crick in his neck. As he straightened he rubbed the nape of his neck.

'Right. If you'd like to get your colleague, Mr . . . ?'

'Mr Papendriou. He's in the back room attending to the accounts.'

'If you could get him please?'

If the reason for their visit to the shop hadn't been so serious, they would have been amused on seeing Mr Barrington taking such long strides with his short legs, an antidote to his small stature. He disappeared through a door marked 'private'.

Honey resumed scrutinising the long established shop, noting the sleek cabinets, the gleaming glass and metal surroundings.

She sniffed. 'Nigel really went to town didn't he; and quite recently. I can almost smell the fresh paint.'

Doherty said that he could too. 'Sad really. It wasn't like this when I came before. It was traditional. Expensive and traditional — as in, it only appealed to the over-fifties — possibly over-sixties . . .'

'So Nigel Tern was trying to widen its appeal. Is that enough of a reason to kill him?'

'It could be, but let's keep an open mind on that.'

Doherty was running his fingers around the cuff of a dark mustard jacket. It looked to be worsted, but Honey was only guessing; she'd never been much good at needlework and knew little about fabrics.

'I'd wear this jacket.'

Honey joined him, running her fingers over the shoulders and down the sleeve. It felt soft.

'It's pure wool,' said Doherty.

'How do you know that?'

Doherty flipped open the edge of the jacket and pointed to the pure wool label. 'It says so. It also states the price.'

Grimacing, he let the sleeve of the jacket drop.

'It is bespoke,' Honey pointed out.

'Well, I haven't got bespoke pockets.' He'd moved away from the jacket. The mirrored panels hiding the window display had attracted his attention instead. He reached for the handle.

'I'm going to take a look. Window displays have always intrigued me.'

'Shouldn't you wait until Mr Barrington returns?'

He shrugged. 'I don't think he'd mind.'

He slid one of the panels back to expose the window display. The highwayman and the russet-coloured jackets were still in situ. The gallows had been taken away for further forensic analysis. The tape the police used for marking off a crime area had been removed and a passer-by was looking in the window. Another one joined him. Word of the murder was obviously spreading. Another stop on the tourist map, thought Honey.

'So!' said Doherty, stepping down into a neat square set lower than the rest of the window floor which was higher than that of the shop to facilitate entry. This brought the level of the window floor roughly at hip level. It was reached up a small flight of steps. 'Nigel Tern was already dead when he was strung up. Strangled.'

Honey frowned. 'So what was the point of putting him on display in the window?'

Doherty shrugged. 'I can only guess. A macabre sense of humour?'

'Unless whoever did it was trying to send a message to someone telling them this is what happens to you if you dare . . . dare . . . um . . . whatever the murderer didn't want you daring to do.'

'Thank you, Professor. Care to elaborate?'

Psychological profiling wasn't her bag, but she made a stab anyway ' . . . dare to become a highwayman?'

Doherty raised one eyebrow. 'Dare to wear dated sports jackets?'

'And plus fours.'

Doherty frowned at her. 'There are no plus fours in the window.'

'I know there aren't. But sports jackets used to be worn with plus fours for shooting and golf and suchlike — didn't they?'

Doherty had to concede that she was right but added a comment of his own.

'I don't believe in murderers sending messages. The motive for murder never moves far from the core reasons: greed, revenge or sex. Sometimes all. Let's get on . . .'

They left the window, Doherty closing the panel behind them.

They were standing in the middle of the shop when Mr Cecil Barrington returned with a tall swarthy man through the door marked private.

'This is Mr Papendriou. My second.'

The man's hand was cool, his fingers spidery. His hair was black and slicked back on his head. He smelled of hair gel.

After a cool handshake, Honey returned her hand to her pocket. Out of sight in her pocket, she fingered her palm. It felt moist. Mr Papendriou had a slimy veneer. She was just telling herself that it didn't mean to say he was a bad man when an almighty crash sounded behind her.

All four of them turned to see the shop door had flown open, revealing an elderly man in a wheelchair. He had grey hair and an unpleasant expression; his gloved hands rested on a tartan blanket over his knees.

'There you are, Mr Arnold,' said a woman behind him, navigating the chair. 'Just sit tight whilst I get both of you in and close this door.'

'She's used to dealing with wheelchairs,' snarled the old man. Even if the woman hadn't mentioned his name, Honey would have guessed this was Mr Tern Senior. She also guessed that not only was the woman used to dealing with wheelchairs, she was also used to bad-tempered patients and bedpans.

Another wheelchair followed the first, this time self-propelled by the very same woman Honey had seen at the presentation — Grace Pauling, daughter of George Pauling, deceased partner in Pauling and Tern.

The old man fixed his eyes on Doherty.

'Are you the police?' he demanded in a loud though wheezy voice.

'Detective Inspector Doherty,' said Doherty, extending a hand. 'We met earlier when I came to tell you about your son.'

'Oh yes. So you did. I've had so many people come in. Some with commiserations plus the funeral director who wanted me to spend a fortune on an oak coffin. What a waste!'

'Honey Driver,' said Honey, offering him her hand. 'I would suggest against oak, it's not environmentally friendly.'

'Never mind that! Did he think I was made of money?'

'I hope you don't mind me coming back here, Mr Tern,' said Doherty. 'I want to leave no stone unturned. I want to go through everything. I promise I will do my best to catch your son's murderer.'

The old man gave a curt nod of his head. His neck was scrawny, the skin reddish and hanging loose from the sinews. Honey was surprised his head didn't fall off.

'Just to let you know, your son's body will be released for burial as soon as possible.'

Mr Tern gave a curt nod in acknowledgement. 'Grace did the identification. She knows him well enough. I did tell you I wouldn't do it. What's done is done.' His voice sounded hollow as though it were coming from inside a metal drum.

Next to him, Grace Pauling made no comment but sat stiffly, her hands gripping the sides of the chair.

Whereas Mr Papendriou had left her hand feeling slimy, Mr Tern left it feeling dry. Out of the two of them Honey felt an instant dislike for this man and for more than one reason. Firstly he didn't seem that upset at his son's death. Secondly he was taking full advantage of being in a wheelchair. Rather than look up at her face his gaze was fixed firmly on her breasts.

'Who did you say you were, young woman?'

Honey bristled at the fact that he was actually addressing her cleavage. Perhaps he had tunnel vision due to his age.

'I'm Honey Driver. I'm working with the police. I was also one of the last people to see your son alive at the presentation.'

'Were you indeed?'

'Did you see your son on the day in question?' asked Doherty.

'No. The doctor had prescribed strong medicine — either that or my son was overdosing me . . .'

'Now, now, Mr Tern. It wasn't always Mr Nigel giving you your medicine, remember, and I was most certainly giving you the proper dose.'

How the woman pushing the wheelchair could smile so cheerfully, was beyond Honey's comprehension. She would have willingly given him a double dose just for a bit of peace and quiet.

'I know nothing of that day, except that I finally woke up not feeling as woozy as I had done. Can you tell me my son's movements?'

Doherty outlined the award, the presentation and the party at the Cricketers that very same night.

'He always did like parties; much more than work. He never liked work, but he did like having plenty of money to spend. Did you go to the evening celebration?' He directed the last question at Honey.

Honey shook her head. 'No. I had a prior engagement.'

'Another man — I hope.' He looked her up and down. 'Understandable. Grace went of course. She never could stand being left out of anything, could you Grace?'

Grace turned bright red. 'Nigel wanted me to go, so I did.'

Doherty turned his attention to the woman in the wheelchair. 'How long did you stay at the party, Miss Pauling?'

The blush had not left Grace Pauling's face.

'I'm not sure.'

'What time did you arrive?'

'About eight thirty,' she said after due consideration. 'Yes. About eight thirty.'

'Do you have your own transport, or did you take a taxi?'

'I took my car. It's customised for my circumstances, and anyway, I wasn't going to drink.'

'And you can't recall what time you left?'

She shrugged, her eyes seeming to dance anywhere except in his direction.

'Probably about ten. Ten thirty at the latest. Two hours was quite enough and things were getting noisy.'

'You weren't there when the fight broke out and the police were called?'

She shook her head. 'No. I was not.'

Mr Tern chuckled. 'Grace lived in hope of my son paying her some attention, but he never did. The poor woman is likely to remain a spinster for the rest of her life!'

Grace Pauling's flush but this time with anger. 'Perhaps I have no wish to marry! Have you ever considered that, Arnold?'

Mr Tern ignored her, turning instead to his employees.

'Mr Barrington. Have you and your colleague had nothing else to do but stand and gawp?'

Cecil Barrington was a vision of humility, positively choking on humble pie.

'I do apologise Mr Tern, but this gentleman here expressed a wish to interview everyone who works in the shop or might have gone to the party.'

'I did,' confirmed Doherty.

'I take it *you* didn't go to the party,' said Arnold Tern, his slack mouth curving into a lopsided sneer as he addressed the senior assistant.

Mr Barrington blushed almost as much as Grace Pauling. 'No, Mr Tern. I did not.' He appeared to know his place, subservient in the presence of his employer. Impressions could, of course, be deceiving; was it possible that resentment lurked beneath his humility? Honey thought. It was hard to tell.

Arnold Tern's sneer widened. 'No. Of course you did not, Barrington. Tucked up in bed with your wife like a good little boy. And you, Papendriou?'

'With all due respect, Mr Tern,' Doherty interjected. 'I'm the one asking the questions here. Mr Papendriou, did you attend the party?'

'Well, excuse me . . .' For a moment the old man tried to rise from his chair. A restraining hand from the woman who appeared to be his nurse stayed him.

Papendriou gave no sign of being as subservient as Mr Barrington.

'In a manner of speaking, sir,' said the shop's second-in-command to Doherty. 'Mr Tern asked me if I would stay on and serve drinks here before everyone went elsewhere to the organised event.'

'And did you?'

'Yes sir. I stayed on and served drinks here, then I washed up. By the time I'd finished, everyone had moved on to the Cricketers. It's not my favourite place in Bath, so I was disinclined to attend. I decided to go home.'

'Do you live alone, Mr Papendriou?'

'No. I live with my partner.'

'And your partner will vouch that you were there for the rest of the night?'

'Yes. He's a light sleeper, so I assure you he would know if I sneaked out of bed in the middle of the night.'

He spoke very precisely. He held his hands in front of him, one crossed over the other round about waist level.

Honey became aware of a slight growling sound from the aged Mr Tern. She didn't need to ask whether he approved of his employee's sexuality. She guessed this was the first time he'd heard of it and wondered what his response might be. It didn't look as though Mr Papendriou cared about his opinion. Perhaps he was considering moving on? It was very likely.

Doherty looked restless. The last thing he wanted was conflict in the middle of a questioning.

One look and Honey knew what she had to do. Divide and rule — in her own way of course.

'Is there somewhere here we can make a cup of tea?' she asked, her face a picture of bright-eyed innocence.

Mr Barrington indicated the door he'd recently entered through. 'Mr Papendriou will show you where everything is.'

'You too, Mr Barrington,' said Doherty.

Papendriou bent from the waist, not in an abrupt way but like a willow, slowly. 'Tea for everyone, sir?'

'No sugar for me, thanks,' said Doherty.

Arnold Tern was not a stupid man. He glared at Doherty. 'No matter. I'll deal with him later.'

Doherty's face was grimly set. 'Mr Tern, I am more concerned with cracking this case than discussing your attitude towards your employees. Your son has been murdered. That is my priority at this moment in time. You can deal with your personnel arrangements when I've finished. Can we agree on that?'

'Agree?' The old man's eyes glared like a snake about to strike its prey. 'Do you think I did it then? Is that why your assistant's going off to make tea whilst you ask me some in-depth questions?'

'Did you do it?' Honey heard Doherty say.

'Have you seen me? I'm in a wheelchair! My son was twice my weight. I'd have had my work cut out. Besides, as Edwina here can verify, I was in bed on the day of the competition and fast asleep that night.'

'Edwina.' Doherty looked at the nurse. 'Edwina . . . ?'

'Cayford,' she supplied.

Leaving Doherty to it, Honey followed the two shop assistants through the door and into a small kitchen where Mr Papendriou took charge of boiling the kettle and setting out cups, saucers, sugar and milk on a very pretty silver tray.

'Very upmarket,' she remarked, nodding at the tray.

'It's Georgian,' said the tall dark man. 'The cups and saucers are later of course, but they are porcelain.'

'Not a mug in sight,' laughed Honey.

'Certainly not,' said Mr Barrington looking positively appalled. 'We offer refreshments to our clients. We couldn't possibly serve it in mugs! Whatever next?'

Honey restrained herself from smiling.

'So. How long have you worked here, Mr Barrington?' she asked pleasantly.

'Thirty-five years. I joined Tern and Pauling after I came out of the army.'

'You were in the army?' Given his height, the fact surprised her.

'I was invalided out. Flat feet.'

Not his height then.

'It's a long time to work in one place,' commented Honey. She herself had owned and run the Green River for only a few years. How many more years she would do this she didn't really know. Variety was the spice of life and that applied to career as much as to anything else.

Mr Barrington adopted his lemon sucking expression. 'I am not the kind of man to flit from one position to another, young lady! If you'll excuse me.'

He promptly left through another door in the corner of the room marked washrooms.

'Don't worry about Mr Barrington,' said Papendriou, making the tea in his slow slippery manner. 'He's grumpier than usual of late, but then he's got reason to be.'

Honey watched as he poured the boiling water into a teapot, stirred it, put the lid on and covered it with a multi-coloured tea cosy. It occurred to her that she hadn't seen a tea cosy for years. Nobody let their tea 'mash' anymore, did they? Then it came to her. He wasn't using teabags. Instead, proper leaf tea. Earl Grey. English Breakfast. Darjeeling.

She focused on Mr Papendriou's comment. 'Is his grumpiness anything to do with work or does he have problems at home?'

Mr Papendriou glanced at her over his shoulder. 'Very perceptive, miss. It is indeed work. Mr Nigel wanted everything in the shop updated and that includes the staff. The young lad, Rossini, and myself he deemed likely to adjust. But Mr Barrington would not fit in. Mr Nigel had decided to terminate his employment.'

'I can see that would make him very grumpy.'

'Indeed. Mr Barrington lives to work for Tern and Pauling.'

'And you do not?'

His deadpan expression was unaltered.

'It is a means to an end. I have managed to save a little cash, plus I've put my parents' house in Pontypridd on the market. They died some months ago and probate was granted. They didn't believe in making a will. Still, I'm the only son so it was quite straightforward really. As soon as the house is sold then I will give in my notice. The fact is that I intend becoming self-employed. I want my own business where I can make outfits, not just sell them.'

'Good for you! Tailor-made suits? Jackets like the ones Tern and Pauling make?'

Mr Papendriou smiled that slippery smile of his. 'Not at all. I intend to make speciality products — well-made speciality products for the leather goods market.'

'It'll be quite a wrench for you, leaving here to go self-employed.'

'Actually I'm quite looking forward to it. I've had enough of working for other people.'

'So how long have you worked here?'

'Three years. Long enough.'

'And your younger colleague, Mr Rossini?'

'Only a year, though I can't see him hanging around much longer. He might have done if Mr Nigel had lived, but I can't see him fitting in with the old guard — Mr Tern Senior.'

From a bespoke tailor to leather goods; Honey considered what he'd said. 'Well a handbag needs to be as well stitched as a made to measure suit I suppose.'

He turned to face her, both hands holding the tray on which were enough cups and saucers for everyone, plus a large white china teapot, sugar basin and milk jug. The teaspoons looked to be made of silver and of good quality — a bit like their clients.

'I will not be making handbags, miss,' he said, his face still deadpan, his voice monotone. 'My intention is to make leather goods for the bondage market. The internet has opened up many opportunities in that sphere.'

Honey stood in the centre of the room with her mouth open. From jackets suitable for field sports to items suitable for sports of a more intimate and sexual nature.

Mr Papendriou stopped at the door.

'Do you think you could oblige?' he asked.

Honey nearly choked. Would she oblige him by modelling a few leather straps, a spiked dog collar and carrying a whip? 'Oblige?'

'The door,' he said, jerking his head at it. 'Can you please open the door?

'Oh yes! Of course.'

* * *

79

Whilst the others had gone off making tea, Doherty had asked the old man some pretty blistering questions.

'Mr Tern. I need some clarification here.'

'I've had enough of your questions. I want some time alone in my shop. I need to brief my employees. There's a lot to be done.'

'We can do it here or down at the station. We have full disabled facilities; ramps, low level toilets, the lot.'

'Only in my presence,' snapped the woman in the wheelchair before the old man had time to answer. 'I'm his solicitor,' she said in as lofty an air as she could manage, the veins in her neck starkly prominent.

Doherty had felt her beady eyes on him the whole time, assessing his actions and waiting for her moment.

'There's no need for you to be concerned,' he said to her. 'Mr Tern is not being arrested; on the contrary, I just want some background information which in turn might highlight the murderer's motives. It might help me in solving the crime.'

'I demand that you only question Mr Tern when I am . . .'

'Shut up, Grace,' the older man snapped. 'You *are* here, or do you wish to inconvenience me and get me dragged into the station. Now Inspector Doherty, what is it you want to ask me?'

By the time the others came back in with the tea, the junior assistant Angelo Rossini had returned with the newspapers. After glancing around like a frightened rabbit, he was told to put the newspapers where they were always placed on a table between two comfortable chairs. He asked about ironing them as he usually did, but was told to do that later.

Mr Tern fixed him with a watery, malevolent gaze.

'In the meantime you will make yourself available. I expect Detective Inspector Doherty will want you to answer a few questions. I have no doubt you did attend the party, young man. I would have at your age.'

His tone was sour, almost jealous. Rossini, a pleasant looking young man with wavy brown hair and very blue eyes, nodded and said that he had.

'Did you stay very long?' asked Doherty.

'I left at about eleven o'clock.'

'Did you go to the party alone?'

'With my girlfriend. Mr Tern said she could come. He said she'd brighten the place up a bit.'

He looked a bit unsettled admitting that.

After only one meeting with Nigel Tern, Honey had it worked out as to why he'd want Angelo to bring his girlfriend. The man had been a class one lecher. And, judging by his fixation with her breasts, the old man might have been of the same ilk in his youth. Like father, like son.

'Were you there when the fight broke out?'

'Yes.' Rossini looked uncomfortable. 'It wasn't really a fight. More a misunderstanding.'

'Did you know the men fighting?'

'Roper I think his name is, the owner of the chocolate shop. And Lee Curtis. I think he runs a gift shop selling naughty things . . . if you get my meaning. He runs it with his mother just around the corner from the Pavilion.'

Honey almost choked on her tea.

'Do you know what it was about?'

'Oh yes,' said a grinning Angelo Rossini. 'Roper accused Lee of fixing things. Said it was him that should have won.' He shrugged. 'It was just a skirmish.'

'Skirmish or no,' said Doherty. 'We'll be having a word.'

'Funny,' said Rossini who was still grinning. 'It was supposed to be a celebration and all around people were arguing and fighting.'

Honey held back. She was gagging to ask a question, but she had to leave it to Doherty.

Doherty was frowning. 'Why do you say that? Who else was arguing?'

Rossini flushed.

'Well go on, boy,' snarled Arnold Tern. 'I want to know too.'

Angelo licked his lips. His face was still flushed and his eyes were flickering nervously.

'Mr Tern was arguing.'

'Who with?'

Again Angelo's eyes slid sideways settling on Grace Pauling.

'Mr Nigel was having a few hot words with Mr Frobisher . . .'

'Ronald Frobisher of Frobisher and Blackwood, estate agents?'

Angelo nodded. 'Yes. And then . . .' This time he held his head stiffly, unwilling to let his gaze wander.

'Miss Pauling,' he said softly.

Doherty nodded. He was nowhere near having found the murderer, but a little ground was being broken, a few things found out.

Like bits of a puzzle, they would take some time to fit together — if at all. Not everything would fit, but the fact was that some would. It was all a matter of time.

Firstly he'd learned that the old man had not been consulted about the revamping of the shop and neither had he been aware of the window display being entered for the competition. It was unlikely the old man was strong enough to kill his son, but he did have a motive. Then there was Mr Roper and Mr Curtis. Both were now flagged up on his 'to interview' list.

The old man evidently perceived what he was thinking.

'Yes. I did have a motive, Detective Inspector. Tern and Pauling have been the purveyors of fine tailoring to the gentry for many years. We do not need to cater for the high street element! My son was a fool. A stupid, irresponsible fool!'

Doherty said that he understood.

Honey was mixing and matching the possibilities. Mr Roper who owned The Chocolate Soldier; Mr Curtis who owned and ran two shops, number one the sex shop where he sold everything from sexy maids' outfits to leather. Then there was Mr Papendriou. He had plans to become self-employed making items for people who liked being tied up. On reflection there were connections all over the place.

Mr Tern's head suddenly dropped forward. He placed his hand over his eyes.

'I'm not feeling too good. Can we finish up?'

His nurse, Edwina Cayford, poured him tea, added lots of sugar and insisted he drink it.

'Your sugar level's dropped. You need every drop of this.' To Doherty she said, 'Mr Tern has been very ill for some weeks. I think he's had enough of this for one day. Despite appearances, it has all been a bit of a shock.'

Doherty chewed the inside of his cheek. He wanted to get this sorted, but not at the expense of the old man taking a turn for the worse.

He sighed. 'I understand but I can't wait forever.'

'No need to,' said Edwina. 'Can I suggest you come to the house if you wish to question him further?'

He jerked his chin in agreement. 'I suppose so. I'm not sure of how much more I need to ask, but I will call in if I think of anything pertinent to the case.'

Edwina attempted to force another cup of tea on the old man, insisting that he could do with more sugar.

Arnold Tern waved the proffered tea away, bending around Edwina so he could better shout at his senior assistant.

'Mr Barrington! As soon as this policeman leaves, I want the door locked and a staff meeting convened.'

Doherty exchanged a look of surprise and exasperation with Honey. The old man was a wily old bugger.

Tense looks sallied from one employee to another. Honey decided she wouldn't want to be in their shoes. However, she was loath to leave just yet. There was one question bugging her.

'Can I ask one more thing?'

Doherty eyed her sidelong. The old man sighed and looked at her somewhat condescendingly.

'What is it?'

'The window display was very impressive. Whose idea was it?'

Arnold Tern slapped the arm of his wheelchair with his bony hand. 'My stupid son of course. Who else?'

Honey persisted. 'But who actually designed it?'

Everyone looked at everyone else. It was Mr Papendriou who provided the answer.

'Vasey Casey. He's from London.'

Honey searched in her bag for her notebook but couldn't find it. She did find a pen and a creased envelope. It would do.

'Do you have an address?'

'No, but I expect it's somewhere in Mr Tern's office. He kept a diary.'

'I think we have the diary,' Doherty said to Honey. 'We'll get it from there.'

To the rest of them he said, 'I think I'm finished for now. I'll be back if there are any further questions. Thank you for your help. We'll see ourselves out.'

'Edwina will lock the door behind you. If you could oblige, Edwina?' Mr Tern looked mightily pleased. Honey wondered on who the axe would fall first; Mr Papendriou or Mr Barrington. She didn't hold out much hope for either of them.

His nurse responded instantly. The door was shut firmly behind them.

Honey shoved her hands in her pockets and like Doherty stood with her head back sniffing the city air.

'So what do you think?'

Stony-faced, Doherty nodded. 'I think I'll stick to the tried and trusted.'

He patted the lapels of his well-worn leather jacket. It was black and scuffed in places, a little the worse for wear but still serviceable — a bit like its owner.

'Talking of leather, Mr Papendriou is thinking of quitting his employment in order to set himself up making leather goods for the bondage market. He reckons he'll do very well online. Interestingly, Lee Curtis, the man who argued with Mr Roper who owns The Chocolate Soldier, owns a sex shop. Is that just a coincidence?'

He looked at her admiringly. 'You have been busy!'

'Plus Mr Barrington was being given the push by his boss. Nigel Tern wanted to refurbish and make the shop more trendy — that included getting rid of those employees not likely to fit in i.e. our Mr Barrington. He's been here for years.'

'Let's get this show on the road,' murmured Doherty.

Once he'd phoned into the police station with instructions to locate Vasey Cascy, they started walking, heading up the alley steps and onto street level. Their footsteps took them into Sally Lunns. Honey ordered breakfast for Doherty and coffee for herself.

'How did you know I skipped breakfast?'

'You did, didn't you?'

Doherty confirmed that she was right.

'So what's the word from forensic?'

He folded his hands in front of his nose, elbows resting on the table.

'Nothing untoward on the DNA or fingerprint front. The shop assistants and Nigel Tern's prints, plus another set which will no doubt turn out to belong to the window dresser, Vasey Casey. Bits of thread and fibre but seeing as this happened in a tailor's shop, it's only what you'd expect.'

A smile came to her face. 'Vasey Casey. Hell of a name that. It can't be his birth name — can it?'

Doherty shrugged. 'Not everybody keeps the name they were given at birth. Things get changed, *Hannah*.'

Honey grinned. 'Touché.'

She'd been christened Hannah, but it was only her mother called her that. Everyone else called her Honey.

'Is that really the guy's name or is it the name of a company?'

'Whichever. We'll enquire about both.'

The waitress set down Doherty's breakfast. Doherty picked up his knife and fork. He was about to tuck in but feeling Honey's eyes on him he paused.

'What?'

'That is a very big breakfast. Most of it looks fried. Bacon. Eggs and TWO sausages. You know a meal like that can clog your arteries, don't you?'

His gaze stayed locked with hers. 'OK. You can have one.'

She pounced on a sausage. 'Damn the diet. I'm starving.'

* * *

Arnold Tern cast his beady eyes over his assembled workforce and thought what a pathetic lot they were and how dependant on his largesse, the jobs he'd given them.

He also couldn't help thinking how his son's plans for a wider clientele base — clients who could walk right in without an appointment as had always been the case, kept his anger boiling.

It suddenly occurred to him that there was one person here who didn't fit in.

'Get out Grace.'

The woman in the wheelchair looked both surprised and offended.

'What? Arnold. I really think I should stay and . . .'

'No, you should not. Get out.'

He did not raise his voice but his tone was cold and to the point.

A pink blush spread up the woman's neck and over her face.

'My father's name is still above the door . . .'

'And that, my dear, is your only connection to this business and property. I bought him out years ago. Now get out. Now!'

Four pairs of eyes turned in the direction of Grace Pauling, each showing various degrees of nervous surprise.

'How come *she's* staying?' Grace Pauling threw a withering look at Edwina Cayford, the woman clinging to Arnold Tern's wheelchair.

'My choice,' returned Arnold Tern in the same dull monotone with its undercurrent of firmness.

He didn't look at either woman. His eyes remained fixed on the three men who had worked for the firm for varying lengths of time. At present they looked — again to varying degrees — like condemned men waiting for the axe to fall on their heads.

Behind him, Grace Pauling was gritting her teeth hard enough to grind them to dust. Her face was puce.

'Right! Then I'm going.'

Mr Tern acted as though he hadn't heard her. She belonged to a different department in his life. First and foremost he was here to sort out the mess his son had left behind. The boy was an idiot. Always had been. He showed no great remorse at his passing, he felt none. His son had never lived up to his expectations. He always got things wrong. He couldn't even do it right and live longer than his father!

Angry at his treatment of her in front of his staff, Grace wheeled herself to the shop door.

Edwina Cayford followed her, one hand reaching out to help push.

Grace bridled. 'I can manage!'

Edwina removed her hand while Grace opened the door just wide enough for her to wheel herself through. She thought about telling him that the will was ready for his signature, but it didn't much matter now. The man who would have got the lion's share of the inheritance was dead. The main heir to the new will would surprise everyone — if the old man went ahead and signed it.

* * *

Resigned to how people could behave, Edwina closed the door softly. Normally she would have thought no more of it, but there was something disconcerting about Grace Pauling, something that niggled at the back of her mind.

She couldn't recall meeting the woman before, certainly not at Mr Tern's house. She knew the family solicitor did make occasional home visits to the old man, but she had never been there when she'd called.

All the same she was sure she'd seen her before. It had to have been at the hospital; quite understandable of course seeing as she was in a wheelchair. But there was something else about seeing her, something irritating at the back of her mind and it wouldn't go away.

She returned to Mr Tern, listening as he outlined his plans to bring in a team of interior designers to soften the stark modernism his son had inflicted on the interior of the Grade II listed building. At least the outside had not suffered and for that he was grateful. But a suitably traditional and up market ambience had to be injected back into the interior.

'Our clients appreciate an air of tradition when they come in for a measuring or a fitting,' he said. 'It doesn't matter that we farm our work out to master tailors in Saville Row etc., our gentlemen clients appreciate the quality of our garments, our service AND our air of traditional continuity. They are not the sort of clients who window-shop. They do not have the time. That is why we keep their measurements and fabric preferences on file. That is why they make appointments and do not call in on the off chance. They do not care for it and neither do we!'

The looks of nervous apprehension lessened. If all that was going to happen was a bit of redecorating, well that was nothing to worry about, was it?

The two younger men, neither of whom had had many dealings with Mr Tern Senior, mainly because they hadn't known him when he was still hands on, looked to Mr Barrington, the senior assistant.

'I take it our jobs are secure?' There was a new brightness in his eyes, a new lightness in his tone of voice.

'No!'

Barrington looked as though he hadn't heard properly, tipping his head to one side.

'I beg your pardon, sir?'

'There are going to be some changes.'

Barrington looked shocked. Papendriou looked only slightly ruffled, after all he had his own plans if he were made redundant.

Young Rossini was also making his own plans. If he got made redundant and depending if there was a payoff, he would have more time to spend with Tracey, his girlfriend. Perhaps he'd get enough for a deposit on a flat; rented of course, but still . . .

Arnold folded his bony hands in his lap and addressed Mr Barrington.

'Mr Barrington . . .'

'Cecil, Mr Tern. Do call me Cecil. We have known each other for quite some time . . .'

'MISTER Barrington. You have given long and faithful service. However, I think it's time that you hung up your tape measure. Your days here are done.'

'But sir?' Sweat had broken out on Barrington's brow. His tongue licked over his bottom lip leaving it wet and flecks of spittle at the corners of his mouth. 'I don't understand.'

'It's quite simple,' said Arnold Tern, his tone as flat and cold as a tombstone. 'My useless son had plans to make Tern and Pauling no different than any other shop in any high street, in any city. That is not and never was this firm's way of doing things. We cater for a more discerning customer. We measure up princes. The fact is, Mr Barrington, nobody thought to tell me what was going on here — including entering a decidedly downmarket, seedy little competition — and all for five thousand pounds!'

'But I . . .' Barrington looked at each of his colleagues, his expression imploring in his search for their support.

'You are the senior assistant, Mr Barrington. It is you who should have told me. But you did not.'

'But you were ill . . .'

'Yes. How convenient,' said Mr Tern, interlacing his fingers in front of his face, his eyes viewing down over the pointed central as though he were focusing through a gun sight. 'You remained silent whilst my son tore this place apart. It's not good enough, Mr Barrington. Not good enough at all. You're dismissed.'

Mr Barrington blustered and drew himself up to his full height. 'I shall demand severance pay.'

'You will get what you're entitled to. No more, no less. Miss Pauling will deal with the details. Now please. Get your things. You can go. You,' he snapped, turning to Mr Papendriou. 'You're in charge, at least until after the decorators have finished putting some character back into this place. I am prepared to overlook your domestic arrangements — at least until this place is put back to its original state.'

Gustav Papendriou was a picture of humility, bending his head, hands clasped in front of him. A cautious man, he said nothing about his plans. He had a house to sell. Once it was sold the ball would be in his court. He would choose his time.

Whilst all this was going on, Edwina Cayford busied herself tidying up the tea things, returning everything to the tray then taking it out into the kitchen.

She didn't actually dislike Mr Tern because he always appreciated everything she did for him. OK, his eyes did focus on certain aspects of her curvaceous anatomy, but at least his hands didn't wander. She'd had some of that behaviour in the past. She didn't like it: she was an respectable woman and as long as Mr Tern acted the gentleman, she would remain in his employ.

Whilst wiping up the tea things, Mr Barrington came out to take his things from the cupboard, namely his sandwich box and a supply of tablets he kept there. He looked totally dejected and she felt immensely sorry for him.

'Mr Barrington. I'm so sorry,' she said, lightly touching his upper arm once she'd put the tea things down.

He didn't appear to notice. His head was bent and the curvature of his upper back seemed more pronounced than usual. Edwina guessed he had joint problems. In a short time he would have a dowager's hump, an affliction that occurred in men as well as women, though not quite so often.

When he finally looked up she saw malice in his eyes. His mouth was set like a bulldog, the corners downturned, his lower lip protruding over his upper.

'My loyalty has been tossed aside, Miss. I have been thrown onto the rubbish heap without a fair hearing, without a by your leave. Thus my loyalty to this establishment is null and void.'

With a flurry of a plump, short arm, he reached for his raincoat and an old-fashioned, but very handsome trilby hat. He set the hat on his head and threw his raincoat over his arm.

'On my way home I shall pop into the police station and speak to the officer who was here earlier. I shall drag all the skeletons I know of out of the Tern and Pauling closet. Thus I will have my revenge, my dear lady. Thus I will have my revenge!'

CHAPTER TEN

The Green River Hotel was situated in a side turning just off Great Pulteney Street. Honey had fallen in love with the place at first sight, not just because of its undisputed grandeur, but also because it was within walking distance of the shops at one end and the Holbourne Museum at the other.

Her belief was that if she felt it attractive to be within walking distance of both the Palladian frontage of the Holbourne Museum at one end of Pulteney Street and Robert Adam's Pulteney Bridge at the other, then the tourists would think so too. OK, the hotel wasn't actually situated in Pulteney Street itself, but the Green River was as near as damn it and the side road just that bit quieter than the famous street itself.

The building had an impressive facade. A grand portico stood astride the entrance. The rectangular windows were set in neat rows, one above the other all the way up and along the building except for the arched window situated immediately above the main entrance.

Attending the scene of the murder, she'd forgotten about the woman who'd looked as though she were about to fall out of the window but on entering reception at the Green River Hotel, she was immediately reminded of it.

'Mum, Mary Jane is camped out on the landing. She says she intends to keep vigil all night.'

Just the word vigil was enough to set the alarm bells ringing. Honey's vibrant footsteps halted abruptly. She did a quick left turn heading towards the reception desk.

Lindsey, her fresh-faced daughter, looked up at her with a bemused expression on her face. Her eyes were twinkling. Honey felt an immediate sense of disquiet.

'Blow it. Running a hotel is hard enough without playing host to a committed ghost hunter!'

'Before you accuse me, Mum,' Lindsey said calmly. 'I didn't tell her you'd seen a ghost. Blame Smudger.'

'I didn't say I saw a ghost,' Honey protested. 'I said that I thought I saw a woman looking as though she were about to jump.'

'There was nobody on the landing, Mum. Plus that smell of jasmine in Mary Jane's room; it had to be something to do with it, occurring so suddenly as it did. Come on, you did smell the jasmine, just as the rest of us did.'

'It doesn't prove anything. It might not have been down to her. I mean, a woman about to throw herself out of the window wouldn't douse herself in perfume first. She'd leave that to the funeral directors or whatever . . .' She stopped herself from going any further.

'Mum, you're waffling.'

Lindsey tapped something into the computer. When it came to computers, Honey stood back and let her daughter get on with it. It sometimes unnerved her that Lindsey could browse the world so easily, leaving her feeling like a dinosaur. That's how she felt now, as though she was being left out of the loop. What was Lindsey looking for?

The glow of the computer screen lit her daughter's face. Her eyes were positively dancing with amusement and a secretive smile hovered on her wide pink lips.

Unable to think of anything else to say, Honey side tracked. 'How come Smudger told Mary Jane about the ghost?'

'I think Mary Jane was at a loose end. Her beloved Caddy is in for a service. To her it's like mislaying a friend. She's been wandering around here kicking her heels and unfortunately she made the mistake of wandering into the kitchen. Smudger was not amused, but Mary Jane made the excuse that she was writing a book on ghosts and did he have any experience of the supernatural. In other words, had he ever seen one?'

'And he said . . .'

'He spoke without thinking. I think he was in the middle of making meringues. If he doesn't get them right they end up looking like sick pads! Flat and gooey instead of fluffy and light.'

Honey grimaced. Like the majority of chefs, Smudger Smith was very sensitive about his cooking. He was rubbish at taking criticism and furious if things didn't work out to a certain standard. Flat meringues would not be tolerated. According to Lindsey, not wishing to shout at Mary Jane as he did most of the unfortunates who ventured into his kitchen, plus the kitchen staff of course, he'd told her that the boss had seen a ghost looking out of the arched window at the top of the stairs.

'Are you going to tell her that there is no ghost?'

There was an unspoken message in Lindsey's eyes. It was easy to read. She'd found evidence online.

'Who was she?'

'Opinions differ. Some say she was the wife of a nobleman who had cast her aside for a younger model.'

Honey thought of Candy Boldman. It was more than likely she had replaced an earlier older model. No change there then!

'And the other theories?'

'Daughter of a nobleman, mistress of the Prince Regent, kitchen maid . . .'

'She was too well-dressed to be a kitchen maid.'

'OK. We'll discount that one. Others say that she'd escaped from an asylum and murdered the man she'd been sharing a room with.'

Honey shook her head. 'I've never heard of anyone being murdered here.'

'I can check if you like.'

'I don't think I want to know.'

'If Mary Jane gets wind of the possibilities — especially that somebody might have been murdered here, she won't let go until the puzzle is solved. I think, Mother dear, it might be best to let sleeping dogs lie. Let her camp out and do things in the old-fashioned way. Pretend it just isn't happening.'

Honey thought about it. Getting involved in murders in an investigative capacity was one thing because the murders happened elsewhere. Having one happen in the hotel was another matter entirely. It could affect trade. Nobody wanted to sleep in a room where murder had been committed.

'You're right,' said Honey nodding enthusiastically. 'If she's occupied up there keeping vigil, she's happy. Anyway. I've got things to do.'

As usual the paperwork was piling up, the bank manager was asking her to come in for a review of her account, and Doherty was going to be preoccupied with the present investigation. There were certainly a lot of demands for her time and she didn't want any more.

'I'm pooped,' she said to Lindsey. 'I don't think I could take on anything else — or speak to anyone else today.'

'I'm afraid you have to. Caspar rang. He said he couldn't get you on the phone.'

Caspar! He'd want an update. Was the murder solved yet? It was almost as though Caspar expected the word 'murderer' to be written on the forehead of the prime suspect. Not that they even had a prime suspect. Not yet anyway.

Honey took out her mobile phone. 'Whoops! Low battery.'

Speaking of the devil, the double doors of the Green River Hotel let in a blast of cold air with most people plus the noise of the city. She didn't know what it was, but Caspar St John Gervais could open a door without a sound coming in with him. His footsteps were soundless too; like a cat he seemed to pad around, sleek and shiny in tailored jacket, pressed trousers and highly polished shoes.

Honey pasted on a smile. 'Caspar! How nice to see you. Can I offer you a cup of coffee? A sherry? A glass of wine?'

His response was swift, his expression slightly disdainful. 'I'll forego your offer of coffee. Ditto wine. I am partial to a sherry of course, even at this time of day. It isn't Cyprus sherry is it?'

'No. Harveys Bristol Cream.'

Caspar sniffed. 'It's acceptable, but just a small one please, Lindsey.'

He flashed a charming smile at Honey's daughter and with a wave of his walking stick, nose in the air and without being invited, headed for Honey's office.

Once the door was safely closed behind them, Caspar spun on his heels turning to face her, chin held high, one well-manicured set of fingers combing through his mane of white hair.

Honey guessed what the opening line would be.

'How are things going with the murder of Nigel Tern?'

His frown was very deep and his mouth was no more than a thin slash across his face.

Honey shrugged and tried not to show her discomfort. Caspar was always so demanding. He expected things wrapped up as quickly as possible.

'There are no leads as yet, though I get the impression that he made enemies quite easily — especially amongst his staff. He had pretensions of making the firm less exclusive and more modern. To that end he had given the senior assistant, Cecil Barrington, his marching orders.'

'Could it be him who committed this nefarious deed?'

Honey shrugged. 'Possibly, but Mr Barrington is rather plump, in his mid-sixties and quite short. It would have taken a strong man to heave Mr Tern into the window and then string him up by the neck.'

'But it's possible?'

'Anything's possible.'

'Are there any other likely suspects?'

'Well, I . . .'

She didn't really know whether there were officially, but Caspar did like to hear the positive side of things. Luckily Lindsey came in with the drinks before she had chance to respond; at least it gave her time to think.

'There you are,' said Lindsey setting the schooners of sherry on Honey's desk. To Caspar she said, 'Are you running the Bath Marathon this year?'

Caspar visibly blanched. 'Indeed I am.'

'I'll see you there then. I'll be up front — poll position. Bet I can beat you over the first four miles.'

Caspar rose to the bait. 'Five pounds.'

A cry of fifty came bouncing back from Lindsey.

'Done,' said Caspar. They shook hands.

'You will be,' said a grinning Lindsey. 'You will be well and truly done.'

Humming a happy tune and wearing a smug smile, Lindsey took her leave.

Honey looked amused. This was the first time she'd heard of Caspar running in the Marathon.

'I didn't know you were entering,' she said to him.

'I don't say I'll finish the course, but it is my dearest intention to compete. Anyway, I'm asking people to sponsor me, a small donation per mile; for charity of course. And I will not be suggesting that you take part, my dear girl. It's too late. No matter how hard you prepared, you just wouldn't be fit enough in time. There's no room for saggy muscles and batwings in competition you know.'

Although her first instinct was to tip the sherry over his head, she refrained and smiled. After all, she had to remember that it was Caspar who'd given her the task of Crime Liaison Officer on behalf of the Hotels Association. In gratitude, he often sent overspill from his hotel, thus keeping her room lets up. Grateful for the extra business, she held her tongue.

Caspar took another sip of sherry before asking again. 'As we were saying. Are there any suspects?'

Honey outlined Doherty's intention to interview other shopkeepers who had entered the competition, especially Alan Roper, plus locating some of the women Nigel Tern had been involved with.

'Doherty is also attempting to locate the window dresser. Somebody called Vasey Casey — though that could be the name of the company.'

'We need this cleared up quickly,' said Caspar in a low voice, almost as though he were afraid microphones were hidden in the room or somebody in MI5 was hiding behind the filing cabinet taking notes.

'The police are doing their best. I will keep you informed.'

'Of course you will. Contact me immediately when you have something positive to report. Jeremy Poughty is my current hotel reception manager.'

'Potty?'

'He's left his past behind him and prefers to be known as Jerry now,' said Caspar in a crisp tone.

'Of course.'

Jeremy Poughty, a lean figure with high cheek bones, used to run a market stall where all kinds of herbs and other substances were for sale. Just one sniff of the stall was enough to send anyone high. Reading between the lines Honey concluded that Jeremy had split up with the guy who had been both his business and live-in partner. It wasn't beyond belief to assume that he and Caspar were now an item, though not necessarily living together. Caspar was a very private man.

'Did you know Nigel Tern personally?' asked Honey. 'I mean, socially?'

'I had my jackets made there. We did not socialise.'

In one way his answer surprised her. Caspar was a sucker for dinner parties favoured by the higher strata of Bath society. Nigel, as tailor and confidante to the aristocracy, seemed ideal dinner company for Caspar, and yet he was quite adamant that they were not acquainted. She couldn't help suspecting another reason for his negative response.

Obviously her expression betrayed what she was thinking.

'The other side of the sexual coin,' Caspar suddenly remarked.

'Of course,' said Honey. He had to be referring to the fact that Nigel was most definitely heterosexual. Not until much later did another conclusion enter her mind. Not until she remembered what kind of shop Lee Curtis owned and what sort of business Mr Papendriou was going into.

So how about Nigel Tern? Was he into leather and bondage? Her mind went back to the window display itself. The highwayman. It *was* a highwayman, wasn't it? Charlie York had thought otherwise. He'd been convinced it was Adam Ant, a pop star from way back. He can't have seen the gallows. She couldn't recall a set of gallows in Adam Ant's act. However, she had to concede that it was a coincidence worth pursuing.

With that in mind she swooped on Lindsey.

'Darling daughter, I have a favour to ask. You know there are a whole host of Elvis Presley look-alikes out there. I understand they have clubs where they all turn up looking like the King.'

'Loads,' said Lindsey. 'Anyone we know thinking of joining? Doherty perhaps? Caspar?'

She grinned.

Honey grinned too. 'No. I'm not looking for an Elvis Presley impersonators' club. I'm looking for an Adam Ant club. Do you think you could check if one exists?'

'Go have a coffee. I'll get back to you.'

CHAPTER ELEVEN

'You are joking!'

It wasn't like Doherty to choke on his drink and thus risk spillage, but there were exceptional circumstances when he couldn't help it. This was one of them.

They'd managed to snatch some time at the Zodiac Club, just enough to indulge in a couple of drinks before they both went to their separate beds — at least that was the plan. Hope, as they say, springs eternal. They might get up the energy to sleep together tonight.

Sharing his disbelief, Honey shook her head and laughed. 'It's true. Elvis and Abba are not the only impersonators going the rounds. I spoke to the organiser. Nigel Tern was most definitely a keen Adam Ant impersonator. They have conventions and everything, just like the Elvis lot do. Elvis has the biggest following. Abba do pretty well too, though of course they come in foursomes and you do have to have to cavort around in platform shoes. BIG platforms too. But there are Adam Ant impersonators too. Quite popular apparently.'

'I would never have believed it! Not that I knew the bloke at all. I only met the man once. That was the time I've already told you about when the Chief Constable was being fitted up for a penguin suit for some posh bash he was attending. Nigel Tern looked nothing like Adam Ant. In fact the very thought of him wearing tight britches is enough to make me turn to drink.'

As if confirming the fact, he swigged back his Jack Daniels.

Honey nodded at the barman. 'Another, please for both of us.'

The entertainer at the Zodiac Club was belting out 'Goldfinger', the old James Bond number best belted out by Shirley Bassey.

The female impersonator looked the part with his gold lamé dress, killer heels and a curly black wig. However, his voice wasn't a patch on the Welsh diva.

Doherty watched the performer from over the top of his newly filled glass. On second thoughts his figure wasn't as good as Shirley's. He had no waistline, his boobs were obviously false and he had a voice like gravel. He didn't care for dressing up himself and that included fancy-dress parties.

'He's quite good,' said Honey.

Doherty grunted and half-heartedly agreed.

'Not attractive though. I thought the highwayman was attractive, though I'm not so sure now. It didn't occur to me that he resembled a pop star from the eighties. I wonder whether it occurred to the window dresser.'

'We'll ask him when we find him. Either he's an enigma or he's emigrated to Australia.'

'If Charlie York hadn't thought of the connection, we wouldn't have followed up the Adam Ant lead.'

'Cheers to Charlie York,' said Doherty. They raised their glasses in a toast.

'Highwaymen ended up on the gallows. I can see that connection, hence not getting the Adam Ant thing. He did sing the song 'Stand and Deliver' just as a highwayman would do. That's about it. Nice touch in the background. Gallows and highwaymen went together,' said Honey.

'They also figured pretty high as the means of despatching Mr Tern.'

CHAPTER TWELVE

The next day Honey had a surprise visitor at the Green River Hotel.

Lindsey informed her that a Mr Barrington was waiting for her in reception.

Honey frowned. 'Why here?'

'Is he something to do with the case?'

Honey nodded. 'Senior assistant at Tern and Pauling, though not for long. Apparently the deceased had given him notice to quit.'

'That's a motive.'

'Yes,' said Honey. 'It is. I'd better see him in my office.'

Mr Barrington was a picture of nerves. His brow was furrowed, the corners of his mouth were downturned.

He sat down gratefully, his feet swinging a few inches from the floor.

'I did have it in mind to march along to the police station, but I lost the nerve. You see I've never entered a police station before. I have lived a quiet respectable life and the very act of entering those doors filled me with fear. I couldn't do it. Mr Papendriou mentioned that you were a civilian and I might be able to approach you direct. A friend gave him your address. I do hope you don't mind.'

Mr Cecil Barrington looked at the floor as he spoke, though raised a quizzical eyebrow when he'd finished what he'd wanted to say.

Honey smiled. 'Of course not.'

Honey studied the little man sitting on the other side of her desk. She had planned to deal with some paperwork today — mostly bills and officious letters from the council informing her of the latest regulations with regard to listed buildings. The Green River was Grade II, which meant nothing could be drastically altered on the outside. The inside was a different matter though she didn't think it would be too long before the officials had something to say about that too.

'Right. So there's something relevant to the case that you want to tell me. Do you mind if I write it down,' she asked whilst pulling a pad towards her and picking up a pen.

He looked slightly alarmed.

'For the sake of my memory,' she added hastily in order to ease his consternation. 'I forget things if I don't write it down. It's not official — like a police statement. It's just for me.'

He nodded and seemed to relax a little but did not touch the tea Lindsey had brought in for him. He'd also declined the coffee from Honey's percolator, which was always on the go.

'So,' she said, her pen poised for action. 'Where would you like to start?'

Mr Barrington sighed heavily and shook his head. 'I cannot believe it has come to this. I just cannot believe it.'

He continued shaking his head.

'I take it you're enjoying a day off,' she said in a friendly manner she hoped would put him at ease.

'And why not?' he said somewhat huffily. 'I am not obliged to work out my notice.'

'Your notice. I thought it was Nigel who gave you notice and seeing as he's gone . . .'

She purposely left the sentence hanging in mid-air guessing that Mr Barrington would fill in the details.

She was right.

'Mr Arnold has decided that I am too old to continue. My dismissal and subsequent retirement is to stand.'

She felt for him. He was a figure of dejection. His life had been given to his employer and now the employer had done the dirty on him.

Honey maintained her pose. She had done everything possible to put him at ease, hence the tea. She had also instructed Lindsey that they were not to be disturbed. 'And that includes your grandmother,' she'd added in a low voice so Mr Barrington couldn't hear her.

Mr Barrington fingered the teaspoon sitting in his saucer. His eyes were downcast. His mouth moved nervously.

'This is difficult. So difficult,' he muttered. 'I feel like a traitor coming in here like this.'

'Rest assured, Mr Barrington, no one is going to behead you and stick your head on a spike. This is the Green River Hotel not the Tower of London.'

Her attempt at humour failed to illicit a response. Mr Barrington was an employee of the old school having loyally stayed with the same firm for years. She wondered how much he was paid. She guessed not very much.

He was taking his time and she could understand him feeling guilty. He'd worked for Tern and Pauling for a long time. However, she did have a hotel to run. She glanced at her watch. He saw her do it.

'I'm sorry for taking up so much of your time. It's not easy. Not easy at all.'

'Take your time.' She immediately wished she hadn't said it. Time was precious and the officials at the European Union waited for no man.

'The fact is I've nothing appertaining to the slaying of Mr Nigel as such, but I can give you some background information regarding the family and Mr Nigel's lifestyle and . . .' He paused in his search for the right word. 'Other things. Things that are not quite normal . . . not respectable. They might have some bearing on the case. Or they might not.'

Honey nodded. This was all very ambiguous, but there might be something in what he had to say — when he got round to spilling it out.

She smiled reassuringly. 'Well we have to start somewhere. Have you always got on well with your employer?'

'Yes. On the whole. Mr Arnold ran the business somewhat autocratically. By that I mean he was always in charge — there were never any familiarities but everyone knew their place. He was always Mr Arnold or Mr Tern Senior. And it worked the other way too. It was old-fashioned but respectful.'

Honey nodded in understanding. Tern and Pauling had maintained a rigid workplace environment. There was no intermingling between management and staff. Mr Barrington would have fitted well into times past, a typically Victorian style old retainer. She tried not to colour her judgement by thinking that Mr Arnold Tern had more in common with Ebenezer Scrooge and made an unlikely signatory to the Employee Protection Act.

'Excuse me for saying so, but Arnold didn't appear terribly upset at the death of his son.'

Cecil Barrington shifted nervously in his chair. She guessed he was beginning to regret dropping in.

'You mustn't take Mr Arnold at face value. He's a very private man. He never showed any emotion when Deirdre, his wife, died. It isn't, I think, that he doesn't care it's just that he considers death to be part of life. Nothing is fair in this world so get used to it, that's what he always used to say.'

Honey frowned. She'd only met Arnold the once and had disliked him on the spot. However, it wasn't for her to judge. Mr Barrington had put himself out to come. He deserved her undivided attention.

'Still. It was his *son*. How long ago did Nigel take over from his father?'

'Only six months ago when Mr Arnold took ill. Up until that time Mr Arnold came into the shop for a few hours a day, although ostensibly, Mr Nigel was supposed to be running it.'

'Ostensibly? That's an odd word to use. Do you mean he wasn't really running it, or wasn't running it properly?'

Mr Barrington sighed. 'Far be it from me to criticise, but . . . it wasn't the same. He was always popping in and out. Things got mislaid. Clients questioned why he wasn't there. Mr Arnold made a point of being there for his most important clients.'

'But Nigel did not.'

'No. He did not. He was, shall we say, erratic to say the least. Very erratic and unreliable. Mr Nigel, I have to say, was not a reliable man.'

'So Arnold stopped popping in six months ago when he became ill. What was the matter with him?'

Mr Barrington grinned weakly. 'Everything an old man is likely to suffer from. Prostate problems, arthritis, a weak heart. He was rushed into hospital with suspected prostate cancer, but was then allowed home. Then he went in again and then out again. On the last occasion he went in it was found he was suffering from pneumonia. He demanded to be sent home even though he wasn't fully recovered. I understand he had something of a relapse and was unconscious for some time — very ill indeed.'

'And he didn't go back into hospital?'

'He refused and Mr Nigel didn't insist.' He paused as he gathered his thoughts. 'I'm afraid that Mr Nigel's attitude to his father reflected that of Mr Arnold to his son.'

Honey recollected the way the old man had stared at her breasts when speaking. Not once had his eyes fixed on her face. Nigel Tern had been much the same at the prize-giving and publicity event outside the shop. The phrase like father like son came easily to mind.

One particular thing niggled Honey. 'You seem to know a lot about Arnold's illness, Mr Barrington.'

'I phoned the hospital and I asked Mr Nigel every time I saw him. I also phoned the house. Mrs Cayford works at the hospital part time when she isn't at the house, so knew everything that was going on.'

'Mrs Cayford was the lady at the shop the other day?'

'Yes.'

Honey was thoughtful. Had Nigel wished his father dead? Very likely. But how about the other way round?

'Seeing as they didn't like each other very much, you don't think Arnold might have murdered his son?'

For the first time since she'd met him, a touch of humour lit Mr Barrington's face.

'He's hardly likely to be strong enough to do that. Not physically anyway. They didn't like each other, but Mr Arnold was no killer. In fact he was a pacifist during the Korean war era in the early fifties. He still had to do his national service, but was able to get a desk job in Catterick. I think he was an invoice clerk attached to the quartermasters stores.'

Honey nodded thoughtfully. 'Did he dislike his son enough to get somebody else to kill him?'

Barrington shook his head emphatically. 'No. Absolutely not. That isn't the way he does things. He's most certainly not a killer. The way to bring Mr Nigel into line was financially. Mr Nigel liked . . .' Mr Barrington paused. 'He enjoyed a playboy lifestyle. A threat to cut off his salary and allowance, perhaps even threaten to cut him out of his will, would have had more effect. However, As I have already intimated Mr Arnold was ill for six months so Mr Nigel had free rein.'

'I noticed when we were in the shop that he — Arnold — was very angry. Have you ever seen him that angry before?'

'Oh yes. Although Mr Arnold is a gentleman and prefers the company of gentlemen, he does have a temper. Of course he does not show this when in the company of clients, especially titled gentlemen and royalty.'

'What did Mrs Tern die of?'

'Oh, she drowned in a boating accident. Mr Nigel was at boarding school at the time. He was about nine years old.'

'I understand Mr Nigel was quite a ladies' man. Do you know who those ladies might have been?'

'No.'

His response was very emphatic. She didn't believe him.

'Did he have any enemies that you know of?'

'Plenty. He was not a likeable man.' Mr Barrington frowned. 'I only wish I'd stood up to him, but he was the boss and I let everything flow over me. He liked being in control. He kept the shop assistants under his thumb, his family and the subcontracted tailors. Some of them plain hated him, but nobody turns down work of this calibre. You see it's such a feather in the cap. Some of them can boast of making a sports jacket for a prince — and I think you know who I mean without a name being mentioned.'

Honey thought of Highgrove. It wasn't far away. Boasting that you'd made a jacket for the heir to the throne was a definite marketing advantage.

'How about Mr Pauling? I believe he died some time ago?'

Barrington nodded. 'He died some time ago in a skiing accident. Miss Grace was injured in a skiing accident. That's why she's in a wheelchair.'

'Two accidents!'

'Indeed.'

'At the same time as her father?'

'No. Sometime later.' He frowned suddenly. 'No. I'm wrong. It was at the same time. I've only just realised it.'

It occurred to Honey that Tern and Pauling, tailors and outfitters to the gentry, were accident-prone.

'Was there anything else you think might be useful?'

Mr Barrington shifted uncomfortably in his chair. 'Yes. Floyd Bennett-Simpson. He offered to buy the property in Beaufort Alley a while ago. He kept pestering Mr Arnold to sell but Mr Arnold would have none of it. But Mr Nigel has had lunch with him a few times following Mr Bennett-Simpson's visits to the shop. I think Mr Nigel was willing to sell. He kept it from his father of course.'

The day was rolling on and this interview was taking longer than anticipated. Honey kept her cool. She suspected that Mr Barrington was privy to a lot more than he was letting on. He'd seemed quite expansive at first, but had become more withdrawn the more the interview had gone on. However, she thought, it didn't hurt to press on.

'Nigel seemed to have his own agenda with regard to the shop.'

'He did.'

'So tell me if I've got this wrong; Arnold knew nothing about the refurbishments or the fact that Nigel was considering selling. Is that what you're saying?'

He seemed to think about it before nodding. 'I think so.'

Honey frowned. What would be the point of refurbishing a shop situated in a building you were thinking of selling?

'Am I right in thinking there are residential apartments above the shop?'

'Yes. Six in total.'

'Do any of the staff live there?'

Mr Barrington chuckled. 'None of us earn enough to afford the rents. Some of the residents have lived there for quite some time. Others are newcomers, friends of Mr Nigel. Some of them are women.'

'I thought you said you didn't know any of his women.'

Mr Barrington shifted in his seat. 'I think I should leave now.'

She shrugged. 'No matter. They'll be questioned.'

He nodded curtly as he slid off the chair looking quite relieved when his feet hit the floor.

'I'm sorry you lost your job, Mr Barrington. I think some of what you have told me might be helpful. It's not evidence, but it is useful background information. Thank you again for dropping in.'

* * *

Honey phoned Doherty the moment Mr Barrington had left.

'I've had a visitor. Mr Cecil Barrington popped in. He wants the police to know but doesn't wish to be seen entering a police station.'

'I don't blame him. A right den of iniquity!'

Honey laughed.

'So what did he tell you?'

'Mainly general stuff, though I can't help getting the impression that he knows more than he admits to. Mr Nigel Tern dismissed him from service and to his great surprise, the old man has followed suit. Obviously he was angry and came in here determined to take revenge on being dismissed, but his courage ran out. He told me a few bits and pieces, though nothing that won't keep. Any progress your end?'

'We've interviewed the residents in the flats above the shop and in the other buildings too. Nobody saw anything.'

'From what Mr Barrington told me, some of those flats are let to Nigel's lady friends.'

'We need a list of them from him, then. Nobody actually admitted to knowing Nigel intimately.'

'I take it the alibis for the employees check out.'

'As far as we can tell, though it's early days. Did Barrington give you any leads to anyone who might have had a motive?'

'Not really, except there was a developer interested in buying the property. He'd already approached Arnold Tern who'd promptly turned him down. Apparently Mr Nigel Tern was more amenable and quite friendly with him, lunched with him a few times. It did seem as though he was interested in selling, though I have to ask why Mr Tern would modernise the shop if he was thinking of selling it.'

'He wouldn't. I wouldn't.'

'Although of course the Tern Trust does own a number of other properties in Bath, though I doubt Nigel was in a position to sell whilst his father was still alive . . . which begs the question…'

'Was Nigel anticipating his father's imminent demise?'

'It's worth a thought.'

Honey considered what she might do if she were considering selling the Green River Hotel. A lick of paint, perhaps, but Nigel Tern had carried out a total revamp. To her mind it suggested that he anticipated carrying on trading. She voiced her thoughts to Doherty.

'My thoughts exactly.'

'I take it Nigel was the old man's sole beneficiary as the only son.'

'We're checking on that, though it's hard to pin his solicitor down. Her time seems to be split between hospital and client appointments.'

Honey remembered the woman in the wheelchair. 'Are we talking about Grace Pauling?'

'The very same.'

'I wonder how close she was to Nigel?'

'They'd known each other for most of their lives. She isn't unattractive.'

She cut the phone connection. Her mind went back to the presentation. John Rees had seemed to know quite a bit about Grace Pauling. She decided to give him a call; better still, how about a walk? You could do with some fresh air, she told herself.

Rifleman's Way was crowded with people, milling around with blank-faced enthusiasm and cameras hanging around their necks. Honey wondered how they managed to do much sightseeing if they were forever taking videos and photos. She concluded that they didn't really get to enjoy where they'd been until they got home, visiting the places again by proxy via a computer screen.

The brass bell above the door jangled approvingly. Unlike some lone shopkeepers, John Rees had not been tempted to get rid of the old bell and put a pressure sensor under the doormat. The décor Nigel Tern had adopted for his gentlemen's outfitters wouldn't suit him at all.

Lean, rangy and looking dishy without meaning to, he was serving a Japanese couple but managed to mouth a swift hello in her direction. Honey hovered by the door, waiting for him to finalise his business.

'Mercator charts are very collectable,' she heard him say.

The Japanese couple nodded their heads silently as they poured over what he was offering them, the man's spectacles perched half way down his nose.

Deciding that things were likely to take a little longer than anticipated, Honey wandered further into the shop. She occasionally took a book from the shelf, more attracted by its spine that its title. There were exceptions of course. She came across an old copy of *Fanny Hill*. She was no expert, but it looked like a first edition. It felt good in her hands, the cover a little rough.

Fanny Hill! Now there was a girl who had unswervingly exploited her looks, the only real asset that she'd owned.

The rustling of a paper carrier bag — John refused to use plastic — and the tinkling of the till drawer, was followed by the bell jangling as the couple left clutching their purchases.

Honey smiled at John from the far end of the shop. John smiled back.

'A good profit I hope.'

'I got what I wanted. It was an old map of Japan — before too much of it was properly charted. They loved it.'

'And you loved the price they paid?'

'You bet I did. Can I get you a glass of wine? I've got a bottle to finish off, then I'm off out to spend the proceeds of the sale replenishing my cellar.'

'You don't have a wine cellar.'

'I have a cupboard! And a fridge.'

Honey smiled. 'You always offer me wine before anything else.'

'I do have coffee, but it's a bit stewed.'

Honey glanced at the glass percolator. 'It doesn't look stewed. It's still dripping.'

John grinned and shrugged his broad shoulders. 'Oh well. That's my excuse scuppered. Join me in celebrating my sale. White or red?'

She chose white.

'Ah yes,' he said opening the small fridge that was neatly hidden behind the counter. 'You always prefer white at lunchtime.'

'Even though it's not quite lunchtime,' she replied wryly.

She quite enjoyed the clink as they touched glasses. There was something reassuring about it. For a start it made her forget that blasted paperwork.

John had a pleasant smile. 'I take it your visit is not just for pleasure — although of course I live in hope.'

She just about controlled her urge to turn pink. While Doherty was her daily bread, it didn't hurt to fancy a bagel now and again — as long as it remained nothing more than a passing fancy.

'I suppose there's no point in asking if you are aware of the demise of Nigel Tern.'

John gave a sideways tilt of his head as he continued to pour. 'Nobody could fail to be aware of it. What a way to go! It could almost be described as a live performance — if it wasn't for the fact that he was dead.'

Honey pulled a face. 'That's not funny.'

'It wasn't meant to be.'

John asked her to give him more detail. 'I can't help being interested. I mean, was he a one-off or is there a serial killer on the loose with something against shopkeepers. Worse still, am I next? You see. I can't help being interested. Everyone is interested.'

Honey outlined the scene in the shop window — the way it was after the gentlemen's outfitters had won the window display award.

'I saw it earlier in the day. It was dramatic, perhaps even a bit melodramatic, but there was no swinging body. Oh sorry, I should say there was no dead body hanging from the gallows at least.'

'You saw it that morning?'

He nodded. 'Yep. Then you saw it.'

'You were one of the judges.'

'Correct.'

'Who was the third?'

John shrugged his shoulders. 'Beats me. Everything was normal when me and Lee Curtis swept past. It ticked a few boxes for me, though not all. I preferred the display in the window of The Chocolate Soldier.'

'Really?' Honey frowned. 'I gave it top marks. You gave The Chocolate Solider top marks then?'

'Yep. That's about the size of it.'

'I'm presuming our third judge was of the same opinion as me and voted for Tern and Pauling.'

'You'd have to ask him or her.' John finished his tipple and poured himself another. Honey declined a top up.

'So who was the first person to see the body hanging there?'

'A street sweeper found him. He was a bit shocked to say the least. I mean nobody expects to find a murdered man in a shop window. I keep thinking the killer was trying to send a message but the police are having none of it. The thing is if it was the old man swinging from the gallows, the finger would be pointed at his son simply because he would inherit everything. As it is, the old man still has everything and might very well be at a loss as to who to leave his money to.'

John frowned. 'I think there are relatives, though not close relatives. I don't think the old man was one to encourage visits from relatives he had no time for.'

'You know that for sure?'

John hitched a 'swimmer' from the glass with his pinky. There were a lot of midges around this year and a few seemed keen on dive-bombing into a cold Chardonnay or plum-red Shiraz.

He nodded slowly, one arm across his chest, hand tucked into his armpit. He gestured for Honey to take a seat behind the counter whilst he leaned against the end of a bookcase.

'His wife had family. None of them were welcome when she was alive so they certainly weren't after she died. I think Mr Tern Senior may have had a sister. I don't know the details except that she approached him at one time with regard to him helping her out money-wise. I'm not sure whether she was married, but I did hear rumour that she got 'in trouble' as girls were said to do back then, and needed his help. Needless to say, he sent her packing.'

'How do you know all this?'

John's grin widened, his hand holding the wine glass at shoulder level. He looked impishly naughty, a factor that sent a shiver down Honey's spine.

'One of the hired help — in his house, not in his shop.'

Honey regarded him quizzically, aware of the weight of her hair on her shoulder as she tilted her head.

'Not a nurse by any chance?'

He hid his smile in a sip of the white wine remaining in his glass.

'I'm a sucker for a nurse in uniform. The old type mind. Not these scrubs. They may be more hygienic and convenient, but hey, starched aprons crackled when a nurse bent over to plump your pillows. You'd never get that with a set of scrubs. And that was besides the black stockings . . .'

Honey raised her hand in a traffic stopping gesture.

'Hold it there, cowboy. Can we keep to the subject in hand?'

He sighed. 'If you must.'

'It wouldn't be Edwina Cayford you're talking about would it?'

He laughed. 'You've found me out.'

'She doesn't wear a nurse's outfit, at least not when she's working for Mr Tern Senior. She only cleans for him.'

'No. She doesn't wear it at the hospital, but she will make an exception for close friends with a liking for stiff caps and starched aprons. I think it's something of a sideline. You know, rent-a-gram, rent-a-nurse, rent-a-snakecharmer. I hear it's good money.'

It hit Honey hard that John fancied other women and not just herself. It almost made her jealous. She'd quite liked the thought of having a bird in the hand and one flapping about nearby. She'd already been told that Edwina Cayford worked at the hospital as well as for private clients. She wondered at her financial circumstances. Would she do anything for money? And why was that? Was she in debt? Did she have family commitments? It was worth looking into.

'You pointed Arnold Tern's lawyer out to me, the woman in the wheelchair. How well do you know her?'

He made a casual half wave with the hand that held the wine glass.

'Well enough. She collects first editions. We have exchanged books for cash.'

'Grace Pauling collects books?'

'She does indeed.'

'You don't know her on a personal level.'

A quirky grin lifted his mouth. The direct look he was giving her made her toes curl.

'I know her. I've had lunch with her and although she gave me very strong signals, I did not take it further.'

'She propositioned you?'

'Don't sound so surprised. Women do like me you know.'

'I don't doubt it.'

His grin widened. 'Go ahead then. Proposition me.'

'Am I in with a chance?'

He put his glass down. 'You know the answer to that. Now stop fishing for compliments and get down to business. Grace Pauling is the daughter of Arnold Tern's partner, but you know that already.'

'Any idea who might be the beneficiary of Mr Arnold Tern's will?'

John shrugged. 'It would obviously have been Nigel Tern. But now . . .' he shrugged. 'It's anybody's guess. Could be a relative. Could be the Cats' Protection Society. Or it could be the dedicated nurse who he would be sure to ambush if he were a few years younger.'

She perceived a secretive look in his eyes.

'Would your Miss Cayford know?'

'*Mrs* Cayford. She's divorced. She's got two kids. One in his twenties. The other a teenager.'

'Is she likely to know who would benefit?'

'What makes you think I know her that well?'

'Do you?'

'Some.'

'Perhaps when you see her next . . .'

The mischievous glint in his eyes resurfaced.

'What makes you think I'm still seeing her?'

She slapped the wine glass into his hand and grinned wickedly. 'Because you're not seeing me. I've seen Edwina Cayford and believe she's the consolation prize!'

His laughter rang out behind her along with the jangling of the shop bell. She couldn't help smiling and blushing to think she'd been so brazen. On top of that she must have sounded so superior. Consolation prize indeed! If ever there was a parting of the ways between her and Doherty, John was her consolation prize.

CHAPTER THIRTEEN

Doherty had called into the Green River Hotel. Over fresh coffee and croissants oozing with Ricotta cheese and jam, they'd discussed the probabilities of the will, though of course they could only guess at its contents. They also discussed Grace Pauling who acted for both the deceased and his father, Mr Arnold Tern.

'Seeing as she acted for the Terns, I wonder whether she knew that Nigel had been approached to sell the property.'

'If we ask she'll quote the rules of confidentiality between client and lawyer. It could be interesting though. So could this business with Alan Roper. But was it the shop property Nigel Tern was up for selling? It could have been another one held by the Trust. We need to question Grace Pauling about it.'

'She's not the friendliest of people,' remarked Honey.

'She's a solicitor. They rarely are! Give me some time and I'll see if I can finally tie her down to an appointment. Can we meet up tonight and discuss it then?'

'The Zodiac?'

'Yep. Close to the witching hour.'

'Great. I'll bring my broomstick.'

After stacking the crockery and taking it along to the kitchen, Honey did her best to take herself in hand, which in layman's terms, meant getting back inside her office and tackling that damned paperwork. But before doing that there were important questions to ask and Lindsey, her daughter, was the one with all the answers.

'Is Mary Jane still camped out on the first-floor landing?'

'No. She's gone to the research library on College Green to check on old legends regarding this house.'

Honey groaned. 'I wish she wasn't doing that. Anyway, it's a *hotel* not a house.'

'It was built as a house first. A gentleman's town residence as they were so fond of saying back then,' said Lindsey as she sorted a pile of pamphlets, some advertising the delights of the Royal Crescent and others the Roman Baths. They needed to be separate.

'Lindsey, it was not a ghost! I'm sure of it.' The fact is she didn't want it to be a ghost. They had plenty enough already.

'How sure?'

Lindsey had a forthright way of looking at her mother — of looking at anyone come to that.

'Well . . .'

The truth was Honey didn't know for sure who the woman was that she'd seen hovering behind the arched window on the first floor. What she did know that advertising the fact could bring in a horde of amateur ghost hunters and having one in residence — i.e. Mary Jane — was quite enough.

'You don't fancy the fact that somebody committed suicide upstairs.'

'Or downstairs for that matter. I mean she might very well have slipped and it wasn't that far to fall anyway. She might have survived. Not a good plan if she was trying to commit suicide either now or in the past.'

'But you just said yourself that you didn't think it was a ghost. If it wasn't, who was it and where are they now?'

Lindsey had a knack of getting to the point that made her mother feel very uncomfortable.

'You have a point. If it wasn't a ghost, then who was it? A reflection?'

She thought about it. The windows of the Green River Hotel had been reflecting the sky and the buildings opposite. So perhaps the woman had jumped from there. She frowned as she thought about it. There had been no reports of anyone jumping or falling out of the first-floor window opposite. Still, it wouldn't hurt to pop over there and find out.

Lindsey had already turned back to her computer screen. 'I've done a bit of research on Mary Jane's behalf. She wouldn't do it herself. She's not keen on computers. She reckons some of them can capture your soul.'

'I think it's Xbox that does that,' murmured Honey. She knew these things. She had friends with children who lived their lives through computer games. 'I'm not even sure my son can even talk,' one of her friends had said to her. 'He never speaks to me.'

'I'm thinking of going on a trekking tour,' Lindsey suddenly said.

'Devon again?' Honey remarked as she flicked through the post on the desk. Her spirit lifted at the carefully written enquiries for winter breaks. Some, like these, came through the post, mostly written by older people. The majority came by email though yet again mostly from senior citizens enquiring about weekend winter breaks especially around the time of the Christmas market.

'No. Nepal.'

Honey stopped flicking through the post. 'Isn't that in India?'

'North of India. Squashed between India and Tibet.'

'Are you sure that's safe?'

Lindsey sighed in that patronising way younger people had, as though parents had never had adventures — which was true, well, at least not in Nepal. Honey had never been there.

'As safe or perhaps safer than Bristol City Centre on a Saturday night,' said Lindsey.

Honey was far from reassured. She might have had something further to say if her phone hadn't rung.

'I've got a list of Nigel Tern's girlfriends,' said Doherty. 'There are no women officers to accompany me on interviews. It seems they're all down with colds or on holiday. I reckon bikinis have got a lot to do with it.'

'Could be due to Brazilians,' said Honey. 'Everyone who buys a tiny bikini makes a date to have a Brazilian.'

'Brazilians? I didn't know Bath had had an influx of Brazilian tourists.'

Doherty sounded totally confounded.

Honey refrained from bursting out laughing. She wasn't about to go into detail about women exfoliating in the most intimate places once they'd tried on the new bikini.

'I'll explain later. Trust me. In the course of time, all will become clear.'

'If you say so. I've arranged to meet these women in their homes with the exception of Anne Kemp. She works nights and would prefer we either call in before she goes to bed, that is first thing in the morning or in the evening at work. She starts at nine p.m., so I'm opting for interviewing her at work.'

'Fine with me. When is this happening?'

'Tomorrow morning. In the early hours. Well, just after midnight I think will be best. Are you OK with that?'

'Fine. Do I need to do any research first?'

'Yep! The merits of an underground drinking den after the hours of darkness.'

'OK. Zodiac Club, as we said. Ten this evening.'

'Fine. After that we move on to the Lucky Lady Pole Dancing Club.'

'Either you're trying to encourage me to change career or Anne Kemp works there.'

'She does indeed.'

'I'm popping over the road to Dennison and Dimply,' said Honey once she'd severed the connection with Doherty.

'The solicitors?'

'That's them.'

'Not our own solicitors.'

'No. There's something I need to ask them that our own solicitors couldn't possibly help with.'

She smiled brightly.

When Lindsey narrowed her eyes her mother knew she was under close scrutiny.

'I won't be long,' she quipped, mainly in a bid to avoid further questions. She was going to ask the firm of solicitors across the road about the woman who might have jumped, just in case the fact hadn't travelled through the grapevine.

A grey-haired lady smiled at her when she entered.

'I need to speak to one of the senior partners — I think.'

'Can I have your name?'

'Mrs Driver. Mrs Hannah Driver, I own the Green River Hotel, just across the road there.'

'Oh really,' said the woman as though not quite believing her, as well she might. Nobody from the firm had ever crossed the threshold of the Green River Hotel.

The woman scribbled something down. 'And what is the matter for which you need legal advice,' she asked.

Honey suddenly felt tongue-tied. 'Well . . . actually . . . I don't need advice as such, I just want clarification of . . .'

Aware that she was beginning to ramble, she took a deep breath. Gathering her thoughts wasn't easy, but she did her best.

'The fact is I thought I saw somebody fall from the first-floor landing window in my hotel. I was standing admiring the building's proportions, when suddenly . . . there she was . . . arms outstretched . . . falling . . . or jumping . . .'

The woman looked up at her open-mouthed.

'I'm not mad,' said Honey. 'I really did see somebody at my first-floor window. That one,' she said, pointing out of the ground floor window of the solicitors' office.

'Ah,' said the woman, still looking at her strangely. 'We wondered where she'd gone.'

Now it was Honey's turn to look perplexed. 'What do you mean? Wondered where who had gone?'

'Emily Bennett. She used to haunt here, but Mr Dennison had had enough of it. She was always running along the landing and throwing herself out of the window. I know she's only a ghost, but it got a bit wearing especially when one was with a client. I mean, you know how those Regency gowns were; muslin and almost see through. It was most embarrassing, so Mr Dennison got an exorcist in.'

Honey stood with her mouth open, barely believing what she was hearing.

'Are you telling me that this woman has decamped to my hotel?'

The woman jerked her pert chin in what passed for a nod. 'Lady Emily Bennett. She fell in love with the wrong man, a right scoundrel so legend has it. She lived here and he lived over there — in the days when your hotel was just a house. He let her down badly apparently. Got her into trouble and broke her heart in the days when a girl was easily ruined like that.'

Suddenly Honey felt a great sense of unease. 'You don't happen to know what his name was, do you.'

Honey already had a gut feeling of who it was likely to be, but she had to hear it from this woman who worked for the man who'd hired an exorcist to get rid of the spectre.

'Sir Cedric somebody or other,' said the woman. 'Can't remember the rest of his name, but the first bit was definitely Sir Cedric.'

CHAPTER FOURTEEN

Honey didn't breathe a word of her other investigation to Doherty. Determined to deal with it herself, she focused her mind on the job in hand. The murder of Nigel Tern was at the top of her list and here she was about to gain entry into a pole-dancing club.

The gorilla at the door rolled his shoulders and told them they couldn't come in.

'Members only. Ladies can come in unaccompanied or with fully paid-up members.'

'She's with me,' Doherty said firmly.

'Sorry mate, but I do need a look at your membership card.'

'I haven't got one.'

'Then you can't come in either, buster!'

Doherty flashed his warrant card.

'I think you'll find this card covers our entrance permission and fees. The name's Doherty. Detective Inspector Doherty. I need to speak to Anne Kemp. That's why I've got a woman colleague with me.'

The man with the bowling-ball head and the polyester suit scowled but stood aside and waved them in.

The lighting in the Lucky Lady Pole Dancing Club was very low, so much so that Honey tripped over a protruding foot. Normally she might have ended up sprawling on the floor, but instead found herself hanging onto a pole, one of the ones semi-nude dancers usually did their thing with.

'Honey, stop messing about,' Doherty muttered, but did nothing to help her.

It might have been fine if the plinth the pole was slotted into hadn't suddenly elevated from the floor so it was like a miniature stage, about four feet up from the rest of the floor. Apparently all the dancers' plinths did that, a signal for the next act to begin. All eyes looked expectantly in Honey's direction.

Cheek by jowl with the shiny pole, she found herself caught in the glare of a powerful spotlight.

Blinking into the murky gloom, she espied hairless heads shiny with sweat and male faces turned in her direction, each one wearing an expectant expression.

There was a breathless hush.

Somebody shouted. 'Come on. Get your clothes off!'

'Yeah. Come on. We've paid to see you dance not hang around as though you're waiting for a bus.'

Typical. There was always a comedian.

'I tripped. I'm not supposed to be up here.'

'We don't mind amateurs. A pair of tits is a pair of tits!'

'You moron!' she shouted back. 'Do you hear any music playing?'

'Who needs music!'

'Honey,' Doherty said in a loud whisper. 'I told you to stop messing around. Get down from there!'

Doherty offered his hand. She took it with both of her own and let him help her down.

'You were almost the star turn,' he whispered, his smirk hidden by darkness. 'I've asked for Anne to join us. In the meantime let's get out of the limelight shall we?'

They ended up sitting at a table in the darkest part of the room. The spotlight was suddenly dimmed, though not for long. The darkness was the dancer's cue to step onto the plinth and grind her stuff.

Up came the lights, focusing on the nubile young woman who had stepped onto the plinth Honey had been on earlier. To the sound of Nicki Minaj, she began gyrating against the pole. Honey felt the onset of a hot flush. If ever a song imitated in lyrics and beat the sex act, it was that one.

A roar of approval went up from the crowd. All eyes were on the young woman, her supple body glistening with oil, her breasts bare, her buttocks divided by nothing more than a strip of black lace thong. The music matched the movements.

The young woman, who she had no doubt was Anne Kemp, placed her legs to either side of the pole, dipping and stretching, humping and weaving around it.

Doherty had fallen to silence. So had Honey. Both of them were staring at Anne Kemp. Surely she was far too alluring and young to be a girlfriend of Nigel Tern?

Still, thought Honey, *the Alpha male has it all their own way*. No matter if he had the looks of a smashed bus, he had the status and the money. To a girl like Anne Kemp that was all that mattered.

Despite the dim lighting, Honey could see enough to discern that she was the only woman in the place. Wall to wall men as far as the eye could see. Her cheeks burned.

Her mouth turning dry, she glanced at Doherty. The outline of his face dipped into shadows as he glanced down at his watch. His attention went back to the girl for a moment. He leaned closer and whispered into Honey's ear.

'I know I invited her to join us, but my time might be better served elsewhere. I'm going backstage. I fancy asking a few questions about Anne Kemp. Just some background stuff. Who knows what might come up?'

She started to protest. 'You're going to leave me here,' she hissed.

'Yes. You'll be fine. When she's finished, follow her out. OK?'

'I'm surrounded by seedy-looking men,' she hissed back.

'How do you know that? You can't see them.'

He was right of course. The brightest spot in the place was the plinth and the nubile girl doing her stuff. She was probably in her mid-twenties. Honey thought then that she had seen her somewhere before, though goodness knows where.

It was hard to see. Honey put it down to the dim lighting, though Anne herself had a lot to do with it. She wound around that chromium pole like a snake in the Garden of Eden. Her body was supple and toned, tanned and glistening. Her G string didn't cover very much at all.

The Nicki Minaj number was replaced by something similar though more upbeat. Honey couldn't think of the name of it.

Once the second piece of music finished, the podium settled back into the floor, the girl giving a final twirl whilst holding on with one hand.

The men shouted and clapped. The girl waved. Honey prepared herself to get up from her chair and follow her backstage to the relative safety of the changing rooms. It appeared that Anne Kemp had other plans, heading straight for her.

She was tall and smelled of exertion. She was also breathless. Her dark hair swung around her shoulders. Her eyes were brown.

'Mind if I sit down?'

'Be my guest.'

The girl's white teeth shone thanks to the purplish glow of the table lamp. Its light distorted the girl's facial features, though not enough to make them ugly. Anne Kemp was beautiful.

'Nice to see you again,' said the dancer, her broad smile only slightly smaller than the wisp of material covering her pubes.

'Have we met before . . . ?' asked Honey. Anne's question confirmed her own suspicions. She racked her brains. Not in another nightclub that was for sure!

'You wouldn't remember me. I was wearing a lot more than I am now. I was a bridesmaid at my sister's wedding. We held the reception at the Green River Hotel. That's where you're from isn't it? Aren't you the owner?'

Anne spoke in a North Country accent. Honey wasn't sure whether it was Yorkshire or Lancashire.

'Your sister! What was her name?'

'Beverley. Beverley Kemp though she became Beverley Simpson when she married Brian. He's a footballer you know. Plays for Bristol City.'

'Of course. Brian Simpson!'

Actually she regarded football to be as interesting as watching paint dry, but it paid to have some knowledge of the game, at least on a local level.

She glanced over Anne's shoulder to see where Doherty had got to. What a turn-up! He'd gone backstage in the hope of talking to people who knew Anne for the low down on her lifestyle and Anne had plonked herself down at the table in front of her. Not only that, it wasn't the first time they'd met. Her sister had held her wedding reception at the Green River Hotel.

Anne was bubbling with friendliness. Honey considered it quite refreshing. She was also totally bereft of embarrassment.

'What a coincidence! And guess what, we've got something else in common,' said Honey. 'A mutual friend in fact.'

'Is that right? Who's that then?'

'I was one of the judges for the window display competition. I voted for the one with the highwayman in the window. You know, Tern and Pauling? The gentleman's outfitters down in Beaumont Alley. Of course, it was just a display then,' said Honey, her voice softening. 'Mr Tern was enjoying himself when I saw him. He was still alive, not strung up on his own gallows. I understand you knew him.'

'Ah yes,' said Anne sounding genuinely sad. 'I did. We were an item for a bit but Nigel was too flighty to stay with anyone for long.'

'So you knew Nigel Tern well?'

'No need to be shy. I knew Nigel very well, as in *knew* in the Biblical sense,' Anne replied nodding in a decidedly disagreeable fashion. 'All his girls *knew* him.'

'Would you say you were close?'

Anne sighed. 'We were for a time. That was when I thought it was the real thing and that he really cared for me. He even took me to one of his club nights, or society nights as he called them. I think I was the only girl from the club he ever took there.'

'Society? What kind of society?'

Honey maintained a non-judgemental expression. She was anticipating some kind of swingers' club, sadomasochism even. Her imagination was going wild. What she hadn't foreseen was Anne's surprising answer.

'The Adam Ant Impersonation Society. I only went with him the once.' She threw back her head and laughed as she remembered. 'You ought to have seen them! All these middle-aged overweight geezers wearing tight pants and stuff; a bit like Johnnie Depp in *Pirates of the Caribbean* but twice the size.'

'He dressed up like that?'

'He did,' laughed Anne. 'He should have remembered how young his idol was back then. Should have remembered how young he'd been too.'

'But it was a highwayman in the window,' said Honey.

'Oh yes. I saw it. To my mind it looked better at night when everything around it was dark.'

Honey got up early, but not as early as Charlie York. He was up before it was light. The window display would have been at its most dramatic, confined by the lights, dawn only beginning to light the sky. No wonder he'd been shocked what with the music he was listening to plus the sight of his idol in the shop window.

'He loved dressing up, especially in that highwayman gear,' Anne mused. 'Once I knew his secret, he was dressing up all the time — you know, in private, before we got it on — if you know what I mean. The silk was nice. And the velvet. Really soft.'

Her smile said it all.

Honey nodded. She knew very well what she meant.

'It was his passion. His true passion,' Anne went on. 'He'd been a huge fan in his youth. Couldn't see the attraction myself.' Anne shrugged her naked shoulders. 'But there you are. Each to their own. Can't hold dressing up against him, can we.'

It struck Honey that Anne was totally unphased by the fact that she was sitting there topless. Funnily enough Honey had also forgotten the fact herself. Wasn't it usual to put a top on once the dance had ended? She must be frozen but Anne remained oblivious.

However, the male audience, or at least a portion of it, seemed suddenly to wake up to this fact. A member of a stag night crowd, the intended bridegroom most likely the one sprawled across the table top completely out of it, came staggering over.

'Can I buy you ladies a drink?'

He was holding a bottle of beer in one hand. Judging by the way he was swaying, his knees had turned to jelly due to the amount he'd drunk.

Unperturbed by the state of him, Anne smiled and said she would like champagne. 'A bottle please. For me and my friend.'

She nodded at Honey.

Tottering one pace forward and one back, the young man leered at Honey.

'Yeah! Right. You gonna give us a good show later on love?'

'I'm afraid not,' said Honey. 'Prior engagement.'

The stag night stud persisted. 'Gonna show us yer tits?'

Honey smiled at Anne. 'I think it's time I was going.'

'No need to rush off,' slurred the wobbly young man, his hand pressing down on her shoulder so she was forced to sit back down. 'Plenty of time for you to get your kit off. In fact, how about you undress here? We don't mind lads if she gets 'er kit off 'ere, do we,' he shouted at his friends.

There was much jeering from the row of tables. Some applause.

'Get it off! Get it off!'

Judging by the amount of wine and beer bottles ranged along the tables they sat behind, the stag night crowd were in no state to even remember why they were here, let alone appreciate a striptease.

'I think you should be back with your mates,' ordered a male voice. Doherty was back.

The drunk winced as he tried to focus. Doherty wasn't overly big, but he could adopt a menacing presence when he wanted to.

The drunk's smile disappeared as he attempted to harden his expression and focus on the man talking to him.

He saw a man standing before him dressed in black; black T-shirt, black leather jacket, blue denim jeans that probably looked black to the drunk anyway.

He drew in his chin when he looked at Doherty and swallowed a belch.

'You a bouncer then?'

'No. I'm a copper. I'm here to escort this young lady home.' He was referring to Honey.

The lad sneered. 'Nabbing the best fer yerself, are you? Well I think the young lady will have more fun with me. Not some sodding copper! Is that what you said you were?'

'Yep. I'm a copper.' Doherty reached out to Honey. 'Ready?'

The young man grabbed his arm and sneered into his face.

'Copper. Bouncer. All the same to me. I don't care what you are. You ain't telling me what to do. I don't take any lip from anyone.'

Doherty sighed. 'Sit down or I'll make you sit down.'

The young man wobbled close, his face only inches from that of Doherty.

'You and whose army?'

Doherty poked the thrust-out chest with one finger. The drunk's legs buckled. He sank down to the floor.

Honey smiled at Anne as she got to her feet.

'Thanks, Anne. See you again some time. Enjoy your champagne when it comes.'

'I will.'

Doherty cupped Honey's elbow. 'Let's get out of here whilst the going's good.'

Honey glanced over her shoulder. The young man was otherwise engaged trying to get up from the floor on legs that refused to do so.

'It is good,' she said to him as they navigated between assorted tables and headed past the bar. 'He's suddenly noticed that Anne is sitting there topless.'

'That should sober him up,' said Doherty, but didn't look back.

CHAPTER FIFTEEN

Caroline Corbett, who lived in the second floor flat above Tern and Pauling, held a glass of water in one hand and two tablets in the other. She was about to swallow the latter and take a sip of the former when the intercom buzzed.

Placing both items down on top of a bookcase, she made her way to the window, drew back a portion of muslin curtain and looked down into the street. A man and a woman. It had to be police.

She let the curtain fall just before the man took a step back and looked up. She sank back against the wall, her heart thudding behind her ribs. They wanted to ask her about Nigel. Unfortunately they'd picked the wrong time. She didn't want to talk about him. Not yet. Not until she'd got over the shock and also sorted out what she was going to tell them; certainly not the whole truth. She couldn't possibly do that. She would just say they had been close. Close, she thought, knowing how they would interpret close and what she meant by it. But not yet. She couldn't divulge anything just yet until she'd taken her pills and slept.

She picked up the pills first then paused, surprised that she'd left them immediately in front of his photograph. It was a face and shoulders shot and he was leaning forward slightly, smiling out at her like the old-fashioned Hollywood legends used to do, a casual though at the same time, glamorous shot.

He looked warm; affable, the kind of man that every mother wants her daughter to marry. Yet beneath that veneer . . .

She popped the pills into her mouth and then the water.

'Not that it stopped me loving you,' she whispered, following the contours of his face with her fingers.

When the phone began ringing, she ignored that too. She knew who it was and what they would want, what they would tell her to do. But she wouldn't do anything else to help them. Whatever they wanted they would have to do for themselves.

Once the phone went to voicemail she switched it off and headed for the bedroom. She wanted to sleep. Just sleep. And she didn't care if she never woke up.

* * *

Like an old man with aching joints, the coach house Honey shared with her daughter grunted and creaked as it settled down for the night.

Doherty was sharing her bed. The shutters were drawn. Lindsey was staying the night with a friend. Honey had an inkling it was a male friend, but had refrained from asking questions. Her daughter was old enough to expect privacy and they were both grown-up about things like that.

Propped up in bed, they were halfway through a bottle of dry white wine when they settled back against the pillows, the bottle sitting temptingly on a bedside table.

Their conversation turned to the case in hand, discussing the fact that Nigel Tern had had many girlfriends, some of whom he was fonder of than others.

The fact that Nigel Tern dressed up as an eighteenth-century highwayman, or more specifically like Adam Ant, a singer from the early eighties, added a certain new light-heartedness to the case. It made the victim seem so human, so open to dramatic suggestion.

'The idea for the window display had to be his,' murmured Honey. 'Vasey Casey was just following his instructions. Have you got the name of the person who came down to erect it?'

'Dandy Simcox. She sounded quite a nice person and was happy to help.'

'Did he try to hit on her, do you think?'

'He didn't actually. She says a woman oversaw the whole thing. She couldn't recall her name off the top of her head, but remembers she was very upmarket and had fair hair held back with an Alice Band and a very cut-glass accent. She'd going to check her files to see if she made a note of her name.'

'Somebody at Tern and Pauling might remember?'

'That is true. Are you doing anything tomorrow?'

'I could be.'

He leaned over and kissed her.

'That's my girl.'

Honey smiled. 'You'll have to do more than that to show how grateful you are.'

He grinned. 'Give me time. I'm only warming up.'

He lay back on the pillow, one arm tucked behind his head.

'What bugs me is that the gallows were far more authentic and strongly built than they needed to be,' he continued. 'They really could take a man's weight. Surely if they were just for display, they didn't need to be built that well.'

Honey yawned as she thought about it. The busy day was catching up with her. She lay back tucking her hands behind her head, burrowing into the pillow.

'The question has to be asked, was it built with murder in mind, and if so, what was the murderer's motive?'

'Right. So far we haven't found one. We need to find out who actually nailed the thing together; was it the window-dressing company or a local craftsman?'

'One of the shop assistants might know. When I pop in tomorrow I'll ask them that too.'

'If you don't mind. The window dressers had to have been there for a while. Somebody in that shop is bound to know. If nobody does remember, perhaps you can pop round and see old Mr Barrington too, the loyal — now pissed-off — old retainer!'

Honey seemed to have fallen asleep. Doherty turned off the light and frowned into the darkness.

His mind shifted away from the case to personal problems. Rachel, his daughter, had emailed him that morning to say that she was coming down to see him.

He wasn't one for premonitions like Mary Jane, the Green River's resident professor of the paranormal, but he couldn't help feeling apprehensive.

Rachel was like her mother. When she made up her mind to do something, she went all out to do it, in the process of which she tended to ignore and trample over what everyone else wanted.

So far he hadn't said anything to Honey about her imminent arrival. They'd barely met, but he knew Rachel wasn't thrilled she was getting a stepmother.

'So what about the will,' Honey said, suddenly.

It took him by surprise. He'd really thought she was sound asleep.

'Arnold Tern was about to change his will.' His personal problems and the prospect of telling Honey hovered in the background. It suited him better to concentrate on the job in hand. All the same his apprehension wouldn't go away. 'I finally pinned down Grace Pauling. She was reluctant to tell me until I reminded her that the last will and testament of Arnold Tern might have a direct bearing on the case. She already knew that of course, but like every solicitor I've ever dealt with, she likes to play power games.'

'Hmm.' Honey yawned again. She was soft and malleable when she was tired.

He gritted his teeth. Now, he said to himself. Now is the time to tell her. Go on. Are you a man or a mouse?

The mouse got sent for cheese.

'I had an email from Rachel this morning. She's coming down to see me. Perhaps all three of us could have dinner together. She'll be staying with me — I suppose. What do you think?'

There was no reply from the other side of the bed, just a gentle snoring.

CHAPTER SIXTEEN

Mary Jane came dashing down the stairs. The clothes she was wearing constituted a total fashion faux pas, but somehow seemed to suit her stick thin frame.

'Honey. The woman in white. I think I know who she is.'

'Re . . . ally?' Honey replied hesitantly. She'd said nothing about the information gleaned from Dennison and Dimply across the road. Perhaps I should, she thought. If their exorcism had moved her over here, perhaps there was a chance that if one was held in the Green River Hotel, she might move on somewhere else. Or back over the road. The thing was she felt quite sorry for the woman — Emily Bennett. However, mentioning it to Mary Jane was likely to be tricky. After all, it was Mary Jane's relative, Sir Cedric, who had let the lady down.

'I see you're in white yourself, so I've obviously chosen the right moment,' said Mary Jane.

Honey narrowed her eyes and pulled a face.

'I'm not sure about that.'

She was wearing a large white apron that almost went round her twice. Dumpy Doris, their breakfast cook and mistress of all trades, had phoned in sick. Apparently she'd gone down with a virus. Honey suspected she'd overindulged on a takeaway curry the night before. Doris tended to overindulge forgetting that spicy foods disagreed with her.

Lindsey peered over the top of the reception desk.

'It's a book by Wilkie Collins. *The Woman in White.*'

Lindsey had just returned from her friend's and whoever the friend was, the stay had obviously agreed with her. She looked as fresh as a daisy.

'How did you get on over the road, Mother? You didn't say.'

Mary Jane looked from mother to daughter and back to Honey.

'Is this relevant? What's the building over the road got to do with anything?'

Honey squirmed. 'I thought I might just have seen a reflection, something not too clear reflected in the windows across the road. I thought it wouldn't hurt to ask.'

'Did they know anything?'

Mary Jane's deep blue eyes were piercing at the best of times but when ghosts were mentioned they glittered brighter than gemstones.

Lying was out of the question. Mary Jane would know, that's what those glittering eyes were saying to her.

'Well . . . actually . . . they had heard tell of a ghost who threw herself out of one of their windows back in the days when it was still a house.' She purposely left out mentioning her name.

'No way!' Mary Jane was mesmerised, her eyes seeming to explode to twice their normal size; her voice hushed, awe-struck. 'Did they say why?'

Honey cleared her throat. This was the awkward bit. She didn't want to upset Mary Jane, but on the other hand she didn't like to lie if she could avoid it.

'She had man trouble.'

'Isn't it always man trouble,' mused Lindsey, slapping down piles of leaflets the length of the reception counter.

Mary Jane shook her head sadly. 'Poor girl. I suppose he jilted her?'

'I suppose so,' said Honey who was already making tracks for the kitchen. Mary Jane kept pace with her. 'Supposedly her husband was hanged leaving her pregnant with nobody to turn to.'

'How do you know this?'

'I did the research. I think her name was Dorothea Finchley. She was an honest girl from a poor background who fell in love with a Captain John Finchley. They got married but the family didn't approve so her husband was cut off without a penny.' The lies poured easily off of her tongue. All in a good cause, she told herself.

Honey paused in front of the kitchen door. She could hear the clattering of pans on the other side and somebody whistling. Smudger Smith, her head chef had arrived for the day. So also, it sounded, had some of his minions. Hopefully Clint, their erstwhile washer-up had also arrived. She'd cooked breakfast for around twenty guests, but didn't have time to do the washing-up. Doherty had set her a task which was becoming more attractive by the minute, anything rather than contradict Mary Jane's findings about the spectre she'd seen. Anything rather than mention that the young woman had been jilted by Mary Jane's long dead ancestor.

It was common for either Doris or herself to do break-fast thus giving the chef a break. Split shifts, prepping and cooking lunch and then a break before the evening shift was hard enough without dragging any of them in to cook some-thing as simple as a full English breakfast. But washing-up? Clint was the most proficient washer-up she knew. And he was cheap. Cash in hand of course.

'So, was it really a reflection you saw?'

Honey winced. She didn't much like the thought that somebody had thrown themselves out of the landing win-dow. 'I prefer to think she threw herself out of their window and I merely saw the reflection.'

Mary Jane frowned. 'Are you sure about this? I mean, how come we've all been smelling jasmine so strongly? Something else had to be going on.'

Here it was. Should she lie or should she tell the truth — or at least part of it.

Honey cleared her throat and dived in. 'I understand that the senior partner at the firm of solicitors across the road brought in an exorcist.'

'It was successful?'

Although Mary Jane's eyes still twinkled like stars in her wrinkled face, she sounded sceptical. Honey put that down to the fact that nobody had asked her to carry out the exorcism.

'I'm not sure. What I mean is . . .'

'Jasmine! I bet my bottom dollar that they carried out the exorcism on the very day we first noticed the smell of jasmine here in the hotel! Hah!'

Honey did her best to look baffled. 'And that means . . . ?'

'She's moved in here,' said Mary Jane firmly.

Honey cleared her throat and prepared an evasive response – not exactly a lie – just a dismissive retort.

Mary Jane got in first. 'Whoever she is, has moved in here after being driven out from across the road. It stands to reason that's what's happened.'

More ghosts were something Honey could well do without and said so.

'I don't care if it does stand to reason I want this ghost out of here. One ghost is quite enough. Two is one too much.'

'Or even three,' said Mary Jane, fascination shining in her eyes. 'Yes. We must exorcise them. I think I've already made some progress in identifying whoever the woman — or at least one of them is. I took the small table from my room and along the landing and made use of the balloon backed chair you've got placed there.'

'You did table-tapping.' Honey couldn't help sounding sceptical — not that Mary Jane appeared to notice. Table-tapping was one of Mary Jane's favourite ways of contacting the spirits of people who had 'passed over'.

'I did it very quietly so as not to disturb anyone, but you know how it is. Sometimes the spirits get carried away because they're so frantic to get through. The table rocked all over the place. Even Sir Cedric complained, said something about a man at eternal rest should be left there to rest.'

Honey fixed her with a direct look. 'Did anyone else complain?'

'Oh, just some man from number nine along the landing. I can't see how he heard anything really unless he had his ear to the door.'

Honey closed her eyes and counted to ten.

'What time was this?' she asked pensively, dreading what the answer would be though knowing it could not be avoided.

Mary Jane heaved a sigh. 'After midnight of course! Table-tapping and contacting the spirits is always best done after midnight. Things are quieter then.'

'Unless you happen to be table-tapping.'

'I tried to keep the noise down.'

'Not down enough if a guest complained.'

'Only one guest and unnecessarily. There was no need to be so grouchy!'

Honey fixed her with a stern gaze. 'He had rights to be grouchy. You disturbed his sleep.'

'I didn't mean to. And he couldn't have been that put out. He only came along to complain once so he must have fallen asleep again.'

Honey sighed. Sometimes Mary Jane was plain hard work.

'Everyone has been down for breakfast except for one. I'm guessing he was the one you disturbed with your table-tapping session. Was anyone else with you?'

Mary Jane shook her head. 'I did invite your mother to come along, but since she remarried, she takes less interest than she used to in the paranormal. Too wrapped up in that husband of hers.'

Honey had to concede that Mary Jane was right. Her mother didn't visit half as much as she used to before she'd met and married Stewart White, her fifth husband. In Honey's opinion it was great that she had somebody else to boss around. Life was peaceful nowadays — with the exception of Mary Jane's exploits.

Exasperated, Honey combed her fingers through her hair. Was it her imagination or did her hair and clothes smell of fried bacon and Wiltshire pork sausages?

'I can smell bacon and sausages,' Mary Jane remarked, sniffing the air.

Well that answered that question.

Honey sighed deeply. The day had only just started and she was already feeling drained.

'Mary Jane, can I ask you not to table-tap in the public areas. It's not fair on the other guests. Or on me for that matter. I was the one cooking breakfasts this morning and no doubt the guest concerned will be in a foul mood when he gets round to checking out.'

'Such a shame he missed breakfast,' trilled Mary Jane sounding without a care in the world. 'It was very good. Far better than Doris's.'

Against her better judgement Honey fell for the flattery. 'Thank you! I'm glad you liked it.'

'Well actually I only had the toast. But it was quite superb. Lovely and crisp.'

So much for the flattery. 'Just toast.'

'Shame about that poor young woman though. She must have been beside herself when her husband was hanged. I mean, what else was he to do when he'd married beneath himself, his wife was pregnant and the family had cut him off without a penny? The only recourse left open to him was to become a highwayman.'

Honey had been about to push open the kitchen door and escape, but mention of a highwayman stopped her in her tracks. 'A highwayman?'

'That's right,' said Mary Jane with a nod of her head. 'According to my research he had no other option but to become a highwayman. He was quite successful at first, or at least it seems that way. It was a year before he was caught. Perhaps he might have got away with it but on the last occasion he'd robbed a coach and four on their way to Marlborough, his pistol went off accidentally killing the local magistrate who happened to be travelling with some local aristocrat. The recoil from the pistol knocked him backwards. He hit his head on something so was easy to arrest. The fact was that if that hadn't happened he would have inherited his family's wealth a few days later when his father died. The old man had never altered the will . . .'

Honey pushed open the kitchen door. 'Interesting. Tell me, they didn't have pole-dancing clubs back then did they?'

Mary Jane failed to pick up on her sarcastic tone. 'No. Of course they didn't. I mean, can you imagine Jane Austen pole dancing? Of course not. Ladies of the late eighteenth and early nineteenth century just didn't do things like that.'

'Could have had something to do with the lack of central heating,' said Honey smiling as she passed through the door and into the kitchen. *Congratulations*, she said to herself. You got away with not going into depth about the other suspected suicide from over the road. Not the one Mary Jane had been researching — whoever that was — but the one who'd been ruined by Sir Cedric, the ghost who appeared to live in Mary Jane's closet.

The man who had been disturbed by Mary Jane's table-tapping grumbled when he paid his bill.

'The woman's mad. She should be locked up.'

Lindsey apologised profusely before conjuring up the tale that Mary Jane was all alone in the world and they'd only taken her in out of the goodness of their hearts.

'She is related to aristocracy,' she added.

She didn't explain that the lord Mary Jane was related to was long dead and just happened to haunt the room she resided in — hence her reason for being there.

As it worked out, Lindsey had made a sound judgement of the man. He wasn't exactly happy but he was just a little impressed.

'I once worked for Sir Edward Potterton-Jones,' he said adopting an air of superiority. He too was a little eccentric. 'I believe some of his relatives spent most of their lives in a lunatic asylum. Only to be expected of course. It's in the blood you know. Inbreeding has a lot to do with it. Also, I missed breakfast. I hope you're not going to charge me for it.'

'Of course not, sir.'

'Just as well. I wouldn't have paid it anyway.'

She didn't enlighten him with the fact that breakfast was at an extra cost. He was pacified. Hopefully he wouldn't put word around that the Green River Hotel was inhabited by a mad woman from America who made a racket out on the landing in the early hours of the morning.

'I doubt I'll stay here again. Unless of course you give me a different room on a different floor and at a knock-down price.'

Lindsey smiled sweetly. 'We'll see what we can do, sir.'

He bid her goodbye.

'You win some, you lose some,' Lindsey muttered to herself once the irate guest had left the building.

The doors opened, he exited and a young woman entered.

'Good morning. I'd like to book a birthday party please.'

Lindsey smiled at the round-faced young woman. She had a very pale complexion and dyed black hair. Her lipstick was bright red and her cheeks were plump. She looked the sort who thoroughly enjoyed junk food and didn't give a damn who knew it. Her clothes were black and fitted her like a glove. Unfortunately even a very large glove would have trouble covering her figure of eight shape. But her smile was full of confidence and Lindsey liked her immediately.

'For how many?'

'Oh, I think at least a hundred. It's for my dad's birthday. He's sixty-five. I think . . . still . . . it's the thought that counts isn't it.'

'Would you like to see the function room?' asked Lindsey.

'Yes please.'

Lindsey asked the new girl, Irina from Moscow, to take over reception whilst she showed the young woman around.

Irina was tall, slender and had the features of a Snow Queen; pale blonde hair and skin to match. Her eyes were an icy blue. Rodney (Clint) Eastwood, their washer-up who had other dubious pastimes that they weren't quite sure of and never asked him about, had tried to hit on her. She'd frozen him out.

'One icy glare and everything seemed to shrivel,' he declared to all that would listen. Nobody ventured to ask what particular parts had been frozen, though most could guess.

Confident that Irina would do a sterling job, oblivious to diversions of a romantic nature, Lindsey took the daughter who wanted to give her father a birthday bash to the function room.

'It's for your father you say. How old did you say he would be?

'Fifty-five. Whoops! I did say sixty-five didn't I. But it's fifty-five. I'm sure of it.'

'I'm sure he'll appreciate it, whatever his age is. Dancing till midnight I bet.'

'Very likely. He's dead fit is my dad. He puts it down to his job. He's outside in all winds and weathers.'

'Oh really?'

'Yes. He's a cleansing department operative for a firm sub-contracting to Bath and North East Somerset.'

'Oh really?'

The girl giggled. 'That means he's a street cleaner. He sweeps the streets, but you know what these councils are like not wanting to offend anybody.'

The girl laughed. Lindsey laughed with her.

'We want to organise a bit of entertainment. Would that be in order?'

Lindsey smiled and nodded. 'Of course, as long as it's not too noisy and is strictly legal.'

'Oh it's legal all right. My dad's a fan of this old punk star from the eighties. We — that is me and my sisters — want to organise a lookalike singer. Would that be all right?'

'Of course it would. We've had Elvis Presley here a few times — well not the real one of course. Last I heard from some way out newspaper he's supposed to be in a London bus on the moon!'

They'd both seen the rubbishy newspaper so laughed in unison. They were getting on like a house on fire.

'That would be great,' said the girl. 'It's not Elvis, mind. It's an Adam Ant impersonator.'

Lindsey took a deep breath. A coincidence or what? She managed to collect herself.

'We are not biased in any way. You can have who you like, though we might draw the line at Liberace. It's the grand piano and silver candelabra you see; too big to get in the door.'

They laughed again.

'Right,' said Lindsey once they were back in reception. 'If you can give me the date you want the function room and the details . . .'

Irina handed her a notebook and pen from beneath the overhanging counter of the reception desk.

'Next Saturday if possible. I know it's a bit short notice, but we weren't going to have a party, then dad went through a bit of trauma and we all said, hey, this is just the time to have a right knees-up. Our dad deserves it.'

Lindsey did a quick check on the computer. 'You're in luck. It's free. Can I have your name?'

'Heidi York.'

'And your father's name?'

'Charles Spencer York.'

By the time she'd taken all the particulars and Heidi had left her with a deposit, Lindsey knew for sure that she'd just been speaking to the daughter of the man who had discovered the body in the window of Tern and Pauling. Mention of his name plus the fact he'd experienced recent trauma was enough to clinch it. She had to tell her mother.

Leaving Irina manning reception, Lindsey went out through the back of the hotel, across the yard to the coach house. After cooking breakfast and feeling immersed in the smell of fried sausages and bacon, her mother would be having a shower.

On the way there her phone rang.

She smiled. 'You OK?'

'I am now I've spoken to you.'

'Flatterer.'

'I mean it.'

'Steady on, Drury. You know how I feel about getting emotionally heavy. Take a step back. Let's enjoy the moment.'

'Odd you saying that, a girl who's into history. Moments pass and soon become history.'

'Now you're being romantic . . .'

The conversation was over by the time she had entered the coach house. Just as she'd guessed her mother was in the shower, clouds of steam misting up the shower door.

Lindsey sat down on the toilet pan next to the shower.

'I have interesting news for you,' she called. 'Guess who we've got coming here next Saturday for a birthday party.'

* * *

Hearing her daughter's voice through the door, Honey shouted back, 'Not a clue!'

She was enjoying the warm water, the smell of the suds, the fact that her hair was soaking wet and squeaked when she ran a strand between finger and thumb.

'Charlie York. The man who first saw the dead body in the window of Tern and Pauling. It's his birthday. His daughter's just been in to make the arrangements. I don't know whether she knows your pedigree, but I don't think she's the sort to care that you're allied to the team investigating the murder.'

Honey stopped running the soap filled sponge over her body.

'That's really interesting.'

'I thought you'd think so. And guess what, she's ordered an Adam Ant impersonator from a theatrical agency in Bristol who specialise in celebrity look-alikes. Should be fun.'

Honey's soaping action slowed down. So far the investigation had been confined to the city of Bath. It struck her that there were other questions that might only be answered in Bristol, principally questions that only a group of Adam Ant impersonators — or a theatrical agency — could answer.

CHAPTER SEVENTEEN

Doherty phoned to ask if she was available.

'Depends what you're asking me to do,' she replied in a voice she thought sounded like Lauren Bacall.

'A car ride to see a carpenter. The window dresser who also designed the window display told me the gallows was supplied by a recommended contractor he'd not used before but who guaranteed it would be very well made. That he didn't build shoddy. A bit of an artisan so I understand.'

'A well-made gallows! Do we have a name for the man?'

'Donald Parquet. Lord Donald Parquet actually. He also happens to be a client of Pauling and Tern. If you're in, I'll be round in twenty minutes. If not I'll see if I can rope in somebody else whose company I value.'

'I'm in.'

He arrived five minutes after the agreed time, which on the whole was just as well. It took all of that just to get away from Mary Jane and more information about the beauty who'd crashed to her death from the first-floor landing.

Honey told Lindsey where she was going and told Smudger to deal with the meat order himself.

'I've got a date with a lord.'

Nobody batted an eyelid, nobody believed her.

'So where does his lordship reside?' she asked Doherty as she slid into the front passenger seat.

'Parquet Manor, otherwise known as the Parquet Trust Estate. It's the part of the estate that used to be stables and outhouses, now turned into artisans' workshops. Lord Vincent Parquet left his wealth and his title to his eldest son. Lord Donald Parquet is a self-trained carpenter. He works in wood in one of the converted stables. A number of those same stables are let out to other artisans of similar skill and mindset; metalworkers, wool weavers, jewellery makers, painters and potters and bead makers.'

'I get the picture. A kind of happy hippy ever after.'

'Something like that.'

As he drove Doherty outlined events on the evening before Nigel Tern had been found murdered.

'The party began around nine, though of course we already know that not all the staff attended. Mr Barrington left the shop at the usual time leaving Mr Papendriou serving drinks to specially invited guests. We know Mr Barrington did not attend the party. I dropped in on Ahmed who was sorting next door's car at the time. Ahmed confirms he saw him come home and at least whilst he was there, never saw him come back out.

'But Ahmed must have left whilst it was still light. He wouldn't have been able to see what he was doing otherwise. So we only presume Cecil Barrington did not venture back out and I assume only his wife confirms it.'

'True. She does. But we don't know for sure. And Mr Papendriou left the shop after doing the washing-up. His partner confirms his time of arrival home and that they stayed in. Mr Papendriou failed to say that a friend called by and shared a bottle of wine with them. His alibi is set in stone.'

'I thought it might be a good idea to interview a few other Adam Ant impersonators in Bristol.'

'To what end?'

She shrugged. 'A wider perspective on the victim?'

'We'll put that on the back burner for now.'

'OK.'

Doherty glanced at her profile. A strong profile, handsome rather than pretty.

She was staring straight ahead. From past experience he guessed she was having deep thoughts.

'Hey. Are you still with me?'

She turned slowly to face him, a faraway look in her eyes. Her smile was worth waiting for.

'I was thinking. There was no sign of forced entry. The murderer must have had a key — or been invited in.'

'Unless they shinned up the drainpipe at the back of the shop. There is a lane at the back and a bathroom window was left open. It's only about six feet from the ground and there was a bin close by. The bin's proximity to the window plus the outlines of two footprints on it were only noticed today by a beady-eyed young constable. A few years and he'll be after my job.'

'Any details yet — about the footprints?'

'Size seven in English, forty-one European.'

Honey frowned. 'A bit small for a man. Could it have been a woman?'

'If it was, she would have to be tremendously strong to overcome Tern and put his neck in a noose — unless she held a gun on him perhaps, but if she had a gun, why bother to hang him? Why not shoot him?'

Honey frowned. 'You're certain he was knocked out then strung up.'

'It seems that way.'

'And the weapon?'

'Not found yet. Would have been something strong. Not necessarily heavy.'

'So definitely not suicide.'

'No. He was definitely strung up, in which case somebody else was there, though whether he knew they were there or whether he'd invited them, we just don't know. Papendriou said nobody was left in the shop and he took the key with him. Tern had a key. So did Barrington.'

'So Nigel Tern had to have invited the person in.'

'That's my view.'

The gates to Parquet Manor were wide open. A security camera blinked at them, a red light flashing in recognition that their arrival had been noted. Somewhere, somebody was watching them.

A large sign proclaimed *Old Stable Workshops — Parquet Trust*. A green arrow pointed to the right down a gravel drive.

Doherty swung the steering wheel to the right. There was no sign of security guards, just strategically placed cameras.

The tyres made a reassuring crunch as they made their way towards an arch dividing one half of the stable block from the other. Once through the arch the gravel changed to cobblestones. A man came out of what had once been home to a carriage horse or a hunter. The stables had been turned to new purpose.

Donald Parquet was tall, well built and subject to early hair loss. He couldn't have been more than twenty-six though his fresh-faced boyish complexion might have been misleading.

Doherty referred to his phone call.

'Regarding the murder of Nigel Tern, your lordship . . .'

'Call me Donald. Can I see your warrant card please.'

He said it pleasantly enough, but being titled and sometimes headlining a disparaging tabloid article, Donald Parquet was not a man to take anyone at face value.

'Thank you.'

He greeted them warmly, shaking Doherty's hand before turning to Honey.

Doherty took care of the introductions.

'And my associate, Honey Driver. She's a civilian liaison officer. I do hope you don't mind her presence.'

Honey smiled. 'Hello. If you do, I'm quite happy to wait in the car.'

Lord Parquet smiled back at her. 'I don't think that's necessary.' He kept hold of her hand. 'Honey. A pretty name.'

'I was christened Hannah. The only person who calls me that is my mother. Everyone else calls me Honey.'

153

'Ah yes. Our parents like to cling on to what they think they made of us including giving us names we don't like.'

Honey suspected his first name wasn't Donald. It was easy to check. He'd be listed in Debrett's Peerage. Everyone who was anyone was listed there.

He turned back to Doherty. 'Nigel Tern. Damn good jackets and excellent service for those who like that sort of thing. I must say I have made use of his services in the past.' He smiled. 'I don't always amble around in dungarees.'

'You knew him well?'

His lordship's expression was open. 'Quite well. Not a friend by any standards, but decent enough despite his liking for the ladies. Too many ladies probably. And such a shame seeing as he'd just won the window display competition. I'm sure he must have been over the moon.'

'Did you know any of his lady friends?' asked Doherty.

Donald's blue eyes crinkled at the edges. 'Not really. We didn't move in the same circles. Would you like to follow me into the workshop?'

In the workshop the smell of wood shavings permeated the air. There were wooden objects and piles of sawdust everywhere.

'You made the gallows,' Doherty said. 'They seemed very strong seeing as they were destined for a window display. I always thought window dressers never used anything stronger than cardboard.'

'Usually yes but Nigel insisted I build them and of course he knew I only make items to a high standard. I did ask whether he was going into business hanging people with it in between supplying sports jackets for the Glorious Twelfth and blazers for Cowes week.'

Doherty nodded. 'Did he give you any reason for building it so strong?'

Whilst listening to all that was said, Honey found herself enjoying the way Donald's eyes flitted between her and Doherty, his smile widening the moment his gaze flitted to her.

A toy-boy! What a delicious thought!

'Why did he want me to build it so strong?' Donald's smile widened. 'I can't think of any specific reason. He did say that the way his father ran the business and dominated his life was enough to make him use it on himself.' Donald shook his head. 'I didn't believe that though. Nigel loved life. He wasn't the sort to commit suicide. Too sound of mind and body, and whilst the latter was still going strong — with the ladies if you know what I mean — then he was up for it. The old man is getting on anyway and shortly after the gallows was finished, he was taken into hospital. Respite as far as Nigel was concerned and his chance to update the shop interior and the shop window.'

So the gallows were being built before the old man went into hospital? There was no change in Doherty's expression, yet Honey knew what he was thinking. She also had a pretty good idea of what the next question would be.

'Are you saying he had the gallows built some time before the competition?'

'Indeed.'

'Did he say then what they were for?'

A thoughtful look came over his lordship's face. 'I think he said personal gratification.'

Doherty nodded. 'I see. So it wasn't initially for the window display but some highly personal motive. Is that what you're saying?'

Donald smiled and shook his head. 'I was asked to make gallows to certain dimensions and for his own private purposes. That's all I know.'

Honey held back asking the obvious questions until they were back with the car.

The breeze ruffled her hair and sucked the sawdust from her nostrils. Her mind was reeling. The murder of Nigel Tern was beginning to head in one very positive direction.

'Fantasy land,' she whispered across the roof of the car. 'He was into the highwayman image big time. I can just imagine . . .'

She stopped as the picture solidified in her mind.

Grim-faced, Doherty opened the car door on his side.

'He didn't necessarily do this by himself,' Honey said.

'It is possible though, isn't it? Auto-ejaculation is a lonely sport and popular among ex-public-school boys.

'Had he ejaculated before he died?'

'I don't know. I never asked and didn't notice it on the pathology report. I'll check, but . . .'

Once he was sitting comfortably in front of the steering wheel, he phoned for confirmation.

The answer to his phone call was instantly answered.

'No. There was no evidence of sexual activity at all although his zipper was at half mast. He was not a gasper.'

'His hands were tied behind his back.'

'Yes.'

'He couldn't have undone his zip himself.'

'Could have drawn it down halfway — in preparation for a little action — so to speak.'

Honey felt a surge of excitement. 'He couldn't do that with his hands tied behind his back. Whoever hit him on the back of the head might have undone his zip.'

Doherty picked up his phone again and ordered that particular attention be paid to the dead man's flies.

'His zip in particular. Check for fingerprints on the zip tab.'

Doherty's hopeful look disappeared in response to whatever was said on the other end of the phone.

Sighing, Honey sat back and folded her arms. 'His own fingerprints?'

'Smudged fingerprints. Not conclusive.'

He put his phone back into his inside pocket with a quick dismissive flick of his wrist.

Honey frowned into the distance. She'd prepared herself for lewd details. Now it appeared there were none.

At last she said, 'I'd like to take another look at the crime scene if that's possible. There was no overturned stool. No way of Tern putting his head in the noose without one

— whether somebody was there or not. And somebody was undoubtedly there.'

In her mind Honey ran over the details of the murder scene. There were just three stairs, but set forward of where the gallows were positioned, too far away for Tern to have jumped from those and hung himself. Anyway, there was still the tied hands. He couldn't have tied them himself. Somebody had to have done it for him.

'Are you certain he couldn't have tied his own hands?'

'I know where you're coming from. It is possible to self tie — people into that kind of sex do it all the time. But not these knots. The rope was tied round and round again, one knot after another. I've spoken to the experts. It's impossible.'

'When do you think we could take another look?'

'After I've spoken to Grace Pauling again about the will, though it's hard to pin her down. She keeps making excuses about having to fit me in.'

Honey beamed at him and patted his hand.

'Trust your little helper.'

'My what?'

'Me. There's a meeting of the Townswomen's Guild this afternoon at four. I've been invited to give a talk on working in a civilian capacity for the local police. Grace Pauling is a member. I've seen the list of those attending. She's booked her place and paid her ticket price.'

Doherty visibly brightened. 'That's a turn-up. I wouldn't have thought you were quite their type. Do you want me to come too? Will they accept me as an honorary woman for the afternoon?'

'You can if you like. As for me not being quite their type — which I agree that perhaps I am not — my mother is their type. She's a leading light in fact and serves on the committee.'

Doherty's facial expression turned taciturn.

'Then on second thoughts count me out. See you later?'

'Sure. Zodiac Club. Close to midnight. Check the scene, check the gossip, oh, and in return I shall report on my "bumping into" Grace Pauling. Hopefully I can pin her down.'

CHAPTER EIGHTEEN

Rachel Doherty had the same shaped face as her father, the same dark hair, the same forward-thrust to her chin. Her eyes, however, were hazel that in a certain light looked brown, and sometimes, mainly when she was dead tired, looked a shade of sludge green.

She also had her mother's aptitude for dressing well, though she'd toned it down during her university days. Having dropped out it no longer mattered. Not that she was wearing designer clothes. Andrew wouldn't countenance that. He chose her clothes for her. Sometimes she wasn't quite sure whether she liked the clothes she wore as much as he did, but she loved him. He knew so much more than her, in fact he was the cleverest man she'd ever met.

'I think we should have lunch first. I see no point in arriving on your father's doorstep with an empty stomach. We can also discuss tactics over a plate of pasta and a decent white wine. I know just the place.'

Andrew talking about the tactics they would use when confronting her father made Rachel's stomach flutter. She wanted to say that her father was not an enemy general, but wouldn't dare. She knew he would declare that, as a policeman, her father did have a military mindset and anyway she hated confronting him.

'OK, Andrew. Whatever you say.'

She sometimes asked herself why she'd ended up with a man like Andrew. A successful trader in the city, he'd plucked her from amongst the student crowd she'd been drinking with that night in a London pub. When Andrew's eyes had met hers, she'd melted. He had such a piercing look.

'Who's the dude?' one of her male student colleagues had asked.

She'd shrugged. 'I've no idea.'

'He's got a look in his eye and it's all for you,' her friend had said.

Strangely enough she'd accepted his comment as fact. It was how she felt whenever Andrew looked at her then and she felt no different now. Everything had changed when he'd told her to be in that same pub the following night. Not asked her, he'd told her. 'Can you feel it,' he'd said, his moist breath filtering into her ear. 'We're made for each other. We have to meet again. It's written in the stars.'

A girlfriend named Faith had laughed when she'd told her what he'd said. 'As if. Fate in the stars, my arse!'

But from that moment on everything had changed. She'd left university because Andrew had said she was studying the wrong course at the wrong time. He'd set her up with a job in the city. It meant her wearing a suit and a crisp white shirt. She'd felt like a fish out of water at first — still did at times — but Andrew had insisted it was the right career for her even though it was only part time. The rest of the time she spent in the flat they shared together. She cooked and cleaned for him, made sure everything was just the way he liked it.

At first her mother was furious when she found out Rachel had left university but Andrew was charm itself when they'd been introduced. He'd told her how he'd found Rachel the perfect job and how they were living together prior to setting up a home.

'In time we'll get married and have a family, but as I am sure you will agree, it's early days. We're a born for each other couple who are really going places, but ultimately I shall be the breadwinner. In the meantime we have to get used to living together, balancing our jobs and our home life. I truly believe that is the only way to ensure a marriage lasts. Don't you agree Mrs Doherty?'

Of course she'd agreed. She'd even remarked she wished her and Rachel's father had experienced a trial marriage before the real thing.

'Him being a police officer, the job always seemed to come first.'

'I feel sorry for your mother,' Andrew had said later. 'Waiting around for a man with no set routine.'

Andrew had been so understanding of her mother and so attentive, sympathising with the life she must have led before her marriage had broken up.

Her mother adored him and had taken her aside before they'd left for London.

'All I wonder is what your father is going to think, especially you leaving university.'

Rachel had begged her not to tell him about leaving university or about Andrew, or about the new job. Her mother had promised not to breathe a word.

'I have to tell him myself.'

Back in Andrew's presence before leaving, her mother had asked about her job. 'What exactly do you do, Rachel?'

Before she'd had a chance to respond, Andrew had interrupted.

'She's a city slicker and she loves it. Don't you, darling?'

His arm had been around her. She's felt his fingers tightening on her arm reminding her how important it was to consider her answer.

'Yes. I'm at the heart of everything and really love it,' she'd said, her face beaming with enthusiasm she did not feel. The truth stayed hidden inside. The fact was she didn't much like the job at all. She'd never intended to go into an office, especially a job in a financial institution, but Andrew had been insistent.

'I'm disappointed with you,' he'd said on the journey back to London. 'You didn't sound very enthusiastic about your job. You didn't sound very grateful either. I'm upset, Rach. Very upset.'

She hated him shortening her name. She'd told him she hated being called Rach and braved the opportunity to tell him so.

'I like being the only one allowed to call you Rach. I am special to you, aren't I, *Rach*?'

She'd given in. She always gave in.

'Are you listening?'

She jerked her thoughts back from what had happened to what might happen next.

'Your father will be pleased to see how professional you look. As a policeman he'll also be pleased that we're heading for a traditional marriage. That's the basic outline for our meeting. Support me, Rach. Don't forget to support me.'

Rachel nodded over the pasta dish he had ordered for her. She hated pasta, but Andrew insisted that she only *thought* she didn't like it. 'Your palate is uneducated. With my help you will discover how much you like it. Trust me.'

She said that of course she trusted him. He wanted her to be something special and for him she would be. She'd even agreed to become proficient at making Italian dishes because he loved them.

Rachel couldn't help the queasiness in her stomach. Her mother had fallen for Andrew's charm hook, line and sinker. No matter how much Andrew outlined his plans for convincing her father, she couldn't help fearing that in this case he might be wrong.

CHAPTER NINETEEN

The Pump Rooms echoed to the sound of female chatter and tinkling tea cups. A little Vivaldi played by a string quartet competed for air space, but on the whole remained a soft sound in the background.

After her mother had introduced her, Honey took her place up on the rostrum.

Once the applause had died down, Honey prepared herself.

'I never wanted to be involved in crime, but was given the chance — railroaded into to some extent — though on the right side of the law. Crime Liaison Officer on behalf of Bath Hotels Association. As you all know, visitors come from all over the world to our lovely city . . .'

She went on to talk about crime and its effect on tourism.

There was a round of applause afterwards. Honey saw her mother casting a jaundiced eye on those who weren't clapping hard enough. She strode over to the tables of those still engaged in conversation and had a word in their ears.

After the talk came a cream tea. This was the part Honey really had been looking forward to. According to the seating plan, she was seated next to her mother, which wasn't where she wanted to be.

On arrival she'd told her mother that the seating plan didn't fit in with her plans.

'I need to sit next to Grace Pauling. Can you arrange that?'

Her mother's hair was ash blonde and cut in a fetching bob. Her outfit was Jaeger; turquoise top trimmed in mink-coloured satin, her skirt a darker shade of the same colour. The shoes and handbag matched the mink trim.

Her mother had been in the act of greeting a titled lady and a few other women who she deemed a bit more note-worthy than the general membership. Her mother had always been a snob. She couldn't help herself.

Honey waited for rebuttal or disappointment. What she hadn't expected was that what she wanted slotted in with her mother's plans.

'Oh, Hannah, I am so glad you don't mind swapping. Patricia placed The Right Honourable Esme Tolliver next to Grace Pauling.' She shook her head despairingly. 'I don't know what she was thinking of placing a Right Honourable next to a shopkeeper's daughter.'

'A tailor, mother. Her father was a tailor.'

'Yes. With a shop.'

'As a hotel owner, does your daughter rank lower than a Right Honourable . . . ?'

Either her mother didn't hear or as per usual didn't perceive the irony in her daughter's statement. Happy as a lark, she'd immediately set to swapping the name cards. In addition she'd guided the Right Honourable lady to a place at her side on what passed for the head table. Honey was left to find her own way.

The women at the table had introduced themselves one by one, leaning as close as they dared on account of their hearing not being top notch.

Grace Pauling had no need to shout or lean close. She was sitting right next to her in her wheelchair wearing a red dress and eye-popping jewellery — far too ostentatious for daytime. Honey couldn't help thinking that if she wasn't in a wheelchair she'd make a good croupier or anything else in a night club for that matter. She wasn't bad looking and could be better if she wasn't wearing so much make-up.

Honey introduced herself as being Gloria's daughter. 'Though we have met before,' she added.

'You're not one of my clients, are you?'

Grace's eyes seemed to light up at the prospect of how many hours she might be billing this woman sitting next to her.

'No. We were both at the press conference outside Tern and Pauling when the prize was presented. I was also in the company of Detective Inspector Doherty viewing the crime scene. You came in there immediately behind Mr Arnold Tern.'

Grace's smile froze. Her glittering eyes turned glassy as closed windows with the curtains drawn. She could see out but nobody was allowed to see in.

Honey attempted to get a response. 'It was a fantastic window display. Full of drama, don't you think?'

She smiled as she said it, her tone as reassuring as it could possibly be.

Grace's closed expression diminished. Honey deduced that it wouldn't take much for it to return. Whatever she asked this woman had to be cloaked in niceties. Sweetness and light were the watchwords.

'I suppose it was a very good display. Very . . . dramatic.'

'I hear it was designed by one of his girlfriends.'

'You heard wrong,' Grace snapped. 'He designed it himself. He knew what he wanted.'

'That's interesting.'

Grace gave her a cold look. 'Is it?'

'I understand you knew him very well, though of course that's understandable seeing as your fathers were in business together.'

'Up until my father died.'

'A tragic accident I hear.'

She waved a hand over her legs. 'Our family's prone to them.'

Honey chose not to enquire about her accident, judging that if Grace wanted to impart details she would do it of her own volition.

'Would you like more cake?'

The woman sitting on Honey's left hand side pushed the cake stand her way. Chocolate eclairs, iced fancy cakes, meringues and glazed fruit tarts were set out on each tier.

Honey had promised herself not to get diverted by food. After all she was here on serious business.

Her resolve failed. 'Just a small one.'

Grace declined both a cake and tea or coffee. Instead she reached for a bottle of Cabernet Sauvignon and poured herself a generous glass.

'I recall you at the shop now, though can't recall you from the prize presentation.'

The statement came just as Honey was biting into a glazed fruit tart.

'Purely in a civilian capacity. It was really just a coincidence that I was asked to judge the window displays.'

'And you liked the highwayman theme.'

When she came out from draining half her wine glass, Grace was wearing a knowing smirk.

'There's something romantic about a masked man from that particular period of history when women wore silk dresses and tight corsets . . .'

Grace laughed. 'I think you mean sexy and have to agree with you. A highwayman is very sexy. Women like it. We . . . he . . . Nigel that is, guessed it would appeal to female judges. Nigel always did know what buttons to push to get what he wanted.'

'Especially women?'

Grace drained her glass without answering. There was something going on in her eyes that Honey found difficult to read. There was also a strange smile on her face, a lifting of one corner of her lips.

'Oh yes. He knew all right.'

It crossed Honey's mind that Grace could easily be one of those scorned women, motivated by a failed love affair to take her revenge. Although she was in no physical state to do so.

Honey tried another tack. 'Nigel's father doesn't seem unduly upset which seems a little odd for a parent towards their child. Is there any particular reason they weren't very close?'

Grace laughed, at the same time reaching for the bottle of white wine again which she seemed to have claimed for her sole use.

'The thing you have to remember about Nigel and his father is that they are — or rather were — very much alike. The old man might not agree with that, but the proof of the pudding so to speak . . .'

Grace took a gulp of her second — or was it third? — glass of wine.

Honey said nothing. This was a time for sitting and listening.

The wine loosened Grace's tongue.

'They didn't have the same views about how the business should proceed. I mean, Nigel wanted it modernised and the old man wanted it to stay traditional. Loyal to our esteemed clients, as old Arnold was fond of saying. The fact is that Nigel had upset a few clients. The old man said he was too familiar with them, treating them like human beings and believing that approach to be reciprocal. Unfortunately for some people a title is all they have in the world.'

Grace again reached for the wine. There was about a third left.

'Anyone in particular?'

Grace took a deep breath then a large sip.

'Donald Parquet for a start. He's had to turn his hand to woodwork and let his stables and outhouses out to a host of would-be artisans.' She chuckled into her drink. 'People who think they are more skilled than they really are. I would guess that most of them are drawing state benefits at the same time as earning a bit on the side at craft fairs and such like.'

So! Donald Parquet was on his uppers. He seemed like a nice boy and who could condemn him for trying?

Honey rested her chin on her hand, her eyes intently studying Grace's now flushed face.

'Anyone else?'

'Gunther Mahon.'

'Who?'

'He's not titled, or not as far as I know. Gunther comes from one of the Scandinavian countries I think. Not sure how he got his money but he's got a lot of it. He's also very blond and good-looking. So are his daughters. Nigel seduced them both.'

'Naughty boy.'

'He also seduced the mother.'

'VERY naughty boy. I take it Mr Mahon was very pissed off.'

'Very. He swore never to go into the shop again. He also swore he would inform a number of Nigel's other clients. You see Gunther knows a lot of people, not because he has a title, but because he has a lot of money. People go to him for loans. He gets asked to all the best country house weekends, shooting, hunting and all that. He also keeps an eighty-two foot Oyster sailing yacht on the south coast. You can take it that Gunther could cause a lot of trouble with old and new money alike. That was why Nigel decided to update and modernise the business. The only fly in the ointment would be the old man. Nigel didn't dare tell him the reason they were losing clients, namely that Nigel couldn't keep his dick in his trousers.'

The last comment was delivered with a bitter expression, as though Grace was looking inwards and remembering something very vividly.

Honey nodded. 'I see.'

The conversation had delayed her indulging in the remains of the glazed fruit tart, but meaty gossip deserved a just dessert, i.e. something sweet and naughty. She tucked in.

'So he had no choice but to modernise and dare not let the old man know.'

'That's right.' Grace drained the bottle. Honey had never seen anyone finish a bottle of wine that quickly. Was Grace going back to work after lunch, she wondered?

'Luckily for Nigel, the old man took ill. One thing after another resulting in pneumonia. I can tell you, it gave Nigel the jitters when the old man insisted on coming home but he brightened up when it became apparent that the old man was still out of it most of the time.'

'From the illness or the drugs?'

Grace shrugged. 'No idea. Ask the nurse . . . what's her name? Edwina Cayford. The cleaner-cum-nurse.' Her sneer held enough sarcasm to sink a ferry. 'Nurse my ass! I don't know if Nigel had her too; he said not, but that doesn't mean a thing. Dark or fair, he couldn't resist.'

Her voice was subdued, but still some of those at the table heard what she'd said. Decorous bosoms heaved. Wrinkled mouths pursed in disapproval.

Honey didn't need to ask whether Grace thought the nurse was inveigling herself into old Mr Tern's affections.

'Must want something . . . an old wrinkled body like that.' A slow smile cruised across Grace's lips. 'Not worth having. Too old. Too past it. But then, the Tern Trust is awash with property and money. She probably knows that.'

Doherty had been trying to question Grace properly about the old man's intention to change the will but so far she had given him the slip. It wouldn't hurt to play ignorant and ask a few relevant questions.

'I shouldn't imagine Mr Arnold was too pleased when he found out about his son's plans. Parents have altered their wills for less.'

Grace had started another bottle of wine. She'd pushed the cakes away to the far side of the table. Taking Honey by surprise, she leaned close, a loose smile on her face, her arm snaking around Honey's shoulders. To anyone who didn't know them, it might seem as though they were close friends.

Grace whispered into her ear.

'And good old Arnold was no exception! The old man phoned me the day Nigel learned of winning the prize. He was furious. He told me to visit and that he was going to change his will.'

'And did you?'

'Yes, but later, a few days after Nigel was discovered hanging from his own gallows.'

'What a turn-up,' said Honey, sitting back in her chair. 'I wonder who the new beneficiary is.'

Grace poured another glass from the bottle. Honey noticed it was basically empty. She also noticed that Grace hadn't offered her a drop.

Grace raised her glass in a toast and beamed at her.

'This daughter of Arnold's old partner gets the lot! Lock, stock, bank deposits and property. Me. Grace Pauling. He told me the will's drawn up. All Mr Arnold has to do is to sign it!'

'And he hasn't done that yet?'

'No! He bloody well has not!'

Honey laughed and shook her head. 'Nigel Tern was most definitely a very naughty boy — into all sorts of things so it seems.'

Grace frowned and focused her with bleary eyes.

'What do you mean?'

'For instance did you know that the gallows on which Nigel Tern died was built before he'd entered for the window display competition?'

'So what does that prove?' Grace Pauling's face gave nothing away, except Honey perceived the throbbing of a nerve close to the woman's hairline. Grace too was obviously aware of it, touching it before disguising the gesture by running her fingers through her hair. Could have been the effect of the wine of course, or it could be . . .

Honey jumped straight in. 'Was Mr Tern into bondage? Do you happen to know?'

Grace Pauling glowered. 'I don't know what you're talking about!'

'I thought you and he were close.'

'We'd known each other since we were children.'

'But you'd never been lovers?'

'Excuse me, Mrs Driver, but as a civilian, you have no right to be asking me these questions. If you persist, I will have to take matters further. Now please. I have to leave. I have a busy schedule this afternoon.'

Her departure was rushed and she didn't seem to care much about whose feet she ran over on the way out.

Honey repeated all this to Doherty later that night. 'I don't think she's telling the truth.'

'Hmm.'

Doherty seemed relatively non-committal.

'Anything else to share with me,' she asked.

'Um. Yes. Rachel arrives tomorrow to stay with me, plus her boyfriend. Apparently he's Prince Charming in a business suit according to my ex-wife.'

'Really? That's worrying.'

'Why do you say that?'

'It's the sort of thing my mother would say, and you know how wrong she can be!'

* * *

Mr Barrington eyed Doherty with resigned interest as once again he stood in the narrow doorway leading into the shop window.

'Was it anything in particular you're looking for, Inspector?'

Doherty shook his head. 'Not really.'

He was standing in the pit just before the set of stairs leading up into the main part of the window. Dark blue carpeting covered the whole area. The gallows had been erected to his left; the highwayman had been standing to his right. Due to the position of the gallows, the body had been hanging immediately over the stairwell.

Both items were gone now, the window almost empty except for a large notice saying that the business was yet again at the service of the discerning client.

Doherty interpreted discerning as meaning rich; he couldn't possibly afford having a jacket made by these people.

'So how come you're still here?' Doherty asked over his shoulder.

'I'm working out my notice, though I'm not quite sure whether I will be leaving. Mr Papendriou has also given in his notice. Apparently he's setting up an online business catering to a specialist market.'

'Is he now?!' Doherty mused.

He continued to scrutinise the area of carpet between him and the street. He felt he was missing something, but he wasn't sure what.

'It must have been quite a job removing the display from the window. A lot of lifting?'

'Not really.' Mr Barrington was standing right behind him and when he turned sharply around he almost tripped over him. 'We used a trolley,' he said, looking up into Doherty's face. 'It was quite easy really. Mr Papendriou wheeled it up the ramp and Mr Rossini loaded each item on and took it out. He had to do two trips of course . . .'

'A ramp you say.'

'Yes. The items were wheeled in and wheeled out again.'

'Where is this ramp?'

'I'll show you.'

Mr Barrington nudged his way past Doherty and into the area that was four feet beneath the main area of window display. The edge of the floor reached his waistline.

He lifted the edge of the carpet and unclipped two chromium catches.

Doherty watched with growing interest. The set of stairs were removable. Not only that but when Barrington turned them upside down they formed a ramp.

'Very clever, Mr Barrington.'

The senior assistant beamed at him. 'We are not completely backward in the firm of Tern and Pauling.'

* * *

There were messages awaiting Doherty's arrival when he got back to the station. One was from Honey with a few more thoughts regarding her meeting with Grace Pauling. One was from Arnold Tern asking if he could call at the old man's house at his convenience. The third one was from a young man saying he was his daughter, Rachel's, fiancé and could they meet up this evening?

Doherty grimaced. He'd been expecting a call from Rachel telling him the date and time of her arrival. Instead it was her fiancé who had phoned. True to his suspicious nature he had to ask himself, why the fiancé? Why not Rachel? He'd warned Honey that a visit was imminent and that he would let her know as soon as he knew himself. So here it was. He had to phone her and tell her the time had come.

It was pleasant walking through the city in the summer air. As usual at this time of year, the streets were choked with tourists. He would have phoned, but telling her about Rachel's visit was best done face to face.

His ex-wife had phoned him to say that the young man was especially nice and good for their daughter. She'd also warned him not to shout at Rachel with regard to her decision to quit university. All right for her. She wasn't the one paying for it!

But he'd promised not to blow a gasket. He'd be all sweetness and light.

'And Andrew is such a lovely young man,' Cheryl had added. 'He's got her a job and everything.'

He didn't want to think what she meant by 'everything'. *You'll find out all in good time*, he told himself.

Hopefully Honey would have some free time when he arrived and wouldn't be up to her elbows in dirty dishes or unplugging a drain. Also hopefully she would forgive him for leaving this to the last minute. It wasn't his fault, he reasoned. He hadn't been given much notice. Rachel was already here in Bath and so was her boyfriend.

He wondered if he would like him. Then he shook the thought from his head. What the hell! It wouldn't matter if he didn't. Rachel was as gullible and headstrong as her mother. She would go her own way.

Lindsey looked up at him from over the top of the reception counter.

'My, my, Mr Doherty. You are wearing a very serious expression indeed.'

'Serious business,' he said with a rueful smile.

Lindsey knew Doherty well enough to realise that he was playing his cards close to his chest. This time it's personal, she decided. He's got that sheepish, boyish look about him. Lindsey instinctively knew that whatever he was here for it had little to do with work.

Honey was soaking her feet in a vibrating footbath, arms outstretched, head back, eyes closed. Wonderful was not the word for it.

The footbath was like a gift from the god or goddess of aching feet. She'd had the thing for a while, her staff having bought it for Christmas one year. Up until now it had sat forgotten at the bottom of the airing cupboard. Why she'd put it there and how come she'd forgotten about it until now, she hadn't a clue.

She really should have paid more attention to what she was doing. Her staff understood the value of a footbath. Feet were the key to being a successful hotelier, thought Honey, sighing as the warm water curled over her instep and around her toes.

Doherty used his key to get in. Honey remained with her head back and her eyes closed. She smiled.

He kissed her on the forehead.

'You smell good.'

'It's the aftershave you bought me for my birthday.'

'It's a dead giveaway.'

He chuckled. 'Remind me not to try and sneak up on anybody.'

'You do like it, don't you?'

'Did I say I didn't?'

Perturbed by his tone, and by the fact that he'd only pecked her on the forehead and not landed a smacker on her mouth, Honey opened her eyes and shifted her pose.

'What's happened?'

'Ah. Well . . .'

She saw his slight frown.

'Not going to dump me are you?'

He laughed. 'Of course not.'

'In that case with the serious subject out of the way I'm ready for whatever you throw at me.'

Doherty paced to the window. The back yard joined the hotel and the coach house together. Rectangular flagstones formed an alternate pattern with red and yellow bricks. Flowers and foliage tumbled from tall urns made to look like the broken pieces of Roman columns.

The living room, kitchen and main bathroom of the coach house were upstairs. The bedrooms and en suite bathrooms were downstairs. Honey had designed her home this way. Downstairs was dark. Upstairs was lit by a half moon shaped window at one end. The roof was open to the apex and lined with dark wood, the whole thing supported by huge 'A' frames and 'queen posts'. The effect was imposing.

'I was just thinking about Rachel's surprise visit tomorrow. It's completely true to form. Doesn't give any notice that she's about to arrive on my doorstep. She just assumes everyone will come running at the drop of a hat.'

Honey bent forward and turned off the footbath. The low level hum wasn't that intrusive, but she sensed that he would like her to pay full attention.

The light from the window shone around him — like a very large halo — though he wasn't exactly up front in the heavenly stakes to ever win one.

'Well, it was bound to happen at some point. You are her father after all. And you did know she would be coming at some point.'

'It's not just that. I got the phone call from somebody called Andrew, my daughter's intended apparently.'

'Her intended? You mean she's engaged?'

'I phoned Cheryl straightaway to find out what other surprises I could expect.'

'What did Cheryl say?'

She'd never met Cheryl and Doherty rarely referred to her in conversation. When something was no longer in his life, it was never mentioned. He was like that with colleagues; once they'd left or retired, they were no longer part of his workaday life. He rarely spoke of his parents saying it was a private matter but that he missed them. People he really cared for stayed in his memory. She hoped she would; whatever happened.

'She was her usual harpy self at first, tuning back into the past as though we'd never left it behind. Eventually she said again that Andrew was a very nice young man and might be worth Rachel having dropped out of university for,' said Doherty not without a hint of bitterness.

'You suspected she would.'

'I suspected she *might*. I didn't know for sure. I thought the wild parties and hanging about with unsuitable friends might come to an end. Other parents told me that they settle down to work eventually once they can see graduation and having to find a job in sight.'

She didn't need for him to explain that Rachel had got close to graduation but hadn't seen things that way. She could tell that Doherty was disappointed.

'So when is she arriving?'

'Tonight. Her boyfriend is with her — some long-haired layabout no doubt. That's the only kind she finds attractive, although Cheryl told me otherwise . . .'

'So you said.'

'And you told me . . .'

'We women tend to go for the bad boys. It's something in our make-up.'

Honey took her feet out of the warm water and stood up. Leaving wet footprints in the carpet, she went over to him and began kneading the hard knots of tension in his shoulders. Gradually he relaxed.

Honey turned him round to face her. She smiled up at him.

'I think it's time I got to know Rachel. And perhaps Cheryl might be right. Have you thought about that? How about you give Cheryl another ring and get it straight in your head? A second call might help clarify some of the stuff she told you in the first phone call.'

In Honey's opinion her suggestion was a good one. It wasn't beyond reason that his conversation with his former wife had been fraught. They rarely stayed on the phone to each other longer than five minutes because the conversation always fell back on the subject of his job and how he'd spent more time with his colleagues than he had with her and their daughter. Honey guessed it was the truth, but the worse his marriage got the more time he'd spent on the job. The marriage and job had become part of a vicious circle.

'Right. I'll give her a ring.'

Honey wasn't sure whether to sigh with relief or belt out a loud 'yippee!'. Whichever way, she'd succeeded in making her point.

'If you want me to go downstairs whilst you're making it . . .'

'No need.'

'Do it whilst I put this lot away . . .'

Honey began clearing away the footbath, towel, foot gel and moisturiser. With the exception of the footbath, everything lived on a shelf in the bathroom.

The sound of his voice carried from the living room.

'OK, you say he's not a long-haired layabout — which is something of a surprise.'

There was a pause whilst Cheryl said something.

'A nice guy and he's gainfully employed in a bank; you said that before. And now he's got Rachel working in the financial sector. I hope it's the truth . . . OK, OK. I don't always believe what I'm told . . .'

Doherty was always quick and to the point when he spoke to his ex-wife and she was easy to rouse to argument.

Although she couldn't hear what Cheryl was saying, Honey got the gist of what was being said by Doherty's responses. Cheryl was telling him the way things were, and Doherty was responding that he would reserve judgement until he met the bloke and heard Rachel's excuses as to why she'd quit.

The phone call progressed without Doherty hanging up mid-conversation — something of a novelty. Every so often she peeked round the bathroom door to glimpse his expression. He looked surprised, but also relieved. Obviously Cheryl was beginning to convince him.

'You're certain?' A pause followed. 'OK. OK. I'll be nice. I promise . . . I said I promise . . . OK . . . Goodbye. Goodbye.'

Finished! Honey felt the tension drop from her shoulders. She came out from the bathroom. Doherty had gone back to his position in front of the window. This time he faced into the room.

'She's convinced the guy is going to be good for her.'

'Well, there you are then. You can't always be right,' Honey said to him.

Pursing his lips, he said. 'I'm still reserving judgement. She's a mother. You know what mothers can be like.'

Honey pulled a face. 'Yes. I know what mothers can be like!'

'Cheryl tells me that Rachel actually wore smart-casual when she visited and admitted to wearing business suits when she goes to work. I can't believe it.' He shook his head. 'I never thought . . .'

'That she would make something of herself?'

He shrugged. 'Well. You know. She was just a kid when . . .'

Honey gave him a bear hug and smiled up into his face.

'Judging by the look on your face, you cannot quite believe that your darling daughter has mended her ways.'

'I don't quite believe it. When my daughter and her boyfriend went to see Cheryl, she was surprised. She was as annoyed as I am — was — when Rachel told her she'd left university. She was pleasantly surprised that Rachel has a job and was even wearing a business suit.'

'The girl's made good. I'm pleased for her.'

'Her boyfriend is called Andrew Tompkins and he's a city trader. He earns a lot of money. Rachel only works part time. They live in his flat in London but in time are hoping to buy a house and start a family. Can you believe that?'

'Yes. It comes to us all. Wild child turns into warm and wholesome wife. Might even end up married for life though don't quote me on that! And just think! You could become a grandfather.'

Doherty tilted his head sideways. 'Are we still on for having dinner together? All of us? I mean, you, me, Rachel and the respectable boyfriend. I thought Lindsey might like to come too. Has she got a boyfriend at present?'

'Possibly.'

'You don't know?'

'Don't sound so surprised. I don't pry into my daughter's love life.'

'You don't know anything about your daughter's new boyfriend?'

'Did you know anything about yours?'

'No, but then I'm her father so I'm bound to be the last to know. Mothers always get to know first.' Doherty smiled ruefully.

Honey smiled back and hugged him hoping to dispel his worried expression.

'Look, Rachel's a grown-up. She doesn't have to tell you anything and everything. Did she tell her mother right away?'

'No. She didn't.'

He seemed to buck up at the thought of it.

'So I can arrange a meal?'

'Let me know the when and where and I'll be there. I'll check it out with Lindsey. OK?'

'OK.'

'Right. Now let's get back to business. What was the punch-up about at Nigel Tern's party and who were the guys fighting.'

'They weren't guys. They were girls. Two of Nigel's old girlfriends to be exact. One of them was a woman named Caroline Corbett. She's middle-aged, blonde and very presentable. Respectable and basically not involved in any of this. She lives in one of the flats above the shop. A very spacious flat on the first floor. The other was Grace Pauling.'

Honey was astounded. 'She said she knew nothing about it. And besides, she's in a wheelchair! I wouldn't have thought she was capable of fighting.'

'Don't let that fool you. That's not just a way of getting from A to B. It's a lethal weapon. Apparently she purposely ran over her competition's foot. Three or four times so it seems. Caroline Corbett retaliated with a punch on the shoulder and it all went downhill from there. Quite a scrap I understand. No idea who called the police but be in no doubt there was blood on the carpet and despite the fact that both ladies attended Cheltenham Ladies College, the language was definitely downmarket.'

Normally when on a murder case Doherty wore a serious expression. Imagining two women fighting brightened his expression.

Concern for his daughter far outweighed solving a murder case. Honey was glad for him, although just a tiny bit apprehensive. It brought home to her just how little she currently knew about her daughter's latest flame. Oh well, she thought to herself. You're just about to find out.

CHAPTER TWENTY

There were paper streamers, balloons and loud laughter in the function room at the Green River Hotel. There was also a jolly atmosphere, a lot of jokes being cracked, laughter, liquor, dancing and singing, Happy Birthday being sung at least four times.

Honey was helping Charlie York stay upright whilst he waited for a taxi. His wife had grabbed herself a chair and was already asleep, her chin resting on her fist.

Charlie was too excited to sleep. The beer and the excitement would catch up with him later.

There was only one thing that might keep him awake all night and that was the star turn — the entertainment for the evening.

'Can you believe that? An Adam Ant impersonator.'

Charlie York's face glowed with disbelief. He looked the happiest man alive and all because of the entertainment at his fifty-fifth birthday party.

'I still can't believe it. I mean, you know how it is. Kids go through phases. Bloody awful some of them. Nothing you can do is right and they think they know more than you. And now this.' Charlie York shook his head. Honey noticed his eyes were moist. 'My daughter organised everything — the cake, the entertainment — everything.'

'I suppose she contacted the Bristol lot for an Adam Ant impersonator.'

Charlie beamed. 'Not at all. There's a local group that dress up like him and meet on a regular basis. I was that surprised. Over the moon in fact.'

'I didn't know there was one here in Bath.'

'As you say, they meet in Bristol but are from all over apparently. Did you see him perform?'

Honey confirmed that she had. He'd looked a little middle-aged and a little overweight to be that convincing, but there, what sort of shape was Adam Ant in nowadays? The early eighties were a long time ago.

Charlie beamed at the same time as swiping his hand at the corner of each eye.

'Could never be as good as the original, but it brought back memories I can tell ya.'

'I'm glad you enjoyed yourself,' said Honey.

Charlie nodded. 'I did. I did, but there's something . . .'

His chest heaved in a big sigh. His eyes turned downcast as he bit in his bottom lip.

'I know I've 'ad a bit too much to drink, but um . . . could we . . . speak privately . . . there's something I've got to get off me chest . . .'

Honey frowned. The look of grateful happiness had left his face. His nervousness was palpable. Somehow she didn't think Charlie had imbibed as much as it had first appeared.

'Come into my office. We can talk there.'

She closed the door behind them both and offered him coffee which he declined.

'I've 'ad enough to drink. More than enough.' He almost chuckled, but his nervousness got the better of him.

She still wasn't sure he had drunk that much.

His hands delved into the pockets of his off the peg Marks and Spencer lounge suit jacket. It was in a lovely shade of grey; she guessed his daughter might have had a hand in choosing it.

'Do you want to sit down?'

He shook his head. 'This won't take long. The fact is I've got something that might or might not 'ave some bearing on what happened to that bloke in the shop window. I just 'ope it don't get me in any trouble.'

She wanted to ask him what trouble he contemplated and who with. Probably the police, she thought, but declined to say anything.

His hands continued to rummage in his pockets, not as though he were feeling for something, but more as if he were having second thoughts about pulling out whatever it was he had in his pocket.

'I find things when I'm cleaning up. Most of the time just a few coins, sometimes a bit more. The favourite is a five or ten pound note screwed up with a till receipt and thrown away. You'd be amazed at 'ow many people do that without realising. But that morning . . .' He heaved a big sigh.

Honey waited. She had a lump in her throat and a nervous fluttering in her stomach. What had Charlie found? How much of a bearing might it have on the murder of Nigel Tern? Nothing if it was just money. It could belong to anyone.

'Go on,' she urged, half afraid he might change his mind and then she'd learn nothing at all.

'I found a watch. This watch.'

He took his left hand from his pocket and pulled back his coat sleeve.

The item wasn't in his pocket. It was there on his wrist.

The name Bulgari blinked loud and clear from the centre of the gleaming watch face. An expensive watch. Too expensive for a road sweeper to purchase — unless it was fake, bought at a street market and ticking away for only a few months before dropping dead.

But not this one. One look and she knew it was the real thing. She held her breath.

Slowly he took it off his wrist and handed it to her.

She felt the weight of it; saw the precise movement of the minute hand smoothly moving around the watch face.

'You said you found it that morning. Was it close to the shop?' she asked.

He nodded. 'Just by the steps leading up onto the main road. I picked it up and put it into my pocket. You see I was too wrapped up listening to the music to bother looking too closely. Besides, I still had some sweeping to do. It wasn't until I took it home that I realised it was valuable. Once the dead bloke was discovered it gave me the willies. I thought well, Charlie me old pal, who's to say it weren't on the wrist of the bloke that did it?'

Possibly thought Honey. Doherty would be livid. Fingerprints would be smudged. DNA samples almost impossible, obliterated perhaps by Charlie's own DNA. Not that she was an expert, but she knew the basics.

'And you didn't see anyone?'

'Nobody.'

'Did you hear anyone? A voice, footsteps, a car door slamming?'

'I keep thinking about that morning. I 'ad me earphones on most of the time, but . . .'

Honey scrutinised the splendid face, amazed at how smoothly the hands moved courtesy of the tiniest jewels.

'A car going across the cobbles . . . yeah. I'm sure that must 'ave been it . . . the tyres making that funny sound they do when they're turning over cobbles . . .'

Honey raised her eyes. 'Wait. You heard a car?'

He nodded.

'But you didn't see it.'

He shook his head. 'No. I was down at the bottom of the steps in Beaufort Alley itself. The car had to be up on the main level.' His eyes grew rounder. 'You don't think it was the murderer, do you?'

'I honestly don't know.' A shiver ran down her spine and it was hard to stop her hands from shaking when she took another look at the watch. It was a long shot, but what if . . . just what if . . . the murderer had dropped it in his hurry to get away. It would have made sense to go back for it, but rushing off in a panic . . .

She felt a rush of blood go to her head and recognised it as excitement. Well here goes, she thought turning it over. Surely it was too much to expect an inscription? What a stroke of luck that would be . . .

The inscription read 'To Gunther M Mahon on his fiftieth birthday'.

Her blood was up. She phoned Doherty.

'I'll pick you up.'

'It's late.'

'I don't care.'

* * *

It was close to midnight when they arrived at the home of Gunther M Mahon. He lived in a castle. Not a real castle but a Victorian-type gothic mansion near Clevedon. The grounds were extensive. The house was a huge mausoleum of a place. Despite the strategically placed lighting, Honey thought the place looked as far from a comfortable home as it was possible to be.

A security guard at the gate told them to wait whilst he checked Doherty's warrant card. He wasn't that security conscious, however, as he failed to ask Honey for proof of identification.

'Mr Mahon is not available. He asks that you make arrangements to visit in the morning or afternoon.'

'Would you tell Mr Mahon that I am here to ask him questions about the murder of Mr Nigel Tern. Would you also tell him that I wish to speak to him now. If he cannot see me, then perhaps I can make immediate arrangements for him to be picked up in a squad car and brought into Manvers Street Station. It's up to him.'

'Just a minute.'

More words were delivered into the phone. The security guard's face was unreadable. Without saying a word, a button was pushed and the expansive double gates were swung open by virtue of the guard pressing a remote control.

Doherty's car rolled up the driveway. Every so often he spotted a red light blinking on and off in the trees. Evidently Gunther Mahon was security conscious.

Two uniformed men with guard dogs on leashes flashed the torches they were holding in their direction.

'I think they're taking down your registration number,' said Honey.

Doherty nodded. 'Yep. And double checking it with the guard at the main gate.'

The guards carried on with their vigil, passing each other across the house in front of the steps leading up to a portico consisting of sandstone pillars dividing three separate arches. The middle arch was bigger than the ones on either side. The intention, it seemed, was to ape Norman architecture. The Elizabethan-style lead paned windows caught the feature lighting shining onto them. The ornate chimneys, crowned with upstanding Victorian dark red pots, pointed skywards. Ornate ironwork, again in Victorian style, ran along the apex of the roof. Stamford Reach Castle, the name of the place, was loyal to no particular architectural style, but a mish-mash of everything, as though either the original owner, or the architect, kept changing their mind.

More cameras blinked from a parapet above the three arches.

'Imposing,' murmured Doherty.

Honey gulped. 'Home from home — if your name happens to be Dracula or Frankenstein!'

An ornate lantern hanging in the portico formed by the three arches, cast spear shaped light forms down the walls onto dark red terrazzo tiles. The double doors of rich red mahogany remained firmly closed. Was nobody going to let them in?

Honey voiced her concern.

Doherty was circumspect. 'Are you kidding? They've got more security cameras than Dartmoor Prison! They've watched us come all the way up the drive.'

Honey and Doherty got out of the car and ascended the steps.

The keen wind that had been blowing all day was less noticeable here. The arches formed a fine porch, protection from the elements.

Honey eyed the lantern, a huge glass bowl of a thing in a fancy copper frame. Possibly Edwardian, she decided.

A rainbow of light fell outwards as the door opened. More fancy lighting, though this time more modern, blue lights becoming white, then green before going back to blue. Changing like that they reminded her of Christmas lights.

There was nobody there.

Honey looked at Doherty. 'Who lives here? The Invisible Man?'

'Remote control.'

They stepped into a marble tiled hallway of epic proportions. Honey looked upwards to where what looked like an electric current sparked in green and blue around a glazed portico. The ceiling was high. The hallway was huge.

As she looked up the doors closed behind them.

'Automatic doors,' said Doherty.

A man wearing a white suit and a black shirt walked towards them from somewhere to the rear of the hallway.

Honey and Doherty exchanged a bemused look. The place was an altar to designer lighting and electronic security. They hadn't heard a door open or close.

Doherty might have presumed he'd already been out here, just waiting for the front door to open and let them in, but he hadn't seen anyone when they'd first walked in.

The man in the white suit raised his wrist and looked purposefully at his watch.

'Twelve thirty exactly. You must be a punctual man.'

'I always try to be.'

'Glad to hear it.' The man sniffed disdainfully. 'My name's Winston Copthorne. I'm head of security for Mr Mahon,' puffing out his wide chest whilst at the same time holding in his stomach.

A good eater, thought Doherty. He's living in a rich man's pad. The salary's good, the perks even better.

'My name's Doherty. Detective Inspector.'

'Mr Mahon doesn't like to be dragged from his bed late at night. You'd better have a good reason for being here.'

'How about murder. Is that a good enough reason for you?' When Copthorne didn't respond, Honey saw Doherty's expression tense. He wasn't pleased by the other fellow's procrastinating.

'Are you going to take us through or do I have to arrest you for impeding the course of justice?'

'You can't do that.'

'I can if I want to.'

The man looked indecisive. It was a foregone conclusion that he had no wish to be arrested. Head of Security he might be, but in Doherty's experience a close check on such a man's background usually threw up previous convictions — however minor.

For a split second Honey had the impression that he was going to ask for her identity card. If he did, she might not gain entry and she badly wanted to. Charlie York had given her the watch and she felt she had a right to be present. Doherty thought so too. Charlie handing over the watch was likely to be their biggest break in the case so far. He'd also promised that the street cleaner would not be prosecuted.

Holding an expression that mirrored Doherty's she stood with her chin held high, hands behind her back, shoulders taut with tension. Hopefully the guy in the suit would think she was a tasty customer — as a cockney would say, that she could fling a punch as well as any man — and that she too was a copper. He might even think she was armed. A telltale lump bulged against the inside of her pocket — quite a big pocket in fact.

The bodyguard might interpret that bulge as a gun. It wasn't. A snazzy French waspie — no more than a frivolous piece of lilac-coloured lace and whalebone — had attracted no bids at the auction house earlier that day. Honey had dashed in, desperate to take a break from hotel guests, hotel staff and dead people hanging in shop windows, and secured it for herself.

'Are you armed?'

He addressed Doherty.

'No.'

He turned to Honey.

'No,' she said, before he could ask.

His gaze shifted away from her face and her coat pocket.

'Please come this way.'

They followed him down a broad corridor. Although probably dating from Victorian times, the dado rails, the cornices, even the high skirting boards, were all missing, replaced by white and dark purple paintwork. The flooring was light grey.

A series of recessed lighting lit their way. Here and there broad windows looked out over the parkland surrounding the house. Each window was fitted with an iron grille. She wondered at the probability of break-ins around here; most likely nil. Still, some people were paranoid about their personal security. She could understand it in a big old house like this. Most of the rooms would be empty most of the time. Should have bought a caravan, she thought to herself. But it wasn't likely that that kind of advice would be welcome.

Gunther Mahon had receding blond hair and a pink complexion; worse than that he had a pink growth growing on one side of his nose. With all his money, why didn't he get rid of it? One snip, a few thousand pounds and it would be gone.

No matter how hard she tried not to stare, the blemish drew her attention. She couldn't drag her eyes away from it; the growth on the end of his nose wouldn't let her go.

Mr Mahon was standing in front of a set of French doors, his giant shadow falling over them and dispersing the multicoloured light of the room. Like the windows the doors were lead paned and dated from way back. They didn't go with the rest of the room where purple and grey dominated. White leather chairs were coupled with black two-seater sofas. The curtains were some kind of muslin, though weighted with what looked like silver discs along the hems.

There was a white rug in front of a white marble fireplace — the modern kind — the insert a trio of single flames that seemed to come out of nothing — certainly not coal or logs — not even of the imitation variety. Colour in the room was confined to the multitude of designer lighting which Honey estimated had cost a small fortune. Even as they looked at him the colours his shadow dispersed changed from purple to pink, to green and to blue.

Introductions were made.

'I'm sorry to interrupt you at such a late hour, Mr Mahon, but this is rather important.'

'Is it now?'

Mahon seemed less than impressed. His eyes were hard and cold. Without colour, like glass marbles, round and smooth with only a splinter of colour at their centre.

Honey controlled a shiver and to some extent her excitement at the prospect of presenting this man with a watch found at a murder scene, died. Gunther Mahon had the most evil eyes she'd ever seen and his tone of voice did nothing to ease her discomfort.

'I won't ask you to sit down. I wouldn't want to encourage you to outstay your welcome. Not that this should take very long. I believe you told my secretary that you'd found my watch. I really can't think why the matter could not have waited until tomorrow. A watch is a watch, after all.'

He spoke in a monotone, like a robot might speak, certainly not quite human. The pitch was high, totally at odds with such a big, thickset man.

'And a murder is a murder,' said Doherty.

'What's that got to do with the loss of my watch?'

'First we need you to confirm that it really is your watch that was handed in.'

'Let's get this over with. Do you have it with you?'

'No. But we do have a photograph. Perhaps you could take a look and verify that the watch does indeed belong to you.'

Mahon raised one eyebrow. 'Just a photograph? I understood you were returning my property to me.'

Doherty persisted. 'I need you to confirm that the watch we have in our possession is your property. Could you look at the photos, please?'

An angry expression clouded Mahon's face.

'Did it have my name on the back?'

'Yes.'

'Then there's nothing more to be said. I want it back. Now!'

'That's not possible, sir. The watch is at present in the hands of our forensic people. It was found close to a crime scene. Can you tell us where you were on Thursday the ninth of July?'

Mahon's face turned puce.

'What are you insinuating?'

'I'm not insinuating anything, sir,' said Doherty, his level voice professional and firm. 'We need to know where you were that night and what your watch was doing lying in the gutter at Beaumont Alley.'

'I lost it of course! The strap broke! This is ridiculous!'

Honey took a deep breath. To her knowledge the strap had not been broken. She had watched Charlie York taking it off his wrist.

The air was ripe with testosterone.

'The strap of the watch we have in our possession is not broken,' said Doherty.

'Then perhaps somebody mended it,' bellowed Mahon. 'Or perhaps it didn't break. Perhaps it hitched on something and fell off.'

'Beaumont Alley,' Doherty persisted. 'Were you there on the night in question, Mr Mahon.'

Honey could almost smell the tension. The two men were facing each other down, brows furrowed, jaws firmly clenched.

It wasn't like Doherty to let somebody get to him. She sensed instant dislike on his part, possibly on Mahon's part too.

Honey sighed and shook her head.

'Look guys. This is getting us nowhere. Can we get to the point, please? A watch was found in the gutter and handed to me. It's a very expensive watch engraved with your name, Mr Mahon. All we need to know is whether you have recently lost such a watch, where you THINK you lost it and can you please identify it to make sure it really is yours.'

Mahon glared at her from over the ugly lump on the end of his nose.

'Why is this so important?'

'Do you know a man named Nigel Tern?'

'I admit I do. I like well-fitting clothes,' he said, his gaze falling over Doherty with ill-disguised criticism. Doherty was sporting the usual black leather coat, T-shirt and jeans. As usual he hadn't had a head-to-head with his shaving razor for a few days.

'We're investigating his murder. Your help would be very much appreciated.'

'Would it indeed! And what has this to do with my watch?'

'I would appreciate you answering the question first. Where were you on the night of Thursday the ninth?''

Doherty was good at hiding his impatience from people who didn't know him that well but she knew he was getting angry — very angry!

'I would have to consult my diary.'

'Can you do that now?'

'My secretary keeps it for me. Her desk is locked and she has the keys with her. Anyway, I really don't know what this has to do with me. The man made my suits. He was not my friend, merely an acquaintance.'

Honey could almost hear Doherty counting to ten. He was marking time, being patient. It wouldn't last. She had to do something.

'As you must already know, Nigel Tern was found dead and any help you can give would be very much appreciated,' she said in as pacifying a voice as possible. 'He had a lot of very wealthy and well-connected clients. We know, of course, that you are one of them,' flattered Honey, smiling sweetly and trusting neither of them would take a swing at each other.

It was hard to tell whether the flattery had worked. Mahon's heavy jaw, misshapen nose and dead-looking eyes gave nothing away. He might just as well have been carved from a ton of whale blubber.

'I have many watches.' Mahon's voice sounded as grim as his expression. 'Mr Tern's death has nothing to do with me.'

'We didn't say it did,' said Honey, persisting in her sweet tone and smile. 'But as a customer, and seeing as your watch . . .'

'Mr Mahon, where were you on the night of Thursday the ninth of July . . .' Doherty intercepted.

'That is none of your business . . .'

'Mr Mahon. I am a detective. It is my business. I would appreciate you giving me this information on a voluntary basis. We would appreciate your help.'

The carbuncle on the billionaire's nose seemed to pulsate and redden. Honey suspected his anger would get the better of him. Somehow she would prefer to leave before it did.

As a civilian it wasn't her place to ask questions, but there was nothing to stop her from making general comments.

She turned this way and that as though overawed by the modern décor and over the top lighting.

'This is a lovely place, Mr Mahon. You're very lucky to live here. How long ago did you come to England?'

He blinked and looked at her as though he'd just woken up. There hadn't been much time to do research before charging out here, but Lindsey was quicker than most people in finding things out.

Gunther Mahon was supposed to be of Russian descent, his fortune based on what he'd managed to squirrel away when the Soviet regime had fallen. The Scandinavian name and adoption of residency came later. Rumour had it that he'd picked his name out of a Swedish or Norwegian telephone directory. It certainly wasn't Russian.

Doherty showed him the photograph. Gunther barely glanced at it.

'It is not my watch.'

'But it has your name on the back.' Doherty showed him the second photograph.

'No. You are mistaken. It is not mine.'

Honey was tempted to exchange a look of surprise with Doherty, but she controlled herself. She knew beyond doubt that he too had controlled himself. The billionaire's answer was not what they'd expected. They both knew he was lying.

'Mr Mahon, you are saying that you have not lost this watch? May I point out that when I phoned and asked about it, your secretary confirmed to me that you had lost a watch.'

'I suspect it was stolen from me and it was the thief who dropped it.'

'So it is your watch.'

'If it is I don't want it back. It has been sullied by a thief.'

'Is it your watch or isn't it?' Doherty said firmly.

'Are you deaf, inspector? Yes. It is mine, but I did not lose it. I did not visit my tailor on the day or night in question.'

'Can you tell me where you were?'

'Yes. I was visiting my daughter's school. It is a private school. I pay very big fees. I like to know where my money goes.'

'Is that where you lost your watch?'

The big man shrugged. 'It could have been. It does not matter. I can buy another. Whoever found it can keep it.'

'The man who found it can keep it?'

Doherty looked bemused.

Mahon eyed him over puffy cheeks. 'That is what I have just said. Now please. I am a very busy man. I will wish you good night and you will then leave my home.'

'Mr Mahon, the watch is very valuable. If it was stolen, then surely you would wish to give me the details and I can investigate.'

'No. I never even noticed it missing. See? I am wearing another one. I have many watches. Very expensive watches.'

'Can you not tell us when you think it might have been taken? And by whom?'

'I have just told you!'

There was a noticeable rumble in the other man's voice, like thunder sounding in the distance.

Honey could almost feel the vibrations of his vocal chords. She also detected waves of anger coming from Doherty. The man was lying. They knew he was lying.

'Mr Mahon. I still cannot believe that you would not have noticed when the watch went missing,' began Doherty.

'I have told you I have many watches. I can afford to buy whatever watch I want. I make more money in an hour than a policeman earns in a year!'

Doherty ignored this. 'I will need to check your alibi. I want the address of your daughter's school.'

'I will have my secretary ring you. In the morning. Now goodnight. I wish to go to bed.'

Whilst Doherty clenched his fists, fighting to control his rage, Gunther pressed something out of sight, a button beneath the lip of his desk.

The door opened. The bodyguard appeared.

'See these people off the premises.'

'No matter,' said Honey, thinking on her feet. 'A few tests should reveal enough DNA on the reverse of the watch face and strap to reveal who last wore it. I take it your DNA is on a database somewhere, Mr Mahon.'

The fact was that if there was DNA from the last wearer on the strap and reverse of the watch, it would be Charlie York's.

'Get out!'

Mahon's voice was laced with anger, his eyes black with menace.

Halfway to the door, Doherty turned back round to face him.

'We'll wait until we have the DNA results and come back to you.'

'I will not see you. I will give instructions that you will not be allowed in here.'

'Then I will have to insist that you come down to police headquarters to be formally interviewed. I would suggest you come by taxi. Bath traffic wardens are not very keen on limousines taking up space in no waiting zones.'

Mahon turned his back and headed towards what looked like a wall. At his approach a panel slid open. Once he was through it, the panel slid over and covered the opening.

Doherty followed the bodyguard out to the car.

'He's lying,' said Honey as Doherty started the engine.

'Of course he is.'

'He was there in that alley and it wasn't to get measured for a hacking jacket. If he had been, he would have claimed back his watch.'

Raindrops spattered the windscreen. Doherty switched on the wipers.

'He's not a man who walks far. We have a pretty good chance of finding out the truth. The residents of the flat in Beaumont Alley may have seen something, plus I noticed there are a few security cameras dotted round about. There is also the woman Grace Pauling had an argument with, Caroline Corbett. I think both women had a thing for the deceased, though Grace Pauling is saying nothing. It might be nothing, but we'll call in on the other woman. As for our friend, Mr Mahon, from the information we have, I know he has more than one car — all very upmarket of course and most of the time he's driven round by a chauffeur. Limousines do tend to stand out in a crowd. So too do top of the range Ferraris, Porsches etc., We might get something — that's besides the DNA of course.'

'You mean it's really possible,' said Honey, excited at the prospect. 'That's wonderful! It makes me feel so grown-up!'

'You are grown-up, Honey. I can vouch for that fact,' Doherty replied with a mischievous grin. 'However, we don't know for sure that Mr Mahon's DNA was ever taken and kept on a Soviet database. We can hope, but . . .' He shook his head.

'We have to nail him,' said Honey.

'For losing a watch?' He sounded disgruntled.

Honey's excitement dwindled. Gunther Mahon had lost a watch which had been picked up by a road sweeper, but what did that prove?

'He could have lost it at any time,' said Doherty. 'We need to speak to Mr Barrington. They have some kind of appointment book there. If Mr Mahon was there during the day, he would be in that diary.'

She frowned as she thought it through.

'That watch. I don't believe the thief story. I think he was there in Beaumont Alley.'

'But when and why? Even if he admits it was his instead of this foolishness about it having been stolen, there's no proving when he lost or had it stolen. He could easily say the thief dropped it and therefore the thief also murdered Nigel Tern.'

'But do you believe that?'

Doherty shook his head. 'Of course not. The question we need to ask is what would his motive be for killing Nigel Tern?'

'He sold him an ill-fitting jacket?'

He snorted. 'Don't be facetious.'

CHAPTER TWENTY-ONE

Edwina Cayford tucked the plaid blanket around Arnold Tern's legs.

'That's better. You'll be a lot warmer now.'

'I can hardly move,' Arnold grumbled. 'All you nurses are the same. You tuck a man in so tight, he can't move a muscle.'

'Perhaps that's a good thing,' said Edwina, fixing him with a wry smile. 'It gives me chance to keep out of arm's length, you naughty man!'

The old man chuckled. His eyes glittered.

He had been ill for some time, but Edwina wasn't fooled. She had come to the conclusion that the stronger he got the more he attempted to make up for lost time. A lot of old men got to be gropers as they got older and were convinced they could get away with it just because they were old. Given half the chance his hands would be everywhere. She was thankful she'd never been within his grasp when he'd been younger, but then she'd been younger too. One failed marriage, three kids and she was now without a man and enjoying it.

Arnold Tern's eyes were still twinkling. 'How's your love life, Edwina my dear?'

Edwina threw him a knowing look, her smile wiped from her face.

'None of your business, Mr Arnold.'

'Are you saying you don't have a boyfriend or that you don't want one?'

'Both. I can do without a man in my life; much too time-consuming and demanding. I need to relax when I get home after work whether it's here or at the hospital. I prefer to put my feet up and watch television.'

'Isn't there anything or anyone you'd really like to have with you?'

Edwina grinned. 'Not a man, Mr Tern. I'd prefer a new television.' She sighed heavily as she straightened the cushions on the handsome settee, a faraway look in her eyes. 'Never mind a nice-looking man I'd prefer a thirty-two-inch television with remote control and access to Sky TV. A new TV with internet connection would be best then I could stream what I want to watch.'

'I think I'd like to sit in the conservatory a while.'

Edwina could tell by his clipped tone that he was no longer listening to her.

She tore herself away from her daydream about a new television and glanced past the old man out into the conservatory. Sunshine and clouds were the forecast for today. The conservatory was presently bathed in light.

'That's a very good idea, Mr Tern. It looks sunny out there. You should be warm enough.'

'I know that!'

She was used to him snapping at her like a bad-tempered turtle so took no notice. She opened the door so he could wheel himself out, but he didn't.

'I'm feeling weak today,' he said, his hands hanging list-lessly on his lap. 'I'd like you to push me out.'

'Just out into the conservatory?'

'Yes.'

'Not over a cliff.' One side of her lips curled up in a half smile.

'You're a dutiful woman, Edwina. You wouldn't do that.'

'You know me too well.'

Unseen by him, she pulled a face as she wheeled him out into the conservatory.

Sometimes the old man made her exasperated. Sometimes he made her laugh. He had a dark sense of humour that she'd always taken with a pinch of salt. Just lately she'd wondered if he really meant some of the wicked things he said. His son was a case in point. He'd stated categorically that he'd always expected him to come to a sticky end. What was even worse in her opinion was that he hadn't shed a tear. Not one.

'Would you like something to read?' she asked. 'A cup of tea? Something to eat?'

'No.'

'Then I'll go. I need to vacuum and dust your bedroom before I leave.'

'I would like my spectacles.'

'I'll get them.'

'And my mobile phone, plus that newspaper you brought with you this morning.'

Edwina stopped in her tracks. 'I thought you didn't want anything to read.'

'That isn't reading,' he said grimly. 'Reading that rag is nothing but a skirmish with the English language. The printing isn't too hot either. The pictures are grainy and it's full of advertisements for restaurants, hairdressers and flea markets.'

Edwina sighed. She could have disputed his statement, but he'd taken up enough of her time this morning. There was still some ironing to do and laundry to transfer from the washing machine to the tumble dryer.

After fetching and giving him everything he'd asked for, she left the door to the conservatory slightly ajar.

'Shout if you need me.'

The laundry needed her attention now, but she would still hear him if he called out.

Once he was sure he was alone, Arnold Tern put on his spectacles and scanned the advertisements in the *Bath*

Chronicle. It didn't take long to find a full-page advertisement for a supplier of electrical equipment. Placing the newspaper on his lap, he dialled the number. Eventually, after pressing a few buttons that took him to the sales department, he placed his order. Luckily he knew the details of his debit card off by heart. He also knew Edwina's address off by heart. The one thing he had always had and still held onto despite his age was a formidable memory. Edwina would have her new television set. He owed her that much at least.

Edwina took a look in at him shortly after he'd finished his phone call. She was glad to see he was asleep. She could get on with what she had to do without interruption. First on her hit list was his bedroom which was in need of a good clean and polish.

It wasn't her habit to begin upstairs first, but she had more than one reason for going up there.

Reassuring herself that her mobile phone was still in her pocket, she climbed the stairs. The vacuum cleaner awaited her on the landing. She pushed it along and into Mr Tern's room.

After plugging it in, she went back to the bedroom door, poked her head out and listened. All was peace. Mr Tern was still asleep.

Still feeling a little nervous at what she was about to do, she half closed the bedroom door, tiptoed across the floor and sat down in a Victorian nursing chair upholstered in pink velour. The chair was strategically placed in the curve of the bay window where there was plenty of light. She had no trouble tapping in the number, but still her stomach churned. She'd never phoned the police about anything. On the contrary, in the past it was usually them contacting her, turning up on the doorstep. She had two sons and a daughter. Her daughter was married and respectable. Her sons, both younger than her daughter, were another matter.

Heart pounding, she wetted her dry lips and waited. After half a dozen rings, a young woman answered.

'Police. Can I help you?'

'Am I through to Manvers Street Police Station?'

'Yes, madam. Can I help you?'

Although the girl sounded pleasant enough, Edwina still felt an urge to close the connection, plus her head was beginning to ache with the worry of it all. Was she doing the right thing? Perhaps she was wrong. Or perhaps you're right, said a little voice in her head.

She forced herself to plough on and asked for Detective Inspector Doherty.

'I'm sorry. He's off duty at present. Can anyone else help?'

'No! No,' said Edwina. She made a huge attempt to pull herself together. He wasn't there. In a way that was easier than speaking to him and telling him what she suspected.

'Can I take a message,' asked the pleasant voiced young woman.

'Yes. You can. Tell him I think I know who murdered Nigel Tern. It was somebody I saw at the hospital. I saw this person again in the shop when Detective Doherty was interviewing everyone at the shop. Tell him my name is Edwina Cayford and I think I have evidence that could wrap the case up.'

CHAPTER TWENTY-TWO

Early that evening, just as Edwina Cayford was taking delivery of a thirty-two-inch television set that she did not recall ordering, Rachel Doherty and Andrew Tompkins turned up at Steve Doherty's home in Camden Crescent.

If Rachel hadn't been feeling so nervous, she might have noticed the avarice in Andrew's eyes as he eyed the building in front of him. The avarice was still there when he looked over his shoulder at the terrific view which took in many handsome buildings all the way down to the city centre. If Rachel hadn't been blinded by what she perceived as love, she might have questioned the covetous way he looked at both the house in Camden Crescent and the view spilling out before it. She might have construed that he looked as though it all belonged to him or was at least planning that it would be.

Rachel got out her bunch of keys and quickly found the one that fitted the main door. She was about to put it into the lock when Andrew's hand landed on hers.

'No. That would be rude. You should approach your parent in a formal fashion seeing as you haven't seen him for a while. Press the intercom.'

'You think so?'

'I know so.'

Rachel did as he'd ordered her to do.

'He might not hear it,' she said once the keys were back in her bag.

'If he's keen to see his long-lost daughter, he'll be waiting to hear the bell. Trust me.' He kissed her on the top of her head while at the same time squeezing the nape of her neck.

She didn't see his self-satisfied smile or the triumphant look in his eyes. He had her where he wanted her and that was all that mattered.

Andrew Tompkins prided himself on his ability to judge people. Being able to judge the people he'd worked with had been a definite plus in the world of high finance, the trading of stocks and shares. In their case he knew what they wanted to hear and had done his damnedest to make sure he spewed out the right words. Whether or not they were the absolute truth was another matter. Not that many of his superiors or colleagues questioned either his ability or his results. He got the right results — or at least they thought he did.

At first sight Rachel's father reacted exactly as he'd expected; his face lighting up at the sight of his daughter. Once that greeting was over with, Rachel introduced the baby-faced young man standing by her side.

'Andrew Tompkins. Delighted to meet you, sir.'

He made sure his handshake was warm yet firm, his smile, though friendly, touched with just the slightest hint of nervousness. Potential father-in-laws expected their daughter's boyfriends to be in awe of them. He didn't feel that way of course, but he knew how to play the part. He knew what was expected.

Rachel's father took them into a room with high ceilings with the original plasterwork. A cornice ran just below ceiling level all around the room. From the window he espied a splendid view of the city. Like the décor, the furniture and furnishings erred towards traditional, and looked comfortable rather than ostentatious.

Andrew Tompkins felt a warm glow of satisfaction on detecting the unmistakable smell of furniture polish and air freshener. Rachel's father had been busy preparing for his daughter's visit.

Andrew's feeling of satisfaction intensified. He was in no doubt that Rachel's father had put himself out to prepare for his daughter's visit. *Putty in my hands*, he thought to himself. He had it sussed. There was nothing the old man wouldn't do for his daughter. They'd be all right here, at least until something better came along. In the meantime, the old man wouldn't see his daughter without the wherewithal to arrange a wedding. Getting an upfront advance towards the wedding arrangements was why he was here. He'd done the sums. A really decent white wedding was likely to cost around forty thousand pounds and that didn't necessarily include the cost of the honeymoon. This was Bath. The price of properties here wasn't far behind that of London, especially properties in Georgian crescents like this one.

Whilst Rachel's father made tea and sandwiches in the kitchen, Andrew urged her to go out and speak to him.

'You know what to say?'

She said that she did. 'But . . . I mean . . . are we really getting married?'

Poor kid. She looked so nervous and at the same time so happy.

'Rachel. Darling.' He placed his hands on her shoulders and kissed her forehead. 'Did you think I was joking? Of course we're getting married. Nobody is going to stop us.'

Her face shone with joy. She looked so happy he couldn't help but pity her. Life was a lottery. She needed to learn that. He had. You bet he had!

'Dad?'

'I'm not making too much for now. I've booked a table at Graze for dinner. It's next to the railway station. You might have noticed it when you arrived.'

She shook her head. 'I can't say that I did.'

Doherty poured the steaming water into each mug. 'You did say coffee?'

He looked at her. She nodded.

'And for Andrew?'

'Yes. Black. Not too strong. Two level teaspoonfuls. No more.'

'That's very exact.'

'Andrew is very particular. He hates anything second rate. First class for everything.'

Steve Doherty hid his disquiet. He was a man used to judging people on first impressions. His first impression of his daughter's boyfriend was not good.

Give him the benefit of the doubt, he told himself. *Let's see how things go*.

'How about you do it?' He passed her the sugar bowl and the teaspoon, at the same time giving her a reassuring smile. He watched as she carefully levelled each teaspoonful before putting it in the coffee.

'I've invited Honey and her daughter, plus her daughter's boyfriend — whatever his name is. I think she told me. I can't remember.'

It wasn't usual for Doherty to feel lost for words with anybody, but he couldn't shed the feeling of unease. Perhaps it was because he hadn't seen Rachel for a long while, perhaps because he knew she wasn't Honey's biggest fan. Rachel had made that all too clear a few months ago. But now he saw no sign of hostility in her face and was relieved.

'We're talking more seriously about getting married, but going on the way we are seems to suit us well enough. So basically it's a long engagement.' He shrugged. 'I suppose it's an age thing. I mean, we're hardly likely to start a family at our age, are we?'

He laughed.

Rachel managed a smile. 'That would be strange, you know, having a baby brother or sister.'

She couldn't believe how difficult it was to tell him what she wanted to tell him. It seemed silly. After all he would be so happy for her. His little girl getting married.

As it was it all came out in a rush.

'Andrew and me are getting married, Dad.'

Her father took the sugar bowl and placed it to one side.

'Your mother said you were engaged.'

'That's right. We are. But we had to tell you ourselves. Anyway, you're the one who's got to give me away, aren't you?'

For a moment he said nothing, just stared at her as though seeing her for the first time; no longer a child, but a woman.

'That's right. Does your mother know?'

Rachel shook her head. 'She knows about us being engaged, but she doesn't know we want to get married in the next year. Anyway, we wanted to tell you first. I mean, it's going to be quite an expense . . .'

He nodded. 'And it's the father who foots the bill.'

Rachel blushed, not just because of what Andrew had told her to say, but because her father was watching her carefully.

'You're in love with him?'

'Of course I am.'

'And do you like him?'

'Like him?' She looked puzzled. 'I've just told you, I'm in love with him.'

'It's best you like him first. Love grows over time. You do know that don't you? You do know what I'm saying?'

'Of course I do!'

For a brief moment he saw something of the old defiant Rachel resurface.

'Then I'm happy for you.'

He kissed her on the cheek.

All was quiet in the living room. He couldn't help wondering if Andrew was opening the drawer or lid of his writing bureau. A genuine guy wouldn't do that, but he couldn't help suspecting that Andrew Tompkins was not a genuine guy.

Andrew was not dipping into drawers or bureaus, but standing in front of the window admiring the view.

'I hear you want to marry my daughter,' said Doherty after setting down the coffee and sandwiches.

Andrew spun round, his face beaming with confidence.

'That's right, sir. I do hope you'll give us your blessing.'

'Are your parents in favour of you marrying my daughter?'

'My parents were killed in a car crash. I have nobody to tell, except for my sister. She lives in Australia. I prefer to do things in the old-fashioned way. I believe it's customary to ask the permission of the father of the bride before anything else even though we did tell Rachel's mother. Now we have your blessing, I will phone my sister.'

Doherty took in the tailor-made suit, the crisp white shirt, the shoes polished beyond an inch of their life. That had been his first impression of Andrew Tompkins; everything about him was polished, including his manner.

He flicked a thumb across his nose, glanced at the floor then offered his outstretched hand.

'Rachel is over eighteen years of age. All a poor father can do is to wish the pair of you the best of luck.'

Doherty had purposely left his mobile phone switched on so wasn't surprised when he heard it ringing.

'It's work. Sorry.'

After apologising, he went out into the hallway and along to his bedroom.

Andrew turned to Rachel. 'It all went well, I take it. What a clever girl you are.'

In response to his praise, Rachel positively glowed.

'He's very pleased for us.'

'Good.' He looked around the room. 'Well it does look as though he can afford to splash out on a decent wedding for his only daughter. We don't want to scrimp on the arrangements do we? A white wedding with about two hundred guests I think. At least that. Or, even better, make it three hundred.'

Rachel's cheeks reddened. She hated the way he outlined his plans without ever bothering to ask her.

'I'm not sure he could afford that big a wedding.'

Andrew looked disappointed. 'You do want to get the most out of him, don't you? You deserve it after the way he treated you, leaving your mother when you were small. And here he is, doing it all over again.'

Rachel bit her lip. At first, she'd told him her father was a civil servant before telling him the truth. And then her mother had told Andrew that his profession was a very selfish one that destroyed their marriage and left her alone with a child to bring up.

He'd commiserated with her. Later he'd asked Rachel why she'd thought to lie to him.

'Just because he's a policeman? Do you really think I'm frightened of a policeman?'

'No . . . I . . . well . . . it's just that people think once a policeman, always a policeman . . . and feel . . . well . . . awkward about it.'

He enveloped her in a rib crunching bear hug.

'Let's get this straight, Rach. I'm not intimidated by anyone. Get it?'

She'd protested that he was squeezing the breath out of her. She couldn't breathe. Eventually, he'd let her go.

* * *

The civilian telephonist at Manvers Street Police Station was out that evening on a hot date. Calls received and made had been properly logged. The call from Edwina Cayford had been written on a slip of paper for forwarding on to Detective Inspector Doherty. Unfortunately, when she snatched her bag from the drawer, she didn't see it flutter to the floor. The hot date awaited her. Once the door of the office was shut behind her, she tended to shut her mind to everything that had happened that day. Loose bits of paper didn't count for anything.

CHAPTER TWENTY-THREE

'His name's Drury and he's a bit older than me.'

Honey was getting ready to go out. Lindsey was already dressed in a purple velvet skirt, a green and purple shirt and a pair of Roman style sandals with feathers floating around the ankles.

So, thought Honey. *At last I know*.

'Where did you meet him?'

Lindsey brushed imaginary dust from the back of the sofa she was standing behind. She hadn't told her mother about Drury for obvious reasons — not until she was sure — or almost sure of her feelings for said man. She'd now decided their relationship was serious enough to introduce him to her mother.

'He's a civil servant.'

'I see. I didn't think there were many left in Bath.'

'There are still some.'

The MOD had been called the War Office when it had first come to Bath during World War II. Back then it had taken over a large hotel and a lot of land converting the hotel into offices and erecting lots of rough looking buildings on land on the outskirts of the city they had compulsorily purchased from local farmers and landowners.

The sites had been dispersed in over the years, the offices turned into flats, the land auctioned off for housing development.

Honey presumed Drury was one of those civil servants remaining.

She eyed her daughter sidelong. 'Are you sure you don't mind coming along?'

Lindsey smiled. 'Are you sure you don't mind me coming? I've never met Rachel, but she hasn't exactly endeared herself to me so far. I mean, what daughter visits her father only once in a blue moon. If I had a father . . .'

She stopped. Her father had left her mother when she was young. She could barely remember him. And anyway, there was no chance of reconciliation. Carl Driver had been a keen yachtsman, his favourite passage being the North Atlantic. Unfortunately the ocean he loved the most was now his final resting place. He'd drowned and his all-girl crew with him.

Honey stopped brushing her hair and looked at met her daughter's eyes in the mirror. They looked alike: their bone structures were good and their hair glossy, and Honey couldn't help congratulating herself on bringing up such a considerate girl.

'My marriage to your father was doomed from the start. I should have known better.'

'I still feel sorry for Steve,' Lindsey said 'I mean. He was only doing his job. It doesn't sound as though Rachel's mother was very supportive.'

'I've never met her, so I'm disinclined to throw aspersions,' said her mother.

Lindsey held her head to one side. Her expression had turned thoughtful. 'Do you think it may have some bearing on his preference to being called Doherty?'

Honey stopped brushing her hair. 'I didn't know it was a preference.'

'Didn't you? How many people do you know who call him Steve?'

Honey thought about it. She couldn't come up with one single person who called him by his first name. She certainly didn't. Doherty seemed . . . well . . . somehow more fitting.

'There. I thought so,' said Lindsey. 'His name is as much part of his law-keeping identity as his police ID. That's who he is. Doherty the policeman.'

* * *

In an effort to further the cause of community policing and interactive sympathy, Doherty was persuaded by the Chief Constable to pay a visit on Mr Arnold Tern.

'Just so he feels we haven't forgotten him,' said Mumford, a man who prided himself on having come up through the ranks, mainly because he took on board the current fashion in modern policing.

It was no good arguing that he had better things to do, like chasing Gunther Mahon, locating and questioning the deceased's many girlfriends, and pinning down the true use for the gallows. He had his suspicions as to its true use, but there was no actual evidence. Even then, would his sexual predilections have any direct bearing on the case? Who knows.

Then there were his domestic arrangements. Andrew and Rachel were staying at his place. He was feeling a really modern father because he was allowing them to share a bed. His bed as a matter of fact. The one he only shared with Honey Driver.

He wasn't comfortable with his daughter's choice of fiancé, and couldn't ever see himself warming to him. But Honey had told him to stay cool. 'After all, when they are married, are they likely to live close by?'

He found himself hoping they would not. If they did, then he visualised himself being an interfering father-in-law. He loved his daughter and his unease had not gone away.

So he headed for Arnold Tern's big old Edwardian pile with the window open all the way. Hopefully it might clear his head. He didn't usually suffer from headaches, but today he had a humdinger — and it wasn't a hangover!

Although the house had a drive and attached garage, there was no room to park. A small red Honda Civic that he recognised as the cleaner's car was parked immediately in front of the garage. A sleek grey Saab was badly parked behind it, sitting askew and taking up a lot of the room. There was nothing for it but to park against the kerb.

He saw a woman with fair hair come rushing out of the house, get in the Saab and back out. Although there was enough room to park a ten-ton truck, she'd barely missed one of the gateposts as she'd backed out, spun round in the road and sped off, tyres squealing in protest.

Edwina Cayford answered the door.

'I've come to speak to Mr Tern. Is he available?'

'Oh yes,' she said in a hushed voice. Her face was quite pink, as though somebody had said something quite rude and she was still embarrassed.

'I'll take you through and then perhaps we can speak later?'

He said that of course they could if she liked. There was something about her tone that made it sound urgent. He wondered what it was.

He asked her if the old man was well.

'Very well. Better than I thought. Certainly well enough to use a mobile phone and . . .' She shook her head. 'I'll tell you about it later. That man . . .' She shook her head again. 'Never mind that for now. In here.'

The room in which Mr Arnold Tern was sitting smelled of hot food. The curtains were half drawn against the sunlight.

The old man looked up when he entered. 'Oh. It's you.' Both his expression and his tone were disdainful. 'You're not going to tell me that you're apprehended my son's murderer, are you?'

'I'm afraid not.'

'No. I didn't think so.'

'But we are making some progress, though I can't give you any details at this moment in time.'

Arnold Tern scowled. 'In other words, you haven't a clue!'

'That's not really what I'm saying . . .'

'Never mind. Never mind. Now listen my good man. A lady has just left this house who knew my son better than most. Her name's Caroline Corbett. She's the woman he should have married, but there . . . that's water under the bridge. Caroline was the closest any woman ever got to my son. She came here today to tell me she'd suspected he was having more than one affair when he was still in a relation-ship with her. So she hired a private detective to follow him, and that, my friend, is the path we should go down,' declared the old man, wagging his finger at Doherty as though he was a schoolboy. 'My son had a secret life, a sordid life in fact.'

'Are you going to tell me what this detective found out, Mr Tern?'

A row of yellow teeth jutted forward from a face and jaw swiftly taking on skeletal proportions.

'Caroline hired a private detective to follow him. The same one Edwina used to find out what her cheating husband was up to as it works out. His name is Reggie Foreman. Edwina can give you his card and contact details. His report is there. Caroline left it here.'

A bony finger pointed at a manila file sitting on a side table.

Doherty picked it up. It wasn't like him to feel jit-tery, but Rachel and her boyfriend's arrival had upset his concentration.

Forcing himself to focus on the job in hand, he opened the folder and scanned the report. None of the activities Nigel Tern had indulged in came as much of a surprise. That fact was more down to Doherty having seen enough of the world to know how it was, rather than his appraisal of the man in question.

Nigel Tern had liked women. He'd also liked sex. A lot of sex. With lots of different women. OK, that was no big deal. What was a little unusual was the fact that he'd belonged to a large number of sex clubs. Doherty knew there were a few in the city, but not as many as this. There was everything here from clubs for swingers to sadomasochism and bondage. It was the bondage that drew his attention.

Doherty pursed his lips.

'Seems your son liked to dress up and play at being tied up.'

And not just as Adam Ant, he thought to himself.

'Yes. Especially in leather.'

The old man's voice was as thin as a reed, yet full of condemnation.

'You will see there is a membership list for his favourite club — the Shammy Leather.'

'So I see.'

'Do you know that club, Inspector?'

Doherty replied that indeed he did. It was members only, catering for people who enjoyed dressing up in leather; not all-over leather, just strategically placed bits and pieces. He understood a bit of disciplinary practice went on too — which is probably where the gallows might have come in; not for solo sex, but for something anyone could join in with.

'You will see that Caroline's investigator managed to acquire a copy of the members' list.'

Doherty scrutinised the flimsy piece of paper. A few notable names leapt out at him.

'You will see that one of my employees — who will shortly become an ex-employee — is on that list.'

Doherty dragged his attention from a few other names and onto another that he'd spotted. Gustav Papendriou, the man who had declared his intention to become a self-employed online purveyor of select items to a select clientele — leather items.

'You suspect Mr Papendriou of having murdered your son?'

'It's patently obvious, or at least it became so once Grace Pauling had informed me of my son's intention to invest in Mr Papendriou's online business after my death, including giving him a slice of his inheritance. Unfortunately for Nigel and Mr Papendriou, I am still here and Nigel is gone. It is my considered opinion that Mr Papendriou murdered my son. Grace agrees with me.'

'Miss Pauling told you that?'

'Yes. She did. The new will was supposed to have already been drawn up, signed, sealed and delivered even though I was still alive. At least my son had told Mr Papendriou that. Miss Pauling informs me that she had not completed the draft, so it appears my son lied.'

Doherty frowned. 'Not a very nice gesture, drawing up a will even before you've inherited.'

'Not NICE at all, my good man.'

'And you're sure the will wouldn't come into force unless you had died and passed on your inheritance to your son?'

Mr Tern frowned. 'Quite correct, Detective Inspector; I too would have to be disposed of. I think my son was drugging me with a view to despatching me to the hereafter. I always felt better on the days when Edwina was here preparing my food.'

'And on the other days?'

'My son arranged to cook or have something sent in. He had access to everything.'

Doherty closed the file.

'But that would mean that Mr Papendriou jumped the gun. What was the point in him killing your son if you were still alive?'

A sickly grin yet again exposed the old man's yellow teeth.

'I believe my son told him that I was already dead, hence the celebration that night. It wasn't just about winning the competition. It was also celebrating my death.'

Doherty shook his head. 'I'm sorry, Mr Tern, but I think your analysis is flawed, though the business about the will is interesting.'

The old man's brow furrowed with wrinkles.

'At least I have thought through an analysis which is more than I can say for the police!'

Doherty couldn't help disliking the old man. So far he'd seen no sign that he'd cared for his son. For that reason alone there was one question he just had to ask, though cloaked as an observation.

'You didn't seem to like your son very much.'

'Not really. He was not an obedient son. No matter how much I might take the belt to him, he never listened. Defiant. Rebellious. That was the way he was.'

Doherty found himself imagining a young boy being beat into submission.

'Wasn't that a bit heavy-handed?'

'He got the same treatment at boarding school. That's the way it was back then when he was at school. None of this mamby-pamby kid glove nonsense! The school believed in making a man of him and so did I.'

Doherty found himself disliking the man even more.

'You will investigate?'

The old man sounded demanding. Doherty said he would do what he could. From somewhere along the hallway outside he could hear the purr of a vacuum cleaner.

'How often does your cleaner come in?'

'She's agreed to come and work for me full time. I need the company. I need a nurse and besides I pay her twice as much as what she earned working for the National Health Service.'

'Do you mind if I speak to her?'

'Not at all. Contrary to my less than convivial relation-ship with my son, I do wish for his killer to be brought to justice. It's a matter of principle.'

Of course it was. Doherty nodded and got to his feet. He asked if he could have the file drawn up by the private investigator. Mr Tern told him he could.

'Now that your son's dead, everything goes to Grace Pauling, is that correct?'

216

'Indeed it is. Her father was my partner and his father was my father's partner. If I die and my son is unable to inherit, everything goes to Grace. We're like one big happy family, inspector.'

Doherty shuddered at the thought. What a family!

It was interesting to know that Grace Pauling inherited. Normally she would have been interviewed quite thoroughly about the murder, but seeing as she was in a wheelchair, there was no point.

A thought came to him that made him pause before going out to speak to the nurse.

'Are you going to stay on in this house, Mr Tern?'

Again that creepy grin exposed the yellow teeth.

'Indeed I am, Inspector. In fact I may even consider getting married again.'

Edwina Cayford didn't hear Doherty approach and nearly jumped out of her skin when she saw him.

'You gave me such a fright,' she exclaimed after she'd turned off the vacuum cleaner.

'I'm sorry. You said you wanted to see me before I left. Is now convenient?'

She nodded silently. 'I don't think I know anything of interest as such, it's just a small thing that might have some bearing on the case. Would you like a cup of tea?'

He declined her offer, stating that he was off out to dinner that night and didn't have much time.

He sensed she was nervous. He guessed it had something to do with past experience with the police.

'This way to the kitchen.'

'Do you have children?'

He thought he detected her shoulders freeze for the briefest of moments.

She answered him over her shoulder. 'Yes. A girl and two boys.'

'Are they still at home with you?'

She shook her head. She had her back to him so he couldn't see her expression.

'No. My daughter is married and my boys work away from home. Joe has a baby girl. He keeps saying he's going to get married, but he hasn't done it yet. I wish he would. I don't approve of living together and having children without being properly married, do you?'

'I suppose not.'

It wasn't much of an answer. Quite honestly he was divided on the subject. He wasn't sure he wanted Rachel married with a child, at least not to Andrew Tompkins. On the other hand, he wouldn't want her living with him in similar circumstances. In fact . . . he didn't want her with him at all.

But that was personal. He needed to focus.

'How well did you know Nigel?'

'He was my employer. He took me on to tend to the house and Mr Arnold.'

'It was him who took you on, not Arnold?'

'That's right. Don't mind if I have a cup of tea, do you? I'm gasping.'

She wiped her hands down her overall. He watched as she filled the kettle with water, switched it on and put a teabag into a mug.

'Did you like Nigel?'

She shrugged. 'I can't say one way or another. We didn't sit down and talk over a cup of tea or anything and he didn't bother me much. He was always dashing around; dashing off to the shop, dashing off to meet friends during the day. I'm not sure what he got up to at night. I wasn't here at night, not like I am now.'

'You're here at night now?'

She nodded. 'Mr Arnold made me an offer I couldn't refuse. He's paying me double what I was getting working at the hospital and that on top of the original wage he was paying me.'

'That's very generous of him.' He didn't disclose that Arnold had already told him so.

'Yes. Very generous.'

She didn't sound that convinced, either that or something was worrying her.

Doherty thought he knew the reason why.

'Are there strings attached, Mrs Cayford?'

'I don't know what you mean!'

She obviously did know. Even a dark skin can flush quite pink when somebody was embarrassed.

'I mean has Arnold made sexual overtures.'

Edwina Cayford looked at the floor. She was frowning.

'Not in the way you're thinking. Not quite what I was expecting either.'

Still frowning, she looked up at him. 'He bought me a new television. I said I needed a television more than I needed a man. I never expected him to buy me one, but he did. I was amazed. Absolutely amazed.'

'Is this the first time he's been so generous?'

She nodded. 'More or less.'

Doherty sensed there was something else.

'What else?'

She looked at him with her big brown eyes. 'He's asked me to marry him.'

Doherty pursed his lips. 'Congratulations. Are you considering his offer?'

She shrugged and looked terribly worried. 'I got married once and didn't like it. This time it would be different, but still . . . I have my family to think of . . .'

Doherty nodded affably. Arnold's offer of marrying Mrs Cayford had surprised him. Still, if an old man was lonely . . .

'Did Nigel ever make sexual overtures to you?'

She shook her head. 'No. He did not.'

'Did a man named Gunther Mahon ever visit here?'

Edwina thought about it only momentarily before shaking her head.

'I don't think so, but then I didn't know the name of every visitor who came here.'

'Were there many visitors?'

She tilted her head and shrugged her shoulders, her plump lips pouting as she considered the question.

'Not really. Arnold discourages visitors, especially relatives. Not that they've got that many I think. Or friends for that matter, although there did seem to be a few more when Arnold was ill. The old man was out of it, so I think Nigel did have people in.'

'But you don't know who they were?'

She shook her head. 'No, though I do know there were about ten people arriving one evening.'

'How do you know that?'

'He asked me to do the catering — you know — a finger buffet — ham rolls, filled vol au vents, cocktail sausages and things. I asked for how many and he said I should allow for ten people.'

'You didn't stay on to serve these guests?'

'No. In fact he told me to go early because he had things to prepare.'

'You don't know what things.'

She shook her head again. 'No, except that he did spend some time down in the cellar. That's where he keeps the wine.'

'What about Caroline Corbett, the woman I saw leaving when I arrived? Has she been here before?'

'I think she has, but only when Mr Nigel was here. She seemed nice.'

'Do you know where she lives?'

'I think she has one of those flats above the shop. They're very nice. Mr Nigel took me there once to do some cleaning. They'd had a party.'

Doherty thanked her for her time. Asking her about Gunther Mahon had been a long shot, but he'd had his reasons. Gunther's name was on the membership list of the Shammy Leather club only the investigator had made a mistake. Gunther wasn't a member in the strictest sense. He owned it.

* * *

When the policeman had gone, Edwina sat down in a chair and called herself a fool. She had not mentioned what she'd intended mentioning to him and he hadn't referred to the message she'd left at the station. If he had done, her suspicions would have come flooding out. As it was she'd been too nervous to say it out loud. Give it a day or two. He might come back to her, mention her message and then she would tell him what she'd seen. It might mean something. It might mean that her hunch was correct.

CHAPTER TWENTY-FOUR

Honey smiled and thanked Andrew Tompkins for pulling out her chair.

He did the same for Lindsey. She thanked him too.

'All lovely ladies deserve gentlemanly attention,' he purred.

Andrew was trying too hard and Honey didn't miss the way his hands lingered on the back of Lindsey's chair, his fingertips brushing her shoulders.

She glanced at Drury, Lindsey's boyfriend. He showed no sign of having noticed Andrew's lingering fingers, though an amused smile lifted one side of his mouth.

Her attention turned to Doherty. His expression was closed so she found it hard to tell what he was thinking and his eyes failed to meet hers.

She wouldn't know what Doherty thought of him until this meal was over and they were alone. At present he seemed doggedly insistent on being pleasant to everyone. Was his demeanour sincere or was he keeping his cool for his daughter's sake?

Honey was seated next to Rachel and opposite Drury. Doherty sat on the other side of Rachel. Andrew was sitting between Rachel and Lindsey. Not ideal, thought Honey; a young woman on either side of him. For the second time in barely twenty minutes she sensed he was paying more attention to her daughter than he was to Rachel. Ok, Lindsey, looked gorgeous and she wasn't thinking that purely because Lindsey was her daughter.

Their eyes met. Honey saw Lindsey's knowing smile and guessed what she was thinking. Her daughter was no fool; Andrew Tompkins had been weighed up. It was only a matter of time before he got put firmly in his place.

Doherty had already informed them all that the two of them were planning to get married. It was impossible to tell what he felt about that, though he had bought the champagne and led the toast.

'Will you have a white wedding?' Honey asked once the champagne was finished and replaced with a bottle of chardonnay. She directed her question at Rachel, but it was Andrew who answered.

'A very good question, Mrs Driver.' Turning his head he gazed lovingly into Rachel's eyes and patted her hand. 'I am a firm believer that spending a lot on the wedding day is the precursor for spending the rest of our lives together. Faithful for ever. That's what we shall be.' He raised Rachel's hand to his lips and kissed it.

Lindsey used the menu to hide her face. Nevertheless, Honey saw her make a gagging action with her two fingers. The eyes of mother and daughter met in silent understanding. They were of the same mind; neither of them liked Andrew Tompkins.

Conversation about weddings was mixed with Andrew talking about how much money he made in the city. Apparently he was mostly involved in foreign exchange.

'There's a mint to be made if you've got the guts to do it,' he said, his vowels over-pronounced and arrogance in his eyes. 'I receive a very generous bonus each year. In the past I bought sports cars and speedboats, the very latest in every electronic device on the market. But all that is in the past. The money I make will remain in my bank account — or of course invested in a suitable family home. As for the rest of my career, I aim to take full advantage of my opportunities and retire early. At forty-five I think, though I will still dabble no doubt. Especially if we have children — which I am sure we will, and I would insist on a university education.'

It was noticeable that he talked more than anyone else at the table. Honey badly wanted to stick a pin in the little prick's balloon, but out of respect for Doherty's feelings, she smiled sweetly and kept to small talk.

Drury, Lindsey's boyfriend was sitting quietly and she thought he looked interesting, at least more so than Andrew.

'I didn't think there were many civil servants left in Bath,' she said to him. 'You must be one of the few remaining.'

'I work in Cheltenham.' He smiled. 'Not directly for any of the armed forces. You could say that I'm a backroom boy.'

Honey hid her surprise in a glass of wine. If her guess was right, he had to be referring to GCHQ, the place where they monitored the communications of spies, terrorists and unfriendly regimes?

'You seem a man of few words,' Honey said to him smiling.

Drury smiled back, glanced at Andrew, who was still dominating the conversation, and mouthed the words:

'I listen.'

Drury was a kind of James Bond, Honey thought approvingly; not an out and out action man, but one who kept his ear to what was going on in the world; a spook who listened.

She went on to ask where he'd met her daughter. Was it at the gym?

He gave her a thoughtful smile, the kind that made her think he kept secrets or knew things everyone else wished they knew too. However, his response surprised her.

'When I'm not working, I'm a ghost hunter. I was wandering around a medieval house that was said to be haunted. I didn't find any spectral beings, but I did find Lindsey. I don't think I need to tell you that she has a fondness for everything medieval and old things in general.' His smile widened. 'Perhaps I'm one of those old things.'

Despite the fact that he was a few years older than her daughter, Honey decided she liked him. Unlike the cocksure Andrew Tompkins, he possessed presence without self-importance, perhaps a prerequisite for the job he did.

Absorbed in her conversation with Drury, she didn't notice that Lindsey was trying to attract her attention. After receiving a sharp kick on her foot, she finally looked her way.

Lindsey's eyes slid sidelong. At the same time she gave a sideways jerk of her head. Honey looked in the direction to where a vision in pale grey and pink was being seated by a waiter at a table for two. The man with her was dressed in a pale-grey lounge suit with a pale-grey shirt and pink tie. The corner of a pink handkerchief peaked from his breast pocket. Colour coordinated, her mother and her new husband had arrived!

Since finding, falling in love and marrying Stewart White on a Saga cruise, her mother had not visited the Green River Hotel quite as much as she used to.

Honey now believed that there was such a thing as love at first sight and was glad of it. She no longer got dragged into her mother's circle of friends, getting lumbered with incontinent dogs, aged Lotharios and requests to drive her mother to the funerals of old friends. Her own friends were getting older and, hey, nobody lives forever.

Her mother and her new stepfather were talking nose to nose, hands clasped across the table. Sweet! Her mother's handbag — a large sack-like affair with silver studs and a large red tassel hanging from the fastening, squatted on the floor between them at the side of the table.

It was hard to decide whether to go over and say hello or let them have their privacy. The decision was delayed when Drury asked her a question.

'I understand you inherited a ghost when you took over the hotel and it now seems as though you have a second ghost. Tell me about it.'

Honey gave a light laugh. 'Aren't you going to tell me it was just my imagination?'

'No I will not because it's not always true. Sometimes it is down to an overactive imagination, but sometimes it is not.'

His eyes twinkled. They were brown and there were wrinkles at the corners. His smile was sincere.

She told him about Mary Jane and the ghost that haunted her bedroom and was supposedly a long dead relative. Then she told him about the one she had seen. Halfway through her discussion, Andrew Tompkins made his excuses to go to the bathroom. To get there he had to pass close by where her mother and stepfather were sitting.

Honey's eyes strayed in that direction as she spoke about her experiences with the paranormal — though only sounding half convinced. She didn't want her daughter's new boyfriend to think she was gaga.

'I'm not sure what I believe,' she said to him, suddenly unable to hold back her thoughts. 'I just listen to everybody and make my own judgements.'

'I do pretty much the same,' he replied.

Honey's attention drifted back across to where her mother and stepfather were engrossed in each other. Not once did either of them look in Honey's direction. They were in their own world.

Andrew reappeared from the door at the corner of the restaurant which led out into a corridor leading to the toilets. He strode out like a gladiator about to do battle — which seemed odd, seeing as they were there to celebrate an engagement and possible wedding.

The gap between the table for two and a large plant-holder wasn't great. Suddenly Andrew tripped over her mother's bag and almost went sprawling.

Honey stopped talking though she was aware that Drury had asked her a question.

'I'm sorry?'

'You were telling me about this Mary Jane. I understand she's a professor of the paranormal.'

'That's right. From California. Well, she would be wouldn't she? It's known for being home to a lot of far out people.'

'She might not be so far out. She might be absolutely right about everything.'

His tone of voice was so calm, so matter of fact.

Honey looked at him in disbelief. 'But you work at GCHQ. You listen to . . .'

She couldn't quite think of the right description.

'Spy traffic and terrorists who think their way is right and to hell with everybody else,' he finished.

'That's about it.'

He grinned. 'That doesn't mean I don't have some imagination. I think a lot. Probably too much.'

Honey suddenly became aware that in the absence of Andrew, everybody at the table had fallen silent, their attention torn between Honey and Drury's conversation and another — rather louder — one going on over at her mother and stepfather's table. Andrew sounded as though he were tearing them off a strip.

'Mary Jane is totally off the wall, getting on in years and quite wonderful,' said Lindsey. 'I've told Drury all about her.'

Doherty pulled a face. 'I'm guessing you haven't mentioned her driving.'

'I have not.'

'I try not to think about Mary Jane's driving,' added Honey. 'Especially when I'm in the passenger seat. I keep my eyes closed.'

'Something of a speed merchant?' Drury smiled.

'Let's say she doesn't always concentrate on what she's doing.'

Drury nodded thoughtfully. 'We could take the view that it's difficult focusing on this world if you've got more than a passing interest with the next.'

'You could say that,' said Doherty. 'But there are occasions when she's only narrowly missed going there — and her passengers with her!'

The raised voices at the other table continued. Honey tried to ignore them. Her mother was quite capable of looking after herself.

'OK. This is it,' said Doherty. 'Mary Jane believes that the man who lives in her wardrobe is a long-distant relative who died a few hundred years ago.'

'The one I saw standing up at the landing window, looking as though she was about to throw herself out, is a new one,' Honey said. 'Apparently the firm of solicitors across the road got a bit fed up of her and engaged an exorcist to get rid of her. In the event she merely moved house. So now it seems we've got her.'

Drury frowned as he contemplated the matter. He looked to be thinking deeply.

Finally, he pronounced, 'It sounds as though something's happened to trigger her appearance. An exorcism would do it. One minute at peace, the next springing into life — well not exactly life — but essence so to speak and springing across the road. But don't worry. She'll move out again, straight back into where she came from.'

'That's good,' said Honey, immediately cheered by his analysis. 'Tell me, Drury, what made you interested in ghosts?'

Drury grinned. He had an attractive face and an attractive grin.

'I thought I saw things when I was a kid. And I heard things other people didn't seem to hear.' His grin widened. 'Perhaps that's why I enjoy my job.'

'How intriguing. So you listen to things?' said Doherty.

'And I interpret things. That's my job. But the past still fascinates me and so does the concept of another world that's way beyond the one we see and accept, so it's . . .'

Their pleasant ongoing conversation was rudely interrupted.

'Can you believe it! The sheer ignorance of old people!'

Andrew was back, his face red with anger and a haughty jut to his rather pointed chin.

Rachel looked up at him in alarm. 'What is it, darling? Come and sit down.'

Andrew was livid. 'I've just tripped over a silly old woman's handbag. Honestly, some people shouldn't be let out.' He shook his head. 'Still. Never mind. Perhaps the old biddy will opt for euthanasia and give us all a break!' He barked a laugh. 'Now where was I?'

'Crowing,' said Honey. 'Telling us how much you earn in the city and how you've got a lot more money than the rest of us. And now it appears you're stupid enough to make an enemy where you really shouldn't go.'

Doherty sunk down into his arms, his shoulders quaking with laughter.

For the first time since he'd arrived, Andrew Tompkins was looking totally ill at ease.

'Pardon?'

'You were also fondling my knee,' added Lindsey. 'You were fondling my knee and fancying your chances. If Rachel marries you, she's a bloody fool. You'll always be fondling somebody's knee. That's the sort you are.'

Rachel turned pale. Her mouth hung open. Doherty was still immersed in laughter. Drury was the picture of casual amusement. True to his nature, he was taking stock of everything and making his own mind up.

Andrew did his best to laugh it off.

'In your dreams, sweetheart! Why would I want to fondle your scrawny knee when I've got my lovely fiancée sitting next to me?'

He grabbed Rachel's hand. For the first time that night Rachel looked a bit daunted, but Andrew was not a man to be defeated that easily. His eyes locked with hers.

Honey detected a small change in the girl. She suddenly looked less besotted and less sure of her boyfriend than she had been earlier.

For a moment it looked as though something had snapped, but Andrew Tompkins had exerted his control over her long enough to break any sign of resistance.

'Darling,' he said, gazing fondly into her eyes. 'The chairs are a bit close. It was accidental. How could it be anything else?'

Rachel looked at her father who had finally managed to raise his head. He just about managed to control the quirky smile that kept breaking out on his face. She looked round at everyone seated at the table, aware Lindsey was glaring at Andrew, that her father had just recovered from laughing, that Honey Driver was looking downright angry. Lindsey's boyfriend was the only one whose mood was impossible to read. All the while Andrew continued to whisper into her ear.

The incident might have passed, Rachel might have forgiven him and Doherty might have taken the view that his daughter was committed to marrying a waster who at some time in the future would leave her high and dry.

Honey understood what he was thinking. His daughter was no longer a child. He might give her the benefit of his advice, but ultimately the decision was hers and hers alone.

All this might have come to pass, however, Andrew Tompkins had not allowed for Gloria Stewart, formerly Cross, striding across the restaurant and descending upon him like a whirlwind.

'You nasty little man!'

'Madam, I am . . .' He tried to rise from his chair, but didn't get the chance. Honey's mother served him a hefty clout around the head with her handbag.

Honey winced. Her mother carried a lot of heavyweight gear in that handbag — mobile phone, camera, door keys and enough make-up to open a market stall.

'Don't you tell me that I'm too old to be let out, you stinker! You can't fool me with your smart suit and your Eton tie. I've lived long enough to know a worm when I see one, and you're a worm of the worst kind!'

She would have socked him once again but Doherty grabbed her hand.

'Steve Doherty, let go of me.'

'Gloria. This won't be the first time I've mentioned the chances of you being charged with GBH.'

'What's this creep to you? And what are my daughter and granddaughter doing seated at the same table as this moron?'

'We're having a quiet family dinner.'

'That's not what I mean,' she snapped, her anger unabated. 'I mean what do you mean protecting this pond life from a frail old woman like me?'

Honey hid her face in her hands. Her mother did not tolerate other people defining her as old. When she referred to herself as old it meant she was REALLY angry.

Doherty shook his head at her. 'Don't try and play the age card with me, Gloria.'

'Gloria, darling . . .'

Husband Stewart gently put his hands on her shoulders.

'I will not calm down,' she said to him. 'This is important.'

'The thought didn't enter my mind. I was only going to ask you if you wanted me to punch his lights out.'

Honey sighed. Not only did she have a dotty mother but it seemed the man she'd chosen to marry thought along similar lines to her. Could be the next few years would be as entertaining — or exasperating — as the past few years.

Her mother looked enquiringly at her granddaughter.

'Lindsey. Are you with him?'

'No.' Lindsey patted Drury's shoulder. 'I'm with him.'

Drury raised his hands palms outwards in a defensive action.

'Please don't handbag me. I'm more fragile than I look.'

Gloria's angry expression flopped into a smile.

Andrew, however, was looking totally destroyed.

'It appears I've made a mistake,' he said with as much pride as he could muster.

'You have that,' said Doherty. 'You've made an enemy of Honey's mother.'

'Let go of my wrist.'

Doherty released Gloria.

'He's with me,' said Rachel bravely. 'He's my boyfriend.'

Honey's mother drew in her chin and eyed Doherty.

'What are you going to do about it?'

Doherty sighed. 'About what? Him insulting you or you swinging your handbag around his head?'

'You're a policeman. You've got the technology. Check up on him.'

Doherty leaned close and whispered in her ear.

'That, dear Gloria, is a very good idea.'

CHAPTER TWENTY-FIVE

Drury Constantine, a long name for a very nice chap, asked Honey if he could call in during at the Green River Hotel when he had to time.

'I'd like to talk to this professor of the paranormal,' he said to her.

'Be my guest.'

And so it was that he arrived and was properly introduced to Mary Jane. Unlike some people he did not bat an eyelid at her outrageously colourful outfit. Today she resembled a mobile rainbow; multicoloured pants, multicoloured tunic top, ditto the swathe of silk wrapped around her head in turban style.

If any colour predominated, it was her eyes, a vivid blue verging on violet.

'Mary Jane. Pleased to meet you.'

'Drury Constantine. Pleased to meet you too.'

'Don't I know you from the Ghostly Guys site?'

Constantine smiled and said he had dipped in on the site now and again.

'Is that something like ghost busters?' asked Honey.

'Nothing like!' Mary Jane sounded offended. 'We don't bust our ghosts, send them back to wherever; we befriend them.'

Feeling out of her depth, Honey left them to it.

Just as she was about to leave the building, Andrew Tompkins turned up to make an appointment for the wedding reception in three months' time. Although Rachel's attachment to him had wavered, it hadn't been shaken enough to finish the relationship.

'I've been to the Abbey. The vicar was very helpful. We managed to get a cancellation.'

Honey expressed some surprise. People queued to get married in Bath Abbey. She remarked that it was extremely lucky they'd managed to get a cancellation.

'Andrew popped in there at the right time,' said Rachel. 'So he tells me.'

So he tells me.

She didn't sound too convinced. A warning flag fluttered in Honey's brain. Up until now Rachel had expressed no doubt in her boyfriend. Perhaps at long last some cracks were beginning to show in Rachel's supposedly perfect relationship. However, she couldn't see a smug control freak like Andrew letting her get away.

'Sweetheart, I told you I would arrange everything,' said Andrew.

Andrew was cringe-making with a capital C. Honey had a great urge to slap his smug smile off his face. She also had an urge to give Rachel a sound talking-to, but hey, this was not her daughter, it was none of her business.

But, they were paying customers so accordingly she booked them in for a wedding reception on the date earmarked for the wedding.

Seeing as it was for Rachel, she didn't ask for a deposit.

'Right. That's that done,' said Andrew. 'Now for booking the limousines.'

Smudger rang through from the kitchen to tell her that they'd run out of eggs.

'I've been making a lot of meringues of late,' he said, looking slightly panicked.

'No problem. I'll nip round to Waitrose. Anyway, I could do with a breath of fresh air.'

On her way to the supermarket, she phoned Doherty.

'Your daughter and potential son-in-law called in to book the wedding reception.

'Why am I not surprised?' he replied. 'He's very well-organised regarding the wedding. He's made me a list of the sort of affair they have in mind including how much it's likely to cost. He's also asked for a sum up front so he can begin putting down deposits for the event, the cake etc., and the bridal gown of course. In fact he's given me a list of the deposits including the one he gave you. He's asked if I can hand the monies over pretty quickly. As he put it, nobody likes talking about money.'

'He certainly doesn't,' remarked Honey. 'He didn't give me a deposit.'

Doherty fell silent.

'Do I recall my mother suggested you check him out?'

'She did. I've checked the limousine company, the gown shop and the gentlemen's outfitters supplying the morning suits — grey top hats and tails no less!'

'Don't tell me he's been along to Tern and Pauling!'

'He has indeed. A good enough excuse to pop in there again I think.'

'Have you handed him any money?'

'No. He's just given me a list for reimbursement of sums he tells me he's already handed over.'

Honey sensed what was in Doherty's mind. He was a policeman not a fool.

'Money he won't get.'

'He doesn't know that yet.'

* * *

It didn't take long to purchase eggs from Waitrose and promptly take them back to the Green River before Doherty arrived to pick her up.

Stewart White, her mother's new husband — Honey couldn't quite think of him as a stepfather mainly because he was only about ten years older than she was, came armed with a notebook and pen, plus a recording machine.

'I'm writing a novel,' he said to her. 'A detective novel. Do you think that chap Doherty might oblige me with a few authentic case notes?'

Honey pointed out that he was a very busy man. Stewart frowned at this and bit his lip. 'I wouldn't want to get in the way of anything important. The fact is I've always wanted to write a novel based on my days taking bets from the high and mighty you might say. Still, I wouldn't want to intrude . . .'

'I don't know much about betting,' said Honey. 'I don't think I know anybody who bets.'

'Don't you? Well that does surprise me. There are plenty around who do, you know. Your mother was telling me about one of the members of the Townswomen's Guild. Besides being a bit of a boozer, she's a hefty gambler. They've heard rumours that she's run up thousands in debt.'

'Really?' Honey was suddenly all ears. 'Do I know her?'

Stewart shrugged. 'I don't know her name, though I think your mother said she's in a wheelchair. I suppose if you're incapacitated, you have to have your fun somehow. Still. It's never wise to overstretch yourself.'

Honey had no doubt who he was talking about. Grace Pauling was a gambler. Well there was a turn-up for the books.

He might have wandered off if Mary Jane hadn't come along reeling off a list of reasons as to why there was suddenly a second ghost haunting the Green River Hotel.

'I could write about ghosts instead,' exclaimed Stewart.

Honey refrained from pointing out that writing a novel about ghosts was far removed from that of writing about the world of betting and detectives, but Mary Jane looked keen to oblige.

'I'll leave you to it then.'

The air outside the Green River Hotel was brisk and blowy. Her new hairstyle got blown all over the place, though not for long. Doherty was waiting for her.

'Want a lift?'

She got in the car, pleased to see that the hood was up. There was a chance she could rescue most of her hairstyle.

'I've got news,' he said to her. He went on to outline what he'd found out about Nigel Tern from Caroline Corbett, the woman who lived in one of the flats above the shop in Beaufort Alley.

'He was a member of some very salubrious clubs. Sex figured high on his list of hobbies,' said Doherty. 'Caroline would have nothing to do with it, but guess who did make a habit of accompanying him.'

Honey shook her head. 'Surprise me.'

'Grace Pauling.'

'I don't doubt it. In fact I can believe that Grace Pauling was having a relationship with Nigel Tern — a very sexual relationship.'

Doherty sighed, folded his hands behind his head and lay back in his chair with his eyes closed.

'Honey, you don't know that for sure.'

'Oh yes I do. You should see the way her eyes light up when she talks about him. I never really noticed it at first. I put it down to drink, and my word, that woman drinks like a fish!'

'Honey, your gut instinct is not admissible in a court of law. Believe me, if it was I would have made Chief Constable by now.'

'Did you know that Grace Pauling is a gambler? Not just a little gambler either. She's a big gambler. Owes thousands from what I've heard.'

Doherty opened his eyes wide. 'I didn't know that.'

'Probably because you're regarding her purely as a woman in a wheelchair and as such she's got no bad habits — except perhaps for sex. That just cannot be true. Anyway, you've already found out she accompanied Nigel to these sex clubs. Who's to say she didn't indulge big time?'

Doherty was wearing one of his hard thinking expressions. 'She stands to gain everything, but wouldn't have got anything if the old man had died and Nigel had inherited. Nigel gets first shout. That's the way the will has been drawn up. The old man said that Nigel was under no obligation to share with Grace. Grace would inherit everything if anything happened to Nigel, in which case . . .'

Sitting up straight he began to work it out.

'She thought the old man was going to die.'

Honey cottoned on to his train of thought. 'And if the old man died, then Nigel inherited. But if Nigel died too . . .'

'But the old man didn't die.'

They both tensed. Their eyes locked together.

'Arnold is still alive,' said Doherty.

'Can Grace afford to wait?'

Doherty shook his head. 'But how could she kill Nigel Tern? She's in a wheelchair. There's no way she could have physically strung him up on the gallows.'

Honey lay back in the chair again. Her gaze settled on the toe of one of her boots, then the other. One was scuffed. One was not. She was heavy on shoes.

Where the thought came from, she didn't know except that it had everything to do with shoes, in particular the bottoms of shoes.

'The soles of Grace Pauling's boots were dirty. Not just dirty, they looked like the soles of my shoes or yours, not like a pair worn by a woman who spends her life sitting down.'

Doherty leaned forward in his chair, his hands clasped in front of him. It was as though they were thinking as one; they were certainly travelling the same mental path.

'She might have had them a long time. She might even have bought them second hand. Women sometimes do that, don't they?'

Honey conceded that he could be right. The boots Grace wore had designer written all over them. Nowadays it was quite fashionable to buy second hand on eBay, like a shouted statement saying, 'Recycling is me!'

Doherty shook his head. 'But it's still not evidence. Not enough anyway.'

Doherty's phone rang shrill and loud. It was sitting in its clip on the car dashboard. Doherty jerked his chin at it.

'Can you get that for me?'

'He's here with me now,' she said in response to the female civilian telephonist on the other end of the phone.

'I need to talk to him. It's about a received call the other night. I wrote it down then forgot about it. It's about the murder case. Nigel Tern.'

'He's driving. Can I help?'

'It has to be him.'

'Hang on.' She found the switch that put the phone on loudspeaker.

A female voice filled the car. 'DCI Doherty? Are you there?'

'I am. Is that Sally Hadley?'

'Yes. It is. Look, I'm really sorry, but I was in a bit of a hurry the other night and a message I should have passed onto you fell to the floor. Luckily our cleaning contractor isn't quite the ticket so it was still there today. I think it's important. It's from a woman named Edwina Cayford and refers to a woman she saw at the hospital. She said the woman is usually in a wheelchair, but was walking normally when she saw her at the hospital.'

The car swerved when Doherty looked at Honey.

'Good God!'

'And this woman you say was called Edwina Cayford.'

'Yes.'

'Get a car round to her place. If she's in, get them to stay there.'

Doherty swung the steering wheel of the car in the quickest two point turn she'd ever seen. She didn't bother to ask where he was going. They were off to visit Arnold Tern.

Grace Pauling was desperate. She wanted the money and she'd stop at nothing to get it.

* * *

The sun was setting. The shadows across the garden at the back of the house where Mr Arnold Tern lived were growing longer. Very soon the shadows thrown by the tall trees at the end of the garden would totally cover the garden.

'I think it's time you came in now. It's getting chilly.'

The voice of Edwina Cayford was heard by the person watching from the end of the garden where shadows and shrubs combined to make good hiding.

The old man was sitting in his wheelchair at the top of the steps leading to the rear patio of the house. Beyond him were the open doors of the conservatory.

'A few more minutes wouldn't hurt,' grumbled the old man.

'Ten minutes and then you come in.'

'You're a bully,' the old man shouted at her.

Edwina shook her head and smiled. She was used to him calling her a bully but knew he didn't mean it; in fact he enjoyed having her tell him what to do. Nobody else would dare.

A movement at the bottom of the garden caught her eye. She craned her neck in an effort to see better.

'Strange. I just thought I saw someone.'

Arnold Tern gave that portion of the garden a hard stare.

'Nothing,' he said, and went back to his book. He'd enjoyed sitting in the sun all afternoon and seeing as he wasn't long for this world, he had every intention of enjoying it to the bitter end.

'Have you considered my proposal?' he called to her before she had chance to disappear.

Edwina stood framed in the conservatory doorway, the old man's back to her.

'I'm not sure it's a very good idea.'

'I think it's capital.'

He wasn't an easy man to argue with.

'I'll let you know,' she said before hurrying away. She'd found his marriage proposal embarrassing rather than flattering. Back in the safety of the kitchen, she switched on the kettle and fetched a tea mug. It was the only mug in the place. Mr Arnold insisted on porcelain cups and saucers. Just holding one in her hand scared her. Drop one and it broke to pieces, whereas her stout clay baked mug was far more durable — a bit like Edwina herself.

Arnold Tern was a great reader, though closed his eyes every so often when reading was just too much. It was when he was dozing that he sensed somebody was close at hand. Edwina had come back out. Perhaps she'd decided to accept his marriage proposal.

He felt her let off the brake holding the wheels rigid and stopping it rolling off down the flight of steps.

'You're bullying me again. I haven't had another ten minutes yet,' he snapped. 'I want to read another chapter.'

'I don't think so.'

A different voice. Not warm, not attractive. And she smelled different. Thick with perfume.

'You've had all the time you're going to get, Arnold!'

He turned, not all the way, but just enough to gauge the woman's identity.

'Grace! What are you doing?'

'It's my money, Arnold. If you had your way you'd marry your nurse in there and leave it all to her. Well I won't allow that, Arnold, just as I wouldn't allow Nigel to squander it helping Papendriou with his stupid business. Before long it would be all gone or the best part of it. And then where would I be?'

'But . . . You're walking!'

'Yes. I'm walking, but it suited me to be in a wheelchair — until I was ready not to be. All in my own good time, Arnold; MY own good time!'

The old man felt himself go hot and then very cold.

'What are you going to do?' His voice was shrill and he was in danger of wetting himself.

'Well you know that old nursery rhyme? Jack and Jill went up the hill? And Jack fell down. Only here it's going to be Arnold falling down, all the way down that flight of steps to the . . .'

'Grace!'

She paused just long enough for Doherty to grab her. Grace let go of the wheelchair.

'Christ!' Doherty shouted. 'The brake's off!'

The wheelchair lurched forward. That bit fitter and younger than Edwina, Honey got there first, throwing herself over the old man's lap. The wheelchair lurched to a standstill. Edwina grabbed the handles.

When Honey raised her head, she found herself looking into Mr Arnold Tern's bemused face. As far as she was concerned, his hands were misplaced, one on her bottom, the other in the small of her back.

'My dear! Your body feels remarkably firm. Are you wearing a corset?'

Honey got to her feet.

Edwina put the brake on.

Grace was shouting and kicking.

* * *

It was a cause for celebration. Grace Pauling had confessed to being with Nigel in the shop window.

'It was the gallows and dead of night. Nigel wanted to try it out. He was aroused by the thought of being totally at the mercy of a woman — an incapacitated one at that — or so he thought. He wasn't to know that Grace would have no mercy. She wanted him out of the way. She had gambling debts and she had it in mind to start a new life somewhere without her wheelchair. It was a useful crutch with which to keep her creditors at bay and to keep her clients with the practice. Nigel wasn't to know that. She told me he wanted

242

to stand in her lap whilst she was sitting in the wheelchair. He then wanted her to undo his zip and . . .'

'I get the picture,' said Honey. 'Only Grace decided to walk. Or rather she always had walked, it was just convenient to be able to walk and hit him over the head with something heavy.'

'A bicycle pump in fact. She kept it in the wheelchair for pumping up her tyres. She got the drop on him back in the shop, placed him in the wheelchair, turned the stairs over so they formed a ramp, and strung him up.'

'I don't think she was so keen on Nigel's sexual games as he thought she was; that was why she left him hanging there in the window. It was a kind of last minute revenge.'

'Thank you, Professor Driver,' said Doherty.

The steak had been good and the wine was superb.

'I keep thinking of poor old Charlie York listening on his iPod to Adam Ant. He pushes his cart past loads of window displays every day of the week. None of them have ever stopped him in his tracks as this one did, but not because the display appealed to him aesthetically. Neither did the merchandise. Charlie isn't a sports jacket kind of guy; a padded Puffa perhaps, but that's about it. Listening to Adam Ant on his iPod and then seeing an effigy of him in front of him, well . . . it must have been like seeing a ghost!'

'It didn't occur to him that the model was supposed to represent a highwayman. It's a close likeness to be fair. Some might have interpreted the model as being Captain Jack — you know — played by Johnnie Depp in *Pirates of the Caribbean*. The make-up and dress is very similar.'

Doherty agreed with her. 'As far as he was concerned, the display depicted his idol who he'd seen at a pop concert years ago.'

'What do we do about the watch?'

Doherty took another sip of his wine.

'I'm thinking that Mr Mahon will claim it back once he hears a suspect has been charged. Unless he's got so many he doesn't really care. In which case we'll let Charlie know when it comes up for auction. Lost property have them at least twice a year — mostly bicycles, but a few watches.'

Honey pointed out that he'd never be able to afford it.

Docherty grinned. She guessed what was coming.

'It's not a real Bulgari, is it? Just one of the cheap imports you can pick up for pennies at any Sunday market stall. That's how it will get listed anyway.'

'If Mahon doesn't demand its return.'

'I don't think he will. Bear in mind he owns a nightclub with a very dubious reputation. He wouldn't want the police taking too close a look at it, I'm sure.'

Honey conceded that he had a point.

'I still find it hard to visualise Nigel Tern impersonating Adam Ant. I know there are a whole army of Elvis Presley impersonators. I didn't know there were a whole load of overweight baldies out there thinking they looked good in tight britches and face make-up.'

'You've really got a thing about tight britches, haven't you?'

Reluctantly Honey dragged herself away from the vivid thoughts in her head. Doherty had a glint in his eyes.

'What?'

His smile was wicked. His fingers curved around her neck, pulling her closer so he could whisper in her ear.

'I know where I can get a pair.'

'Wow!'

'I promise I'll wear them, but on one condition.'

'Say it. It's yours.'

'That you wear that corset you were wearing when you threw yourself across Arnold Tern's lap.'

'Will it turn you on?' she whispered, her tongue darting into his ear.

'I saw the look on the old man's face. Hope springs eternal. I want some of that!'

The night was set. A night in at Steve Doherty's place with a takeaway, a bottle of wine and binge watching *The West Wing* – or it would have been. Until the phone rang.

He'd turned off his mobile phone but not his landline – just in case of emergencies.

He frowned as he picked it up and heard the familiar voice on the other end.

'Rachel. What's up?'

Honey listened.

'You're where? New York?'

He was laughing when he ended the call and sat back down. His arm wound around Honey's shoulders.

'Good news. My daughter is off with a friend travelling by Greyhound around the United States.'

'I take it Andrew has been given the brush off.'

'Big time. She's left him to cancel the bookings he made for the wedding. And she's cancelled him out.'

'In favour of travelling whilst she still can.'

'That's about it.'

'The girl's seen the light.'

Steve hugged her close and kissed her cheek. 'And we're left to our own devices.'

Smiling she turned to face him. 'Where shall we begin?'

'I'll make the first move.'

He took the glass from her hand, cupped her face in his hands and kissed her long and passionately.

'Good start,' she said once she'd caught her breath. 'How about an encore?'

THE END

THE JOFFE BOOKS STORY

We began in 2014 when Jasper agreed to publish his mum's much-rejected romance novel and it became a bestseller.

Since then we've grown into the largest independent publisher in the UK. We're extremely proud to publish some of the very best writers in the world, including Joy Ellis, Faith Martin, Caro Ramsay, Helen Forrester, Simon Brett and Robert Goddard. Everyone at Joffe Books loves reading and we never forget that it all begins with the magic of an author telling a story.

We are proud to publish talented first-time authors, as well as established writers whose books we love introducing to a new generation of readers.

We have been shortlisted for Independent Publisher of the Year at the British Book Awards three times, in 2020, 2021 and 2022, and for the Diversity and Inclusivity Award at the Independent Publishing Awards in 2022.

We built this company with your help, and we love to hear from you, so please email us about absolutely anything bookish at feedback@joffebooks.com

If you want to receive free books every Friday and hear about all our new releases, join our mailing list: www.joffebooks.com/contact

And when you tell your friends about us, just remember: it's pronounced Joffe as in coffee or toffee!

CPSIA information can be obtained
at www.ICGtesting.com
Printed in the USA
BVHW041319070423
661948BV00003B/453